THE ONLY CONSTANT

LYNNE A. WARMOUTH

Copyright © 2023 Lynne A. Warmouth.

All rights reserved. No part of this book may be reproduced, stored, or transmitted by any means—whether auditory, graphic, mechanical, or electronic—without written permission of both publisher and author, except in the case of brief excerpts used in critical articles and reviews. Unauthorized reproduction of any part of this work is illegal and is punishable by law.

Unless otherwise indicated, Bible quotations are taken from The New King James Bible. Copyright © 1992 by Thomas Nelson.

ISBN: 979-8-88640-633-7 (sc)
ISBN: 979-8-88640-634-4 (hc)
ISBN: 979-8-88640-635-1 (e)

Because of the dynamic nature of the Internet, any web addresses or links contained in this book may have changed since publication and may no longer be valid. The views expressed in this work are solely those of the author and do not necessarily reflect the views of the publisher, and the publisher hereby disclaims any responsibility for them.

One Galleria Blvd., Suite 1900, Metairie, LA 70001
1-888-421-2397

Dedicated to the lives of
Sam Vinton Sr. and his beloved wife, Marie,
and
The Only Constant they served.

The contributions of experiences, historical information, editing skills, encouragements and patience that have been afforded me in the ten year process of creating this book are beyond recording. I can not begin to name all the people who have helped along the way. But I do genuinely appreciate every thread of information and creative skill from every one of you, and you know who you are! I fully trust God will reward each of you in a greater way than I could ever dream of doing. So my thanks has taken the form of prayer, and God will, as always, listen to my heart. Thank you each and every one.

The art sketches attributed to Sara are the work of Kimberly Mangus who I am proud to call my daughter.

Chapter One

The usual collection of grubby men and drunks lined the sidewalk watching idly as a cab pulled to the curb fronting the rescue mission. The driver wondered to himself if this batch of derelicts was leftover from the midday soup kitchen or just early for the evening handouts. He really didn't care, he was just nervous about dropping off his current fare in such a dismal if not dangerous place.

Sara's hazel eyes sparkled with mischief. She knew the driver was uncomfortable bringing her to such a place, but today she didn't feel like explaining that she lived here. It was her home, and had been all her life. Sara Calhoun was a pretty girl, and nearly seventeen. Her long wavy hair couldn't really be called red, but more a rich auburn. She concealed her freckles behind a mask of artfully applied makeup.

Having paid the required fare, she scooped up her packages: several bags from the mall, a thick bundle of mail from the post office, and a magnificent bunch of flowers she had picked up for her Dad.

"Thank you sir," Sara said as she pushed the taxi door open with her foot and scrambled backwards onto the sidewalk. "I'll be fine here, really."

A blurry-eyed drunk recognized her and grinned a toothless greeting. "Hi there, Miss Sara." He lurched to open the mission door for her.

Sara was well acquainted with the foul breath and body odor of the men her parents ministered to. "Thanks, Bob," she said holding her breath and smiling sweetly. "Close the door quietly please. I'm sneaking in, OK?"

"Of course, Miss Sara, flowers for your Momma, eh?" Bob grinned and nodded as if he understood Sara's request, but the door still whacked Sara's backside as she maneuvered her packages inside.

Oh well, better me than the door frame, Sara thought to herself, *much quieter that way*. Now the trick was to get the flowers nicely arranged in a vase and onto the dining room table without her Mom catching her at it.

Dad liked to surprise Mom with flowers. It wasn't their anniversary or her birthday, and he wasn't apologizing for anything. He just liked to shower her with lovely things when she least expected it. Truth be known, Beth Calhoun was no longer surprised by her husband's thoughtfulness. But she did appreciate his attempts to surprise her, and how he roped Sara into the scheme. So she always made a fuss over them.

Hurrying down the hall, Sara stuck her head into the kitchen. Mrs. Schaffer was busy stirring up a batch of brownies and caught the movement out of the corner of her eye.

"Ya Ma's not in here, Sara girl, come on in."

"It's a good thing I don't have to hide things from you!" Sara grinned at the old cook and pulled herself and her bundles through the door into the mission kitchen. She dumped everything but the flowers onto an empty table, and headed for the deep sink.

"The vase ya be needin's in the pantry."

"Thanks, Mrs. Schaffer. Aren't these flowers just the best?"

"Ya' Dad's in his office. When ya get those flowers arranged, put them in the pantry and take the note card to him. I'll distract ya' Ma if she comes down."

"Thanks, Mrs. Schaffer. You're a wonderful partner in crime." Sara disappeared into the mission pantry and banged around, looking for the promised vase.

"Lordy, Chile. Could ya hold the noise down a bit?"

"Mom'll just think it's you making noise in here. If I were quiet, she'd know for sure something's up!"

"Ya Ma has know'd what was up from day one and ya know it."

"Now don't go spoiling the fun of trying to surprise her," Sara laughed. "The illusion is half the fun."

Sara did her flower arranging and hid the masterpiece in the pantry behind the rice bin. Returning to the kitchen she cleaned up the mess she'd made, picked up the tiny card that came with the flowers and headed for her Dad's office. She found him alone.

"Here's the card, Dad. Put your super sappy note on it, and I'll add it to the flowers. They're hidden behind the rice bin in Mrs. Schaffer's pantry."

"Thanks, princess. You're my angel! Anything vital in the mail?"

"Oh, the mail! I forgot it in the kitchen. I haven't looked yet." Sara whirled around and headed back down the hall to the kitchen where she snatched up the mail and scrounged Mrs. Schaffer's kitchen shears to snip the cord holding all the pieces together. She began sorting through envelopes as she walked back to the office. David Calhoun had finished his note when she returned and handed over the business mail. Still she continued flipping through the rest of the mail as if on a mission.

"They've come!" She suddenly squealed, holding a long envelope from Continental Airlines up to the light. "Our tickets are here!" Unable to control her excitement, Sara dumped the rest of the mail on her Dad's desk, and went screeching down the long hallway back to the kitchen. She swung Mrs. Schaffer around, hugging her, "I'm going to Paris, I'm going to Paris," she chanted. Grabbing her mall purchases, she headed for the private freight elevator that led to her families loft above the mission.

Trailing behind, David Calhoun ducked into the pantry to fix his card to the flowers, and returned to the kitchen to shake his head at Mrs. Schaffer. "The energy of the young! It never ceases to amaze me. Is everything under control here? Do you need anything?"

"No sir, Mr. Calhoun, I be doing this job now twenty years. I think I gots everything under control!" The old cook tried to sound cross, but failed. Her boss knew her too well to be fooled by her gruff exterior. She was soft as melted butter, dependable and loyal to a fault.

She'd had a hand in raising his headstrong daughter because keeping the little tyke out of her kitchen had been impossible. As soon as Sara was old enough to hold a crayon, Mrs. Schaffer used that ploy to keep the child out of her hair. But early on she realized the child had a good eye for detail, and Mrs. Schaffer took on the task of teaching her how to draw, color, and paint. Sara was quick to catch on, and the time they spent together became the challenge and highlight of the old cook's day. Tutoring Sara in the arts gave Mrs. Schaffer opportunity to exercise her own self-taught talent. Over the years their shared love of art created a special bond between the two.

"You're going to miss that girl and her mother while they're gone," the boss taunted.

"Ya don't need to go telling me what I'm gonna do, Mr. Calhoun. Ya jist git out o' my kitchen and leave me be!"

Mr. Calhoun knew when it was time to give the cook space and headed back towards the office to finish his day's business.

"Mr. Calhoun," Mrs. Schaffer called after him. Pausing in the doorway, Mr. Calhoun looked expectantly at Mrs. Schaffer.

"Ya'll hav'ta deliver ya own flowers this time. Sara's mind be on that trip to Paris now. Ya know how one-track minded she be."

"I know," he grinned. "Thanks for the reminder."

Chapter Two

The evening meal proved to be one to remember. Dad presented the flowers to his wife when he came in from work. This time she was genuinely surprised because she had become accustomed to Sara sneaking them into place. Then Mom had a surprise of her own to share over the evening meal. "Not only did today's mail give us tickets to Paris, we also got a card from Uncle Ross. He writes:

"Dear Ones, greetings from Cameroon, Africa. Congratulations to Sara for graduating high school with honors, and early to boot! Way to go, Sara! In a couple weeks I'm taking time off the job to make another trip into the heart of the Congo to visit my dear old friend, Baba V. His energy refreshes my soul and makes me feel young again. I'll get you all souvenirs. Love, Ross."

Sara didn't know much about Baba V, but she knew her uncle valued his time with the ancient missionary. Uncle Ross often sent native craftwork from his trips into the Congo. The clever items made interesting room accents. Her favorite gift was an intricate basket which she filled with silk flowers. The contrast between the rough jungle craft and the delicacy of the silk plants appealed to her artistic side. Uncle Ross had taken a picture of the young African woman making the basket, and attached it to the inside of the weave. She was a pretty girl, no older than Sara. She had a baby strapped on her back, and Sara wondered if it was her own or a sibling. The baby was precious, as were all babies in Sara's eyes, and the soft black eyes smiling out of the tiny black face never failed to bring a gentle smile to Sara's face.

"It's too bad Ross can't meet us in Paris," Beth Calhoun commented absently to herself, and Sara knew her mom was trying to think of some way to convince her brother to do just that.

It would be fun to see Uncle Ross again. It had been nearly a year since he took the Cameroon assignment. Sara loved to hear him talk about his adventures and he'd surely have some new yarns to share by now.

Talk turned to the following day's activities and Sara rattled on excitedly about an all-day youth event at church. "Everybody's going. Pastor Ed will bring me home. Can you drop me off at the church by noon?"

"What's the agenda?" David Calhoun asked. "First we're going out for three games of bowling and pizza. Then we're going to play a round of miniature golf and get ice cream. Finally we're going back to the church for a movie there. It's only $20 for everything, and I won't be out really late. Can I go?"

"Tomorrow's the open house over at the community center," her Dad responded. "Bob and Carol asked us to be there to help keep an eye on things. They're hoping a lot of parents will come to see how their kids are spending their community service hours. Maybe we can build a few relationships that way. Your mother and I promised to be there and help out, but I suppose it won't hurt for you to miss it. You don't get to spend enough time with young people your own age. Beth, do you have any objections?"

"No, I know Sara will be in good hands, and I've heard good things about the movie Pastor Ed is showing. It's fine with me."

"You're the best! I'll take kitchen cleanup tonight." Sara rose to clear away the table. Evenings belonged to her parents, at least the evenings they didn't have chores downstairs at the mission. This was one of those rare nights, and Sara wanted them free to enjoy one another's company.

"Thank you, daughter. I appreciate your help, but you're still not wearing my Bronco sweatshirt tomorrow!" Sara glanced up to see the twinkle in her Dad's eye, and knew he was teasing her. He knew full well she wouldn't be caught dead in that horrid baggy old thing, and the game was on.

"But Dad, I *need* that sweatshirt!" she whined.

"Nope. Not going to happen. You'll just have to break in one of those new outfits you bought to wear in Paris."

"Ohhh well, life's tough all over!" Sara grinned and disappeared into the kitchen backwards, carrying the stack of dirty dishes with her.

The following day's activities were as enjoyable as Sara had anticipated. Five of her fellow 'homeschooled' pals had also been there, adding to the energy of the day. She thought nothing of Officer Kelly's squad car parked in front of the mission when she returned home. That wasn't an uncommon occurrence. But the look on Mrs. Schaffer face, standing silently in the doorway, made her heart stop. Tears streamed down the old cook's face, as she rushed to enclose Sara in her arms the moment she got out of Pastor Ed's car.

"What's happened, Momma Schaffer? You're scaring me."

Officer Kelly came out of the mission and escorted the two back inside. Pastor Ed realized all was not right and followed. The mission's chaplain, Pastor Evans, waited inside and gently guided them all into the small chapel at the end of the hall.

"What's going on?" Sara demanded trying to control her mounting panic.

Clearing his throat and twisting his hat in his hands, Officer Kelly began to explain. "There was a drive-by shooting at the community center tonight. We think it was a gang retaliation or initiation. We don't know for sure which. Five people were wounded. A small child and both your parents were killed. I am so sorry, Sara."

Sara stared in disbelief at the officer, then at Pastor Evans, then back at the officer. This couldn't happen in her family. They were good people. They dedicated their lives to stopping pain and suffering. How could they possibly be a victim of it?

"Ya folks be gone, Sara chile', they be gone!" sobbed Mrs. Schaffer.

A coldness clutched at Sara's heart, threatening to squeeze the very life out of her. It spread to her spine. She visibly stiffened and thrust her chin out. Pulling free from Mrs. Schaffer's grasp, Sara walked stiffly from the chapel to the freight elevator.

"Sara, are you okay?" Pastor Ed moved in front of Sara as if to stop her.

Okay? How could anything ever be okay again? She wondered, but she said, "I'm okay, I just need to be alone for a while." Pastor Ed respectfully moved out of her way and let her go. The elevator lifted her to the home above where there was no one to greet her.

She wandered aimlessly from room to room staring blankly at family treasures and reminders of countless family adventures. Time seemed to stand still. A headache set in and gradually grew from a dull throb to a debilitating crush. Finally Sara fell across her parents' bed, aware that they would never rest there again, and that nothing would ever be the same again, and let the oblivion of sleep block out her agony.

Chapter Three

A full week had passed since the shooting and Sara moved through her days as if in a dream. Grief and anger took turns churning inside her.

Only a week prior, life had been as normal as life could be for any homeschooled sixteen-year-old filled with excitement over a pending tour of Paris. Teaching had been Beth Calhoun's passion, and Sara her only student. Sara enjoyed learning new things, and passed her graduation exams with honors. Her parents had been so proud of her. Now they lay side-by-side under a simple marble grave stone etched with the words:

> David and Beth Calhoun
> Faithful Servants of the Living God

Sara had chosen the words herself, as well as the site under a beautiful old oak tree at the Forest Lawn Cemetery.

Now she sat alone, staring blankly out the airplane window into the darkness beyond. She knew in the depths of her heart that her parents had gone to a far better place, but that knowledge did not ease her anger, pain, or loneliness.

Leaning back against the seat she squeezed her eyes shut as the plane backed away from the Los Angeles terminal.

The emptiness of the seat between her and the oversized businessman on the aisle taunted her. Tears burned her eyes and she turned her head toward the window to hide her grief. Thoughts and emotions struggled to escape her stubborn resolve not to cry.

Mom belongs in that seat! We're supposed to be here together! We worked so hard for our tour of Paris. What good is graduating high school ahead of schedule now? I wish gangbangers would stick to killing each other, but no, heaven forbid they leave innocent people alone! Oh no! They don't care who they kill! They just drive away like cowards thinking they are tough! Well they are not tough! I want to slam their cowardly stupid heads together till they're dead and can't hurt anyone else ever again! It's all so useless!

Sara's anger was not eased by her turbulent thoughts, nor did she realize their self-destructive nature until her fingers went into spasm from prolonged gripping of the armrests. In anguish she forced her thoughts heavenward.

Please, please, God, help me through this bitterness. I know you love those gangbangers just as much as you love everybody else, but don't expect me to! Please forgive me and help me find Uncle Ross! I don't want to be alone.

A flight attendant stationed herself in the aisle and began demonstrating the safety features of the aircraft. Sara deliberately shut out the sound of her voice and continued to face the window. *Maybe the plane will crash and free me of this pain. See, I can be cowardly too!*

Deliberately she forced her thoughts to drift to the grandfather who had been farsighted enough to name her parents as trustees and recipients of his living trust, and Sara as his sole beneficiary. Because of this, Sara's training in how to handle money had begun at a very early age. Since the age of twelve she had her own savings and checking account, and was expected to keep two thousand dollars in her checking account to avoid monthly service fees. Dividends were automatically added to her savings from stocks Grandfather had given her for birthdays or special events. That money was to pay for a college education and for travel adventures.

Grandfather had made it possible for her to leave behind all things familiar. The hassle of lawyers and wills were not going to slow her escape. It strengthened her to realize the extent of Grandfather and her parents' trust in her. Grandfather's foresight gave Sara immediate ownership of everything, should anything unforeseen ever happen to her parents. And it had. Now she felt the weight of that responsibility, but wasn't ready to accept it all at once.

I'm only 16, God, she prayed through clenched teeth, *so you'll have to help me. I **am** grateful I'm provided for. Please help me know when, if ever, I misuse Grandpa's money, and help me know how to invest it wisely. I do want to carry on Daddy's mission work of teaching others about you. I know I must do that much!*

Grandfather had died peacefully of old age two short years earlier. She still missed his periodic visits. He always brought her something interesting from his travels. Grandmother, God rest her soul, died long before Sara was born. She had been a wonderful Godly woman of faith, and no one ever replaced her in her husband's affections. It didn't surprise Grandfather that their only child, a son, adopted his mother's passionate belief in, and love for, God Almighty.

Dad tried, but could never get interested in managing his father's overseas clothing plants. For one thing, he hated traveling, something Grandfather never understood. Secondly, high finance and the corporate world were not what sparked life in him. Dad's motivating passion was to help troubled people come to know God.

"Life on earth is short," he always said. "Life after death is forever! I want to live my life in a way that pleases God and prepares me for life hereafter. Eternity is forever, and that goes far beyond our earthbound potential of a measly seventy plus or minus years!"

Grandfather never really understood his son, but he respected his faith. So he arranged for a buyer, pending his death, who was willing to pay a fair price to gain the empire he had built. Upon his death, dividends from his many well-placed investments were set up to funnel into Sara's money market account and a small portion to her savings account, to be used at Sara's discretion.

The bulk of the cash sale was placed in trust for his son and daughter-in-law, as trustees, and remained at their disposal until their death, at which time the remainder passed to Sara, regardless of her age. Grandfather never believed in using his wealth to control or manipulate his heirs. It was legacy enough for him that his only son, daughter-in-law and grand-daughter should never want for anything.

To the casual traveler Sara looked older than 16. The grief etched on her face contributed more to this illusion than the stylish hairdo or her Mom's elegant business suit. Sara had nudged the illusion one step further by kicking up her usual Spartan use of makeup, and using her own face as a canvas upon which to utilize the skills learned from Mrs. Schaffer.

While she preferred the denim blue jeans, comfy t-shirts, and tennis shoes packed in the cargo bay below, Sara feared looking her own age while traveling half way around the world. She settled on wearing Mom's navy blue business suit with a soft no-nonsense white blouse, navy pumps, and carried her Mom's matching purse. As well as lending her some of her mother's confidence, the suit was made for travel, low key yet professional and not prone to wrinkle. Even after two days on an airplane, she wanted to appear neat and sophisticated - not young, crumpled and vulnerable.

The night before her departure, Sara practiced braiding her hair in a double French braid. Her father had been so proud of her wavy waist-length auburn hair that she didn't yet have the heart to cut it. The crown of rolled braids brought the length up and offset her pale, thin face, emphasizing the depth of green in her eyes. Today a bit of carefully placed makeup hid the freckles splashed across her slightly upturned nose, and gave Sara a clear, artfully blushed complexion. But makeup did not put the sparkle back in her eyes.

Mrs. Schaffer did not approve of Sara's deception, but then she wasn't happy about Sara flying off to her Uncle alone either. The woman had known Sara since her birth, and taught her everything she knew about art. Her self-appointed role as protector of the girl held rougher elements in the mission neighborhood at bay. No one dared challenge the woman. She was respected if not feared in the community. Big-boned and tall, she towered over most of the men in the area. She commanded a confidence that made one believe she was as formidable as she looked.

Sara was more familiar with Mrs. Schaffer's tender side, for she had seen her paint the tiniest details of a hummingbird's wing, and daub sparkle into the eyes of a baby kitten pouncing on a ball of yarn. Time after time Mrs. Schaffer had guided Sara's hand while teaching her the same skills. The bond between the two was undeniable, but since her parents death Sara found she could not reach out for Mrs. Schaffer's comfort.

After the shooting Mrs. Schaffer deserted her own living quarters to stay with Sara at the Calhoun loft above Calhoun House, the innercity mission complex.

"Yer parents would never forgive me if I didn't watch out for ya, Sara girl," Momma Schaffer insisted tenderly. "I know ya can take care of yerself, chile', but let me be feelin' useful now! Even if'n *ya* don't need it, I do!"

Mrs. Schaffer knew Sara wasn't up to talking, and gave her the space and privacy she needed to cope with her grief. All week she made certain Sara ate at least one good hot meal a day. When Sara said she was going to visit her uncle, Mrs. Schaffer pressed a phone card into her hand, and insisted that Sara call her often.

"I don't need your phone card Momma Schaffer."

"Now don't ya go hurt'n my feelin's, chile'. I know it ain't much, but I needs to give this to ya. I needs ya to keep in touch with me. One never knows what'll happen when they travel away from home!" Rather than offend, Sara accepted the card.

"You'll keep an eye on the apartment, won't you, Momma Schaffer? Uncle Ross and I will come back to pack everything up and decide what to do with it."

"Of course, chile'. Ya be knowing I will. I jist don't understand why that uncle of your'ens can't be meetin' ya here!" Misgivings for Sara's safety made Mrs. Schaffer's voice sound gruffer than usual.

"The Chicago office keeps Uncle Ross pretty busy." Sara offered only half the truth. She didn't want to lie, but if Mrs. Schaffer knew she was going all the way to Africa to find her uncle, she would most certainly find some way to stop her.

"I'll be OK, Momma Schaffer. God will watch over me." Sara wasn't sure her statement was of any comfort considering how God had "watched over" her parents, but she said the words anyway, then squeezed the apartment keys into Mrs. Schaffer's hand.

"The bank has been instructed to continue paying Calhoun House's monthly operational budget—I told Pastor Evans already. I promise I'll keep in touch with you all by e-mail." Sara had put her arms around the beloved old woman and hugged her—more out of guilt than emotion. She full well knew how hurt Momma Schaffer would be when she learned of Sara's deception.

The plane finally gained the runway and began to pick up speed. The weight of the plane shifting from the wheels to the wings caused Sara to open her eyes and peer through the dark window at the life she was leaving behind. The night sky hid any possible view of the cemetery from her, but it didn't matter. Sara knew her parents were in Heaven with the Lord, only their bodies remained behind in the grave.

She forced her thoughts towards Africa and finding Uncle Ross. He was the only blood relation she had now.

Chapter Four

Kent Cooper tapped his strong fingers on the restaurant's tabletop as his hungry gut threatened to gnaw clear through to his backbone. His impatience didn't hurry the medium-rare steak dinner he'd ordered, or improve his mood. Looking around to ease the boredom, he focused in on the *Los Angeles Times* being read in the next booth.

"Say, you're reading a California paper! Did you just fly in from the West Coast, or do you subscribe to the *L.A. Times*?" Kent spoke just loud enough to be heard by the man in the next booth. No one could ever accuse him of being shy.

Turning sideways to see who was talking, the businessman came face to face with the handsome young man. His annoyance at the stranger's intrusion on his privacy quickly disappeared when he saw genuine interest and a smile in Kent's alert brown eyes.

"Picked it up in California on my last trip through. It's an old paper, just kept hold of it for a specific article I needed for a project." The man waved his fork in the air, "You have people out in California?"

"My folks live out there," Kent stated. "Grew up there, haven't been back for a couple of years. I miss the ocean. Lake Michigan is all right, but it's just not the same."

"I'm about finished here. You want the rest of this paper?"

"Hoped you'd ask," grinned Kent. "It might help me pass the time while I wait for my meal. They are *really* slow tonight."

"I lucked out by just beating the crowd," the man retorted as he turned back to his meal and paper. Within moments he gathered up his belongings and handed the remains of the paper to Kent as he left.

Kent flipped idly through the pages, but couldn't find much of real interest. The front page was old news, the food section didn't help his already growling stomach, and the classified ads certainly weren't entertaining. He was about to give up when a small photograph of a smiling Beth and David Calhoun caught his eye. His blood ran cold when he realized he was looking at the obituary page.

"I know these people," he muttered under his breath. He had met Beth and David at the age of 11—ten years earlier. It had been a very bad time in his life. His Dad had come home drunk and unruly one night, and his frightened mother had grabbed Kent and his sister and fled. She didn't want anyone in their daily life to know what had happened, so she went to the mission shelter, where she often sang for their chapel services. She liked the levelheaded Beth Calhoun, and her husband, David, codirectors of the mission. She knew they would keep her confidence and put them all up for the night. If anyone saw them, she could say they were there to help Beth plan a special project at the mission.

The kindness extended to his mother had made a lasting impression on the young Kent. Beth and David spent their lives serving the less fortunate. Directing Calhoun House, an inner city mission for the homeless, was not Kent's idea of a desirable life-style. Yet it suited Beth and David, and they seemed genuinely happy in their work—in spite of the hardships. Kent planned to repay that kindness some day. Now it appeared he may have waited too long.

Quickly he scanned the tiny article next to the photo. "Services for David and Beth Calhoun, directors of the Calhoun House inner city mission for the homeless, will be held at 5 p.m. today at the Berean Christian Bible Center in Los Angeles. The Calhouns were two of three victims killed in a drive-by shooting at the Jurupa Community Center on Friday evening. Gang initiation rites are suspected as the motive for the drive-by shooting that also took the life of a three-year-old child. . . ." Whew, Kent whistled under his breath. Scanning down he read

> ". . . The couple are survived by their daughter,
> Sara, and Beth's brother, Ross Mann."

Ross Mann! I know a Ross Mann, I wonder if it's the same one.
Ross worked out of the same Chicago office as Kent and was currently supervising construction of the Tarbell road and pipeline project in Africa. *If this is the same Ross, then perhaps I can still do a kindness for the Calhoun family. I'll check Ross' file when I get back to the office. Maybe there's some advantage to being an office clerk after all.*

Thinking back ten years, Kent vaguely remembered Sara. *I was 11, she was around 7, so she's about 4 years younger than me, give or take.* Quickly he subtracted the numbers in his head. *I'm 21, so little Sara's . . . probably still in high school. That being the case, she still needs family to care for her. The Ross I know strikes me as good family...a bit of a free spirit, but definitely good family.*

"Here you go, Sir. Sorry your meal took so long. We're a bit shorthanded tonight." The waitress set a steak before him and Kent laid the newspaper aside.

The steak was a bit overcooked, but he was too hungry to send it back and wait for another one. Besides, he wanted to swing back past the office on his way home and do a little investigative work. If Ross *was* Beth's sole surviving brother, he would fax a copy of the obituary to him at the African office, with instructions to get word to Ross immediately.

Chapter Five

"Would you like something to drink, Miss?" asked the flight attendant, breaking into Sara's solitary thoughts.

For a moment Sara stared at the woman in confusion, then pulled herself together and offered a weary smile. "I'd like a cola, please."

Enough of this, Sara thought to herself, *I've got to focus on the future, not the past.* She accepted the plastic cup of ice and cold can of soda.

"Thank you," she muttered, and looked away. Mom and Dad had been gone a week. The time went by in such a blur Sara hardly remembered any of it. She knew there had been a funeral, and that it was attended by hundreds of people. Those folks would miss her parents' cheerful encouragement, and their constant reminder that with God, all things were possible. Sara trusted that Pastor Evans had taken advantage of the funeral to present a strong salvation message, but she was submerged too deeply in her own grief to have noticed.

Uncle Ross should have a few days left at the job-site in the jungle before his quarterly break. She could not imagine him being able to rush home in time for the funeral, so she did not even try to contact him. It was after the funeral that she decided to exchange Mom's ticket to Paris for an extension of her own ticket on into Africa to tell Uncle Ross about their loss in person.

She'd always loved to travel, and hoped traveling to Africa would give her the much needed change of scenery.

A best friend to talk with in person might have helped. But her closest friends were currently on foreign mission fields with their families. That was the problem with homeschooled student bodies. They were altogether too mobile. E-mail was wonderful for keeping in touch with such friends, but not so good for literal hugs or just silent sharing. The distance between them was almost tangible, making her feel even more alone.

Doing her studies at the mission had provided Sara with little time to get to know the church kids well enough to confide her deepest agony to them. She would work on that problem now. She was through school, and into world travel. Perhaps she would go visit her close friends at their new mission homes. She was now a free agent, with freedom to move about as desired …within reason… after she found Uncle Ross.

Beth Calhoun had successfully turned the mission's top level into a homey loft, secure against the poverty and hardship all around them. But without her folks, the residence was lonely, and Sara just wanted to be away from there. While being a good base of operations, and a familiar place to sleep, the loft offered little else but painful memories.

The tiny kitchen reminded Sara of the times she and Mom had pretended to be great chefs, preparing gourmet meals for Dad. Mrs. Schaffer knew this and short-circuited that reminder by insisting Sara join her down in the mission kitchen for all her meals.

Sara had ignored the telephone messages of well-wishers. She also ignored the multitude of scam artists thinking the family "fortune" was somehow now destined to end up in their own laps. She just didn't have the energy for it. Her finances were for personal living expenses and opportunities to help others come to know God. Mom and Dad would be disappointed in her if she did any less.

To bide her time while waiting to depart for Africa, Sara immersed herself in preparations for the trip. "I don't want to take anything heavy or bulky," she told Mrs. Schaffer. "So I'm replacing all my desk-top heavy tools with lightweight portable electronic ones." And Sara took on the challenge of acquiring everything she could possibly need—yet carry with her easily.

Grandfather's old briefcase was the only item Sara clung to that failed to look snappy and professional. *A new one might be too much temptation for someone to steal,* she reasoned. *Who'd want to steal a worn-out, old tattered briefcase like this one?* She filled the briefcase with her hardest to replace items, and those items most likely to be damaged if slammed around on a conveyor belt, like her laptop computer and digital camera. She carefully smuggled in area maps of Africa, her paperback English/French dictionary, and a small bottle of water purification tablets from their earthquake preparedness kit, being very careful that Mrs. Schaffer not see them, and finally her own note filled Bible and a sketch pad and pencils.

Fearful she might need additional vaccinations to acquire a visa for Cameroon, Sara spent time surfing the internet to confirm her suspicions. Suspicions confirmed, she reluctantly took herself back to Dr. Austin's office.

"I am so sorry for your loss, Sara. Your parents were wonderful people. What are you going to do now?" asked Dr. Austin's nurse with compassion in her voice and eyes.

"I'll be visiting family in Cameroon, Africa. I'm not certain how long I'll stay, but at least two weeks," Sara answered nervously. She sorely missed her mother's calming presence.

Cringing involuntarily she added, "I need additional shots in order to get a visa for Africa."

Dr. Austin examined Sara with a no-nonsense professional attitude that was easier to handle than the nurse's well-intentioned compassion. His brisk manner made answering questions easier. "How many countries are you going to visit, Sara?"

"I don't really know yet. My uncle travels a lot. He travels all over the world on different construction projects. I plan to travel with him. Right now he's in Africa. Next year—who knows?"

"Then I'm going to give you the more extensive series of injections, Sara. You've already had most of the ones you'll need. The remainder I can give you today."

"Okay," Sara grimaced. "I know it has to be, but I really hate shots! Will I get sick like last time?"

"Perhaps. You may experience flu-like symptoms for a day or two, but nothing major." He handed her the yellow International Immunization Record and a prescription for chloroquinine, a malaria suppressant to be taken once a week.

On her way home Sara stopped by the offices where she and Mom had applied for their visas. She produced the updated immunization record from Dr. Austin's office and acquired the additional stamps needed for entering Africa.

Dr. Austin's questions about her travel plans returned to haunt her thoughts. *I do want to travel everywhere with Uncle Ross. He's no substitute for Mom or Dad, but he's all I have! I don't care where we go. It seems anyplace can be as safe as America!*

Sara packed two cases of chocolate power bars in the backpack in her suitcase. Each boasted the nutrients equivalent to one full meal. They were heavy, but the weight would lessen each time she ate one. They were a favorite quick snack, and hopeful insurance against having to eat roasted bugs somewhere in the jungles of Africa! *I've watched way too many survivor shows,* she chided herself.

The water purifier she brought would make any water safe for drinking. She'd learned about the dangers of drinking bad water in foreign lands from her mother. With Grandfather's travels to and from his foreign clothing plants, and Uncle Ross's surveying work taking him to various isolated places, her mother had made it a point to use their travels as geography and world history lessons.

The flight attendant reached Sara with the evening meal cart. "Would you prefer baked chicken or meat-loaf, miss?"

"Baked chicken, please." Sara accepted the dinner and requested another cola to wash it down. Nothing tasted good yet, her emotional state wouldn't allow it. But it didn't taste bad either, and she ate it all, noting she was hungrier than she had realized. It wasn't long before emotional exhaustion kicked in and she fell into a tortured sleep, reliving the senseless murder of her loved ones.

Chapter Six

Surveying and mapping routes for company pipelines was the kind of challenge Ross Mann enjoyed. This pipeline began near the central coast of Cameroon, Africa, and pushed northward 670 miles through rough, primitive terrain, into Chad, at Cameroon's northernmost tip.

The job was taking the better part of a year, and Ross looked forward to the day when an antacid would no longer be an essential course at every meal, and he could go stateside long enough to catch up to the ever-changing American culture.

Ross and his crew started every morning at 5:45, an hour before dawn. They allowed themselves very little time before breakfast to dress and prepare for the long drive over barely passable roads. Days were unbearably hot and humid, the work hard and dirty. Living in the army style camp of tents, with canvas shower stalls, mess tents, chemical toilets, and medics had lost its charm. Armed guards constantly stood watch over men and camp to protect both from the gangs of bandits that roamed the jungles.

En route to the advancing construction site, they passed scores of villages made of mud houses. The native people in the area lived off the land and had only rags to wear, yet the

Cameroonians were a friendly people, waving and smiling at the big white bwanas, in their caravan of Land Cruisers. They always seemed amused at the sight of white men.

From the drop-off point, the crew walked four to five kilometers (2-3 miles) into the bush to pick up the survey line and work their way northward. Two all-terrain vehicles hauled chain saws and survey equipment, medical supplies, fuel and water over small streams and steep slopes into the work area.

Ross' responsibilities included haggling with village chiefs over pipeline easements through their areas. Every tree and bush downed by the bulldozers had to be counted, and village chiefs were paid accordingly as progress was made. Ross enjoyed these lengthy interactions with the village chiefs. Occasionally one would know a little English, or some French, but if not, there were men on his crew to act as interpreter. Local residents constantly popped out of the bush to stand and stare as they worked their way through the jungle.

Machetes were a common sight. Everyone carried one, from the smallest children to the oldest elders. Ross himself carried one to chop away the under-brush or kill poisonous snakes in his path. Village men carried the biggest machetes, and as these wore down in size, they were passed off to the women who used them until they were small enough for the children to use. Once Ross was privileged to see a field of children, supervised by their teacher, wielding their machetes to mow down the grass and clear an area for the games they all enjoyed.

Ross had punched one of his crew, and pointing to the scene, asking, "Can you imagine that happening in America, 30 plus kids all entrusted with razor-sharp machetes at the same time and place? And we think ours is the land of "civilized" people?"

When 3:30 p.m. rolled around, the team returned to the pickup point and rode back to camp where promise of a tepid shower, nourishing meal, and net-covered resting quarters seemed like paradise.

Today held more promise than usual for Ross. He was due for a two-week break while camp was torn down and moved closer to the work zone, and knew that by this same time tomorrow he would be aboard a chopper skimming the rooftop of the jungle back to civilization. He couldn't help whistling as he road along.

"Ross must be due for a two-weeker," one of the men commented to the others.

"How'd you know?" Ross countered with a grin on his face.

"Anyone with enough energy to be a'whistling on the way home must be coming up on time off!"

"Yep!"

"What you going to do this time, Ross, pick yourself up some special little lady of the evening?"

The question brought a frown to Ross's face and he looked straight into the eyes of the man who so enjoyed antagonizing him for his faith in God.

"You know me better than that Eric. I'm picky about the souvenirs I bring home. Women, children, and sexually transmitted diseases aren't on my list. No, I'm going back to see that old friend of mine over at the Kama Station deep in Africa's interior."

"Must be some pretty little filly," Eric couldn't let the gentle reprimand go unchallenged. His jealousy of Ross stemmed from the respect the other men held for him. Eric didn't understand that 'God thing,' and didn't want to.

"Well, I think this ninety-one-year-old missionary doctor is more like a stubborn old mule than a pretty little filly." Ross grinned wickedly, and the other men chuckled. Eric shrugged defeat, looking as disgusted and uncaring as he could muster. If Ross wanted to be socially boring and miss out on the spice of life, let him.

Ross was a big man, taller than most and not unpleasant to look at. The hard work of cutting through resistant jungles had toned his muscles and tanned his extremities without diminishing the gentleness of his features or the dancing blue in his eyes. He was considerably less rugged when he shaved his bushy red beard but it served him well as a swamp cooler and mosquito barrier.

Ross had never married. His job paid well, but his travels did not easily accommodate a wife and family. He didn't want a wife who was satisfied just to share his name and money. He believed a woman should expect to live with her mate. He hadn't ruled marriage out permanently, only until he could settle down and provide a proper home and companionship for the right woman—should he ever find her . . . that was the real trick!

He had a sister in California, with a husband and daughter. They were really good people, and he kept track of them as best he could, but it was difficult when he spent so much time cut off from civilization.

Except for his job, Ross was free to come and go as he pleased. Now it pleased him to use his free time to travel inland to Kama to check on the welfare of the wiry old doctor, Baba V.

Chapter Seven

The lights of New York City were fading into daylight when Sara woke to the pilot announcing their descent towards New Jersey's Newark International Airport. Her fitful sleep had refreshed her some and she felt better able to face the day ahead of her. One quick glance told her that Grandfather's briefcase was still safely wedged under the seat in front of her.

Fixing her attention on the sights far below, she watched the city wake up. Cars scurried about, filing in and out of residential areas and swirling through freeway interchanges. She was amazed at the web of freeways and train rails that wove their paths into New York City. Her heart skipped a beat as the plane banked left and circled to land from the Eastern end of the airport. From that angle she could see a tiny Statue of Liberty standing diligently at the head of the New York Bay.

I bet it wouldn't look so tiny if I were standing at the base instead of seeing from this bird's-eye view, Sara's thought. *I wonder if my problems look that tiny to God.*

Reaching into her Grandfather's tattered briefcase, Sara pulled out her Bible, removed it from its protective case and paused to pray. *Thanks for being here, and for knowing how big my problems feel to me. Please guide me through your word, and this day. Keep me safe in this strange city and bring me safely back to the airport in plenty of time. Show yourself to me today, and forgive my doubts and fears. Amen.*

She opened the book, allowing the pages to fall open where they would. Her eyes fell on a favorite passage, colored over with her own green highlighter. Hebrews 13:5 and 6. "Let your conduct be without covetousness; be content with such things as you have. For He Himself has said, 'I will never leave you nor forsake you.' So we may boldly say: 'The Lord is my helper; I will not fear. What can man do to me?'"

Sara's eyes clouded with anger. Thumping the Bible shut she slammed it back into its protective case, and returned it to the tattered briefcase. *"Man can do plenty to me! They killed my parents and changed my whole life! How can you make such promises, God, when evil rules this world?"*

Conflicted with her own emotions, Sara allowed her attention to shift to the wispy clouds flashing past the window as the plane descended towards the runway.

So now I've got a twelve hour layover before my flight for Paris, Sara confirmed again and slid her itinerary back into Grandfather's briefcase. She was glad her bags were checked all the way through to Douala, Cameroon, Central West Africa. At least she didn't have to drag them around all day. After breakfast, she would check on the flight and be free to explore New York until mid-afternoon. Hunger tugged at her, and the thought of a hot cheesy supreme pizza and ice-cold cola made her long for this flight to be over. Continued soft snores came from the businessman next to her in spite of the increased activity around him. She was glad. She wasn't yet ready to be engaged in polite conversation. She still had some thinking and planning to do.

The plane landed and Sara gathered up her belongings and exited the plane. Gaining the terminal she set out to find that breakfast of hot pizza. Thankfully this International Airport was one of the few that offered pizza at 6 in the morning. After she satisfied her hunger, she located the international check-in counter. Only two others were waiting in line ahead of her, and Sara's turn came quickly.

"What airline are you flying, Miss?"

"Continental."

"Okay, let me check . . . what's your destination and time of departure?"

"Paris, France, and my flight leaves at 6:00 p.m."

The man behind the counter paused a moment to look into the eyes of the young woman standing in front of him. Her clear complexion, upturned nose, and auburn crown of braids appeared very sophisticated and professional, yet her voice sounded much younger. Misgivings flashed across his face, but after the pause, and Sara's unwavering return of his attention, he decided not to chance offending a paying customer.

"You need to check in by 4:00 p.m. Is your passport in order?"

"Yes, I believe so." She handed it to him, he checked it and handed it back.

"Three-thirty should give you ample time then." The man wrote a gate number on Sara's ticket cover and handed it back to her. She thanked him and once again stowed the tickets away. Turning, she made her way out the front of the terminal to a variety of taxis competing for customers.

Turning left immediately outside the doors, Sara walked briskly down the sidewalk, ignoring taxi-drivers' cries to ride in their cab. Her instincts warned her to choose her taxi-driver carefully. Pretending disinterest, Sara watched carefully for the one driver who had a look she thought she could trust. She passed over a dozen cabbies before seeing an elderly, kind-looking gentleman of a nationality that Sara couldn't quite place. He smiled warmly at her, and nodded his head slightly, but did not yell or warble at her.

Stepping quickly over to his cab she smiled back and asked if he was available for an extended period of time.

"Yaw, I can do that," he responded, and opened the back door for her. Carefully stowing her briefcase on the seat beside her, Sara waited for the driver to walk around the cab and get in. Then she introduced herself.

"My name is Sara."

"Yaw, my name is Ted." The driver paused to look closer at the young women in his rearview mirror. She looked very professional and confident, yet somehow he felt things were not as they appeared.

"Where would you be wanting to go, Miss?"

"I must be back here by 3:30 to catch my flight. I'd like to see the Statue of Liberty. Beyond that I haven't decided. Perhaps you'd suggest other historical sites that I'll have time to see."

"How old you be, child?" Ted's question shook Sara's resolve, and for a full moment she looked intently into the kindly eyes reflecting back at her in the mirror before answering his question.

"I'll be seventeen in May," she answered honestly.

Sara saw misgivings and concern expressed in Ted's eyes, and decided to trust him with the whole truth. "My parents were recently killed and I am on my way to meet my uncle." Something prompted her to continue. "I've deliberately made myself to look older as a precaution. I don't want folks questioning why I'm traveling alone. Looking older helps me to blend into the crowds a little easier."

Ted sat a moment, letting the information sink in. "You are a brave lass. I am sorry for your loss." Checking for traffic over his shoulder, he eased into the steady stream of cars moving along in front of the terminal, then continued, "I have a granddaughter just your age. She lives in the old country and doesn't get to visit my Martha and me very often. I will show you everything I have dreamed of showing my Alina."

"Alina is your granddaughter's name?"

"Yaw."

"Alina is Celtic for 'from a distant place'," Sara stated quietly.

"How you know that?"

"Alina's my middle name. Dad named me Sara Alina. It means 'princess from a distant place.' Dad said I was his princess on loan from Heaven." Sara's voice faded to barely audible as the memory of the last time her father called her princess surfaced. It was the day before he died, in his office when she gave him the flower card to sign. Needing to shake off the pain of that memory, Sara blurted out, "Ted is Greek for 'gift of God!'" Before the taxi-driver could question why or how she knew that tidbit of information, Sara quickly added, "My Grandfather's name was Ted. Knowing the meaning of our names was a big thing in my family."

"You are a marvel, child. Don't anyone be telling me God doesn't keep a keen eye for even the most insignificant details in our lives—right down to our names! Statue of Liberty is coming right up."

Ted's reassuring grin in the mirror strengthened Sara resolve to stay strong. *Perhaps this day will be easier than the last seven, and traveling far from home will be the tonic to help me drown out the dreams of what should have been.* Sara squared her chin and focused on the sights out her window.

Chapter Eight

Ross was delighted to learn that Bill Chapman was at the helm of the chopper that set down in camp the following day. He had flown with Chappy before, and liked the man. Chappy was in great demand and rarely available to fly supplies in and out of their Cameroon bush camp.

"Hey, Chappy, it's good to see you again. How's it that you've got time on your hands to come flapping your wind blades over our neck of the woods?" Ross grinned good naturedly at the ruddy-complexioned old man.

"Not much need for pilots over yonder these days. That Congolese government has frozen all independent airports and is closely monitoring the big international jobbies, and military ports. Can't fly much of the interior, so I've migrated back to the coast!"

"I was afraid of that. What's my best bet in maneuvering into Kama to check on the old doctor there?" Ross asked.

"That's a tough question. I don't know as I've got a good answer for ya. The jungle's crawling with rebels that'd just as soon shoot ya as spit on ya! What roads they got are knee deep in mud this time of year, with potholes you have to drive into, cross, and drive out of! I fear you're on your own there, pal."

"You're no help," bantered Ross tossing his gear into the luggage bay he had just emptied of supplies. "Well, let's get going. At least get me as far as Douala."

The talk turned to other topics and for the next two hours they enjoyed one another's company and the scenic views that passed below the chopper. Steel plates rested beneath each seat, a throw back that spoke of Chapman's service during the Vietnam War as a low-flying chopper pilot. The extra steel gave additional protection from small arms fire coming up from below. The whip of the rotor blades drowned out their voices, so they communicated mostly by hand signals and pointing at this or that item of interest. Ross especially enjoyed skimming along the southern edge of the Adamaoua Mountain Range. There was just something grand about peaks, canyons and valleys that caused him to stand in awe of God's majesty. They said their goodbyes shortly after landing at Douala, the largest of Cameroon's three seacoast cities. Shouldering his gear, Ross set out on foot.

The first order of business was to get a room at the best hotel in town. It wasn't much to brag about, but offered private rooms, fairly clean beds, indoor plumbing, and hot showers. His stomach let him know that a hearty dinner should not be delayed. It was too late to go into the office anyway. They'd be shut down for the day. He'd go first thing in the morning.

The hotel lobby boasted a satellite TV, and Ross found himself stationed in front of it in time for the local and international news. He was hoping for some news of the Democratic Republic of the Congo. Chappy hadn't exaggerated the condition of transportation. The airports were locked down. Rebels ran through the city streets after dark shooting randomly at anything that moved and some things that didn't.

With all private planes grounded, Baba V would be stranded, cut off from supplies. Kama was nestled in the jungle near the junction of the Elila and Kama Rivers, 125 miles to the east of Kindu or 205 miles west of Bukavu depending on what direction one came from. Everything in between was jungle, small villages, a leper camp, and roving bands of rebels. This trip wasn't going to be easy.

Rwanda bordered the country on the East, across the border from Bukavu. The political climate suggested that Rwanda was probably responsible for the rebels overrunning the countryside. Rumor had it that powers in Rwanda wanted to overthrow the Congolese government and gain control over their vast and mineral-rich lands.

Most Rwandans were Hutu, farmers of Bantu stock. Less than 20% of the population were of the Tutsi tribe, a pastoral people that dominated politically until overthrown by a Hutu rebellion in the late 1950s. It was rumored that the Hutu tribes still carried a grudge against the surviving Tutsi. Though few and far between, a few pygmies also still roamed the forests as nomads, living off the land.

The news turned to local talk of lesser importance to Ross, and he decided it was time to turn in. The next thing he knew, the morning sun was shining through the window, full on his face.

The muted city sounds were different from the jungle noise he'd become accustomed to, and he took a couple of minutes just to listen. But it was a new day and there was much to do, so he did not indulge in wasting much time, and true to his resolve, he was sitting in front of the Tarbell Construction Office when the clerk arrived to open up for the day's business.

"Hey, Ross. It's good to see you. I've got a packet of mail that's yours. Decided to hold it for you, figured you'd be coming through." Ross followed the man inside the office and thanked him for the fistful of miscellaneous letters, office memos, e-mails and faxes he was handed.

"So, how's life been treating you, Clark?" Ross asked.

"Great. Not much happening to ruffle my feathers. As long as the Congolese and Rwandans keep their spat to themselves, and don't bring it over here, I'll be happy."

"That seems to be all the talk."

"Yeh, will you be skipping your visit with the old doc this time out?" Clark asked, his head tilted to one side as he tried to see Ross' reaction through his bifocals.

"Don't think so. This could be when ol' doc needs a visit the most. After 70 years entrenched in that soil he's been a Congolese citizen longer than most Congolese life span. They call him Baba V, or Daddy Vinton. I'd hate to think what would happen to any rebel that harmed a single white hair on his hallowed head. A lot of people there owe him their lives. God takes pretty good care of that ol' boy. I could tell you stories that would curl your toenails!"

"I just bet you could."

"But not today. Since I'm going, I'd best get to it. Thanks for the mail call. See ya in a couple of weeks."

"Take care."

Ross left the cool interior of the office, and found a shaded bench where he could sit to look through his small stack of mail. When his eyes focused on a scanned news clipping with the likeness of Beth and Dave on it, his heart nearly stopped beating. Quickly he read the note from Kent, a clerk at the head office in Chicago, then read the tiny article next to the photo.

"They're both gone, killed in a drive-by shooting? Of all things!" Ross questioned aloud, hearing but not believing his own words. "This can't be! Where's Sara? Who's taking care of Sara?"

Ross' eyes suddenly focused on the date of the funeral. "Hold it!" he roared, jumping to his feet. "This paper's a week old! I've got to get on the next plane to America. Sara needs me!"

~~~

Kent Cooper waited two days to hear back from Ross Mann in Cameroon. When no word came from Ross, he began to fear his fax had not reached its mark. A phone call revealed that Ross had been through the office, but that he was on his way to meet with an old friend deep in the heart of Africa. Something, the African office reported, he did on most of his two weeks breaks.

Kent also left numerous messages on the answer machine at the Calhoun residence. But while the machine continued to accept his messages, no return call was forthcoming.

Kent's thoughts tortured him. *The Calhouns have been gone over a week now. What happens to kids with no relatives to watch over them? Would the state put Sara in a foster home or orphanage? Surely they would have to search for Ross, but if they are having as hard a time reaching him as I am . . . well, what options do they have?*

Kent decided to make some calls himself, and waited impatiently as phone connections were made and finally answered in Los Angeles. "Social Services, Clare speaking," said a weary voice at the other end of the line.

"Good morning, Clare. My name is Kent Cooper. I'm looking for information on a young girl named Sara Calhoun. She was orphaned last week, and I'm trying to locate her whereabouts for her next-of-kin, Ross Mann. He is currently out of the country and I'm acting on his behalf. Can you tell me how to contact Sara?"

"What exactly is it you need to know, Mr. Cooper?"

"Well, for starters, do you know the whereabouts of Miss Calhoun? Is she is your custody?"

"Can you hold?"

"Certainly." Kent tried to sound pleasant and not too anxious. His frustration stemmed from the lack of a response from Ross Mann and Sara. No sense taking it out on Social Services.

"Mr. Cooper?"

"Yes?"

"I'm sorry, we can not release any information to a non-family member. Are you a direct relative of Sara Calhoun?"

"No. I told you, I'm acting on behalf of Sara's uncle, Ross Mann, who is working in Cameroon, Africa."

"Sorry, Mr. Cooper. I'm not at liberty to speak with anyone who is not family." And the connection went dead. Raw anger and frustration suddenly seethed from Kent's pores.

How can I be of help to anyone when I can't even find Sara or Ross?

Kent had a few personal days due him and a long weekend coming up. He pondered making a quick trip to L.A. With luck, maybe he could catch her at the mission, or speak with someone that would know where the girl had been placed. Perhaps she was even staying with Mrs. Schaffer and that was why he couldn't locate her.

I'll just go there in person, Kent decided and speed dialed the airlines. "I'd like a round trip ticket for one from Chicago to LAX."

Chapter Nine

Five o'clock found Sara aboard her flight to Paris. Her day with Ted had been one she would remember for a very long time. Before leaving the taxi, Sara convinced Ted to give her his address and phone number. "I'll send you and Martha a postcard from Paris, Ted. Then you'll know I made it there okay."

"Yaw," the man responded, "you send us a card when you have met up with your Uncle Ross too! My Martha and I will be praying for you. God will take care of you, I know that. He and I talk a lot. You'll be fine, young Sara. Go with God!" They shook hands; Sara squared her shoulders and resumed her journey.

The man at the customs counter did a double take when he heard her voice, but her forced confidence put off any question asking, and she marched smartly aboard the aircraft as if she'd done it every day of her life.

At seat 17A, Sara saw that she shared her row of seats with two children. Her carefully reserved window seat was occupied by an eager faced, tow-headed lad about seven years of age. Sitting next to him, and leaning across to look out the small window, sat a younger child Sara guessed to be about five. Long blond curls rested on her delicately flowered pinafore. Sara paused to look around to see where the parents of these small children might be. She made eye contact with the couple immediately behind them. An infant seat was carefully strapped in the seat between the man and woman.

"Miss, is this your seat?" The man asked, rising quickly to his feet, nearly bumping his head on the overhead storage.

"Yes, are these *your* children?"

"Yes. I'm Bill Howard. This is my wife, Mary. The boy here is Adam, the girl is Danell. I hope you don't mind children. They can be very energetic, but are generally well behaved. If they cause you any trouble, please, just signal me and I'll trade places with you." The father seemed nice and was obviously devoted to his family.

Perhaps the good in my day hasn't ended yet, Sara thought and smiled at Mr. Howard, "We'll get along just fine. I like children!"

Sara grinned as two pair of little eyes peering up at her. Danell smiled shyly and Adam flashed a grin at her exposing the loss of several front teeth, then turned his attention back to the window.

"I'll let you know if we have any trouble," Sara reassured the parents as she relinquished her right to be next to the window. *I shouldn't be selfish. After all, I've had the window seat all the way from California, and a wonderful day with Ted. Perhaps it'll do me good to share this time with little people. Good distraction. Right, God?*

Sara settled in the aisle position, stashing her briefcase under the seat in front of her again. Danell continued to look at her, and asked, "What's your name?"

"My name is Sara."

"Hi, Sara. Do you like to color? Do you like to read? I have some books here in my travel pack. I'll share with you!" Her smile was sweet and Sara knew she had a new friend. This time when the flight attendant gave instructions for flight safety, Sara paid close attention, and identified the location of the oxygen-masks and exits for herself and the children. *"Please don't let us need these oxygen masks!"* Her prayer was silent, but emphatic.

Liftoff was smooth, and the rapid gain in altitude made Sara's ears pop. Danell twisted her face in an effort to make her ears pop. Sara reached into her purse and pulled out a package of gum. Speaking above the acceleration of the engines and holding the gum over her head, Sara spoke to the parents sitting behind her. "Do you mind if I give your children some chewing gum to help them pop their ears, Mr. Howard?"

"That would be wonderful. Thank you," came the reply from behind.

"May I have a piece for me and one for Adam too?" Danell seemed eager to be the caretaker for her older brother. But Sara continued to hold the gum just out of the child's reach. "First—the rules of gum chewing are this: you may not play with gum **out**side your mouth, and gum is *not* to be swallowed. You must place it in a napkin when you are tired of chewing. Do you both promise to obey all rules of gum chewing?"

"We do," both children chimed together, and Sara nodded her approval, giving one piece of gum to each child.

"Mommy has the same rules as you, Sara!" Danell beamed proudly.

"My Mommy did too," Sara replied softly.

Sara was drafted into coloring Mickey Mouse and Donald Duck pictures across the page from Danell's artistic efforts on Minnie Mouse before the seatbelt signs were turned off. Sara delighted the child by sketching in a caricature of Adam, standing between Mickey and Donald. Adam kept his nose pressed against the window until they were too high and far out to sea for him to see anything below. Then he too watched with fascination as Sara captured his likeness on paper.

The flight attendant arrived with drinks for them all and by the time their drinks were finished, Danell was sweetly insisting, "Would you read us a story, Sara?"

"Well, okay. But if I am going to read to you, I should sit in the middle so you both can see the pictures." The shuffle of seats was quickly accomplished and seat belts reconnected. Danell pulled several thin story books from her travel pack and Sara read one book after another until they were interrupted by the flight attendant bringing their supper.

"You three seem to be getting along famously." Each child was given a special 'kid's meal' and Sara an adult meal. "I bet I could round up three extra chocolate chip cookies for such good travelers as you. Would you like them for a bedtime snack a little later this evening?"

"Yes, yes, yes!" chimed the children, and Sara smiled her acceptance as well. The flight attendant gave her a conspiratory wink and proceeded with the disbursement of the evening meals.

With meals completed and cleanup accomplished, Mr. Howard stepped forward to take the two youngsters to the restroom before settling in for the night. Sara took the opportunity to do the same. Mr. Howard insisted Sara use the restroom first, which allowed her a moment to herself back at the seats.

Sliding into the seat behind her own, Sara spoke softly to Mrs. Howard. "Your children are wonderful, Mrs. Howard."

"Thank you, Sara, for being so patient with them."

"How old is the baby?" Sara asked, peering into the sweet pink face of the tiniest Howard.

"She is only two-weeks-old. I'm still recovering from her delivery. Mr. Howard thought it best if he stayed close to me and the baby. But Darcy has proven to be a good little traveler. It seems we have been truly blessed."

The children returned with Mr. Howard, and Sara followed Danell back into their assigned seats. Adam settled into the aisle seat.

"Would you tell us a story now, Sara?" Danell asked shyly.

"Oh my, tell you a story? Well, let me think." Sara searched her memory for a story to share with Adam and Danell. Only one came to mind easily. She had told it many times to children at the mission shelter for homeless moms and children. "Okay, I know one. Have you ever gone fishing with your Daddy, Adam?"

"I did once! And I caught a little fish too."

"I did too," countered Danell, not wanting to be left out.

"Did you go out in a boat?" Sara asked.

"No, we fished from the side of the lake," the children said in unison.

"Well, this story took place on a big fishing boat. Jesus—do you know who Jesus is?" The children nodded so Sara continued. "Jesus had just preached to thousands of people beside a big lake, and he had fed them with five little loaves and two fishes, but that's another story. Jesus was so tired, that when he was done, he got into a big fishing boat and told his men to take him across the sea to the other side. He needed to rest, and knew that if he was on a boat the gentle waves would help him sleep really well. So he went into the lower level of the boat and quickly fell asleep. They started across the sea and do you know what happened then?"

"They went fishing?"

"No, but I'll bet they wanted to. No, a storm came up, and all of a sudden the gentle lapping waves whipped up into great big waves that splashed over the sides of the boat, and the wind tore at the sails and turned that boat every which way. The men got so scared they thought they were going to die!"

"What happened then?" Adam asked excitedly, snuggling close to Sara as if he were afraid as well.

"Well, the men were so frightened that they didn't know what to do. So they went down into the boat and woke Jesus up, saying, 'Don't you care that we are going to die in this storm?' Well now, Jesus wasn't afraid. He just looked at the men with sadness in his eyes. 'You just saw me feed 5,000 men, plus their wives and children, with five little loaves of bread and two small fish, and yet you become terrified in a little storm at sea?' Jesus shook himself awake, and going up onto the boat deck, he raised his arms like this," Sara raised her arms to show how Jesus might have done it, "and He said, 'Peace be still.'"

"What happened then?" Danell's eyes were big as saucers.

"The storm quieted, the water got as still and peaceful as a smooth mirror, reflecting the night moon and stars. And the men were amazed! They said, 'He must be the Son of God. Even the wind and the sea obey his voice.' The end."

"If Jesus can do that, he can keep us safe on this airplane, can't he?" Danell asked sincerely.

"Yes, Danell, he can."

Adam's eyes were thoughtful. "What do angels look like, Sara?" he asked.

"I don't rightly know, Adam. I've never seen one, but I'll bet they're beautiful. Don't you?"

"Yep!"

"Do angels protect us, Sara?" Danell wanted to know.

"God protects us, Danell, but I think sometimes he might use his angels to help him, don't you?"

The flight attendant arrived with three small paper bags, each containing a carton of milk and a big chocolate chip cookie, just as promised, and story time was over.

Mr. Howard, who had been eavesdropping on the story as it progressed, stepped forward to see what the flight attendant had brought the threesome, and mouthed "thank you," to her. Then he lifted down blankets and pillows from the overhead bin and set them where Sara could reach them easily after the children finished their bedtime snack.

Soon the cookies and milk were gone, and Sara tucked the children in, as best she could. She folded the armrests between them back between the seats, and allowed the children to prop their pillows against her. With all three seats reclined, Sara and the children squirmed this way and that until they found a comfortable position. It wasn't very long before both children were asleep.

I don't understand why you didn't protect Mom and Dad, God. But I thank you for sharing these delightful snugglers with me tonight, Sara prayed. *Thank you, Father God, for such thoughtfulness and care over me. Please see us all safely to our destinations. Amen.*

Chapter Ten

Ross Mann had no difficulty getting a flight out of Douala for Paris. His connecting flight to New York only gave him 15 minutes to change planes, but he was motivated to waste no time in getting where he needed to be. As his plane lifted off from Douala, the thought occurred to him that he should have called the mission. Why Kent read a Los Angeles newspaper was a mystery to Ross, but it was obvious by his actions that Kent had some knowledge of Ross' family, and some level of caring.

There wouldn't be time to call from Paris. Perhaps he would call from New York.

"You're looking a little agitated there, mate," spoke the man squeezed into the seat next to him, "everything all right with you?"

Ross looked at the man a moment before responding, and sized him up to be genuine in his concern. "I'm okay. Just anxious about my niece. I just learned that my sister and brother-in-law were killed over a week ago back in the states. I'm all the family she's got now."

"You been working out in the wilds, yeh? You got that look about ya. No offense meant, I just mean you look ready to take on the whole world."

"I hope it doesn't come to that!" Ross smiled lamely. It was a relief to have someone to talk to about the problem. He hadn't realized how tense he'd become. "Thanks for noticing and speaking up. It helps a bit to say it out loud."

"Awe, I didn't do anything. Only one who can ease this heavy load you be carrying is the Almighty upstairs. Now He's the one to help ya. But I'm happy to listen."

Ross stared silently at the rough traveler for a moment, wondering if the man had any genuine concept of what he had just said. Then he slowly answered, "I guess you're right there, mate. Thanks for calling that to mind."

Ross knew the man was right, and was a bit sore at himself for overlooking such an obvious source of strength. Ross thought, *"Ol' Baba V would not be pleased if he knew how easily I forget his teachings."*

"You have not because you ask not!" The Ol' doc had scolded him one time when he was complaining about some minor thing. "We don't always know what to do, but when we enlist God's help, the work is always easier. God has the answers we need. He has the strength needed with plenty to spare. When you rely on His great strength and wisdom, you don't get so flustered about how the work is going. Talk to God, Mann, talk to God!"

Silently Ross began talking to "the Almighty upstairs." *Lord, I don't know where Sara is, or if she's okay. I only know I wasn't there to comfort her when she needed me most. I can't rightly believe Beth and Dave are gone, but I know they're with you now. It's Sara I'm worried about. Please watch over her, and keep her safe. Help me find her, and help me be there for her when I do. Thank you, Father. Thank you.*

Chapter Eleven

Saying goodbye to her new little buddies was harder than Sara thought it would be. Adam and Danell didn't do much for her sophisticated professional image, but they were great distractions from her loneliness. She helped the Howards get off the plane with all their travel packs, jackets, and children, then wished them God's speed and safety. Danell turned to wave goodbye as they disappeared down the escalator to the baggage claim area below. *Okay, now I've four hours to kill before my plane leaves for Douala.* Sara sighed. *Well, first things first. I promised to get a postcard and send it off to Ted and Martha, and I need to get an e-mail off to Mrs. Schaffer.*

The airport boasted numerous gift shops and a large food court. Sara headed for a shop with twirling racks of picture postcards on display, and spent the better part of a half hour picking out just the right card, writing a note on it, then addressing it to Ted and Martha Cummins. The shopkeeper sold her the necessary postage stamp, and was kind enough to direct her to the nearest mailbox.

E-mailing Mrs. Schaffer wasn't quite as easy, but Sara finally figured out how to plug her laptop computer into a phone terminal, and sent off an e-mail that assured Mrs. Schaffer of her love and well being. Then she tucked her laptop away in the tattered briefcase, hoping no one had noticed her possessions.

Sara's flight arrived in Paris at 6:20 a.m., so no breakfast had been offered. Most of the travelers slept until they landed. It was nearly 7:30 a.m. before Sara decided that food would be a good thing, and headed for the food court.

I wonder what Uncle Ross is up to this morning, she mused to herself. *Lord, I've got to find Uncle Ross safe and sound. I'm an awfully long ways from home, and I've further to go. I've brought myself to a place where You're the only one I know so You'd better be real and here with me. I'm a bit nervous about what I've set out to do, so steady me, and guide my path. You're supposed to know what's best. Let's see what You've got. Please help me. Amen.*

The familiar golden arches of a McDonalds pulled Sara right into line for an Egg McMuffin, but by the time she took her place at the head of the line, she was ready for the "Big Breakfast," complete with sausage and hash browns. Familiar was good.

"I'll have hot chocolate to go with my Big Breakfast, and a large orange juice too, please." Food in hand, Sara searched for an open table, away from the throngs of scurrying people.

I want to sit with my back to the wall, she thought, then scolded herself. *You've read too many Louie L'Amours, Sara girl. You've got a cowboy-on-the-run's suspicion of folks working on you!* Regardless of whether it was street smarts from being raised in a rescue mission and trained to always be aware of her surroundings or the books she'd given the credit, she found a corner and sat with her back to the wall, wedging her grandfather's briefcase between herself and the side wall.

The breakfast was hot and good, and Sara realized once again that she was hungrier than she'd realized. She saved the hot chocolate to savor while reading her Bible. She'd been reading her Bible every day for so long, that just the familiarity of doing so brought her comfort. After flipping idly through several pages, Sara spoke in her mind again, *Lord, I'm not finding my food for thought, today. What would you suggest?*

For several moments Sara sat staring out into space, thoughtful but unfocused. Finally she forced herself to read several passages but her mind kept jumping from Los Angeles to New York, Paris to Douala, till finally she closed the book and replaced it in its case and put it away. *Maybe later I'll be better able to concentrate, but right now my mind is too 'all over the place,'* she apologized.

Gathering up her belongings, Sara joined the crowd milling about the terminal. The sights out big airport windows were the same the world over, planes, luggage wagons being towed behind motored carts, and airport buildings. Finally she returned to the assigned gate and waited for her group number to be called for boarding. Before long she was filing down the passage to the plane and sliding into yet another window seat.

As the plane gained altitude Sara gazed out the window at the night lights of Paris. She'd dreamed of seeing Paris her whole life. But she'd never thought she'd be seeing it for the first time like this.

One more leg of the journey, God. Then I'll find Uncle Ross and my life will begin again.

Ross Mann nodded a farewell to his travel mate, and nearly ran off the plane. He was the first person to reach the gangway and enter the Paris terminal. He had twenty minutes to find and board the flight to New York. He rushed past the food court, smelling the mixture of foods, and wishing he had time to acquire a Big Mac and fries, supersized, from the McDonalds. Hunger gnawed on his backbone, but he didn't have time to stand in any line waiting for food. He rushed on hoping they'd feed him on the next flight.

Lord, please don't let me miss that flight! he prayed fervently, and dodged back and forth through the milling crowd.

Reaching the customs desk, Ross handed his passport and ticket to the clerk. "I don't mean to rush you, Sir, but my flight leaves in ten minutes. I'd appreciate any help you can offer me."

"You'll make your flight, Mr. Mann. It's at gate three, through the corridor to your right." His tickets and passport were returned and Ross thanked God he had had the presence of mind to check his luggage all the way through to Los Angeles. He didn't stop to catch his breath until he was safely aboard his flight.

Thank you, Lord, for helping me catch this flight. Exhaustion overtook Ross, and he was asleep in his seat before the plane lifted off.

Chapter Twelve

Sara's flight south from Paris to Douala was uneventful. Five-and-a-half hours of cloud cover obscured her view. She tried to guess at her progress over France, Algeria, Niger, and Nigeria, into Cameroon on her maps. Shortly before arrival in Douala the cloud cover parted slightly, allowing Sara fleeting glimpses of rich green forests blanketing a rolling terrain.

She missed the companionship of Danell and Adam. Entertaining the two youngsters had been a good distraction, and it was comforting to have them snuggled against her through the night.

"This is the Captain speaking. We will be arriving in Douala, Cameroon, Africa, in ten minutes. The weather in Douala is overcast but warm today. Please return to your seats and fasten your safety belts. Thank you for flying Air France, we trust we will be able to serve you again soon." The message was first spoken in French, and then repeated in English reminding Sara she was far from home.

Sara checked her seat belt just to be sure it was still secure, and put away her maps. "Well, here I come, Uncle Ross!" she muttered under her breath.

The Douala airport was tiny compared to the airports she had visited thus far on her journey. The plane coasted to a stop near the terminal, and Sara watched as a freestanding staircase was rolled against the plane. "I've hit the big time," slipped from her lips, and she instantly regretted the comment. What if someone from Douala heard her snide remark? Quickly she looked around her, but no one seemed to have noticed. As she deplaned, a wet blanket of hot air covered her body. She and the other passengers were led through customs and immigration where their passports were checked and shots and immunization records were examined. Sara was allowed to pass on through to the luggage area and again she answered questions in French concerning the contents of her luggage. Finally she was released to the public area inside the terminal, and made her way to a courtesy desk. "Do you have brochures on nearby hotels? Or, could you recommend a good hotel?"

"You look ready for a hotel, Mademoiselle," smiled the man behind the counter sympathetically, softening any insult Sara may have taken from his comment. It seemed strange to hear an African speaking English with a French accent.

"I am definitely looking forward to a little rest without the drone of an engine." Sara returned the smile, warming to the friendly nature of the clerk. "A hot shower sounds mighty nice, too."

"Well, we only have one hotel for mademoiselle. The Banyon has private rooms, clean beds, inside plumbing, and hot showers. They have a cafe with fairly good food. If such things interest you, the lobby boasts a television. It's really the only hotel I can recommend."

"Point the way. I'm ready to walk off some of this stiffness!"

The clerk drew Sara a small map, detailing directions to the hotel. "It's not far, but since you have luggage you might should hire a taxi."

"I guess that would be a good idea. My bags are heavy."

"May I call you a helper?"

"Would you please?" Sara was letting her guard down, and she knew it. But soon she would locate Uncle Ross, and the relief and excitement made her feel almost giddy.

"Please be careful, Mademoiselle. Know where you are going, and don't wander around needlessly. Enjoy your stay." The clerk smiled and motioned for a young boy to come help her.

Sara nodded her understanding and acceptance of the advice given, deciding to take advantage of the warning. "You've been very helpful. Could you tell me where I can exchange American dollars for francs?"

"I can do that for you, unless you prefer to go to the bank. I'm an honest man. I tell you up front that I'll charge you a small fee."

"I don't mind a small fee. It's only fair if it gets me to that hotel and a nice hot shower quicker." The clerk exchanged Sara's money for francs and sent her off with the young boy. "My name is Sara. What's your name?" Sara asked in French, marveling at the intense hue of the youth's blue-black skin. She had never seen skin so dark. Mrs. Schaffer looked like milk chocolate compared to this boy.

"I go by Joe."

"How old are you, Joe?"

"Old enough to work at airport and carry people's bags."

Sara smiled at Joe's avoidance of her intrusive question. "I can see that you are. Thank's for your help." She followed the small boy to a taxi waiting outside the terminal and pressed several francs into his hand after he put all her bags in the trunk of the taxi.

"I would like to go to the hotel on this map, the Banyon hotel." Sara showed the map to the taxi-driver and climbed in the back seat.

"I know the Banyon," nodded the taxi driver.

I should have time for a shower before supper, Sara determined silently. It didn't take long to get to the hotel. Sara paid the taxi driver in francs and was grateful that her mother had taught her enough about foreign coins to get by.

Fifteen minutes later Sara was being shown to a room on the second floor, near the staircase. The first thing she noticed was that there was no phone or television in her room. But she'd seen both in the lobby, so she wasn't going to let it concern her. The furnishings of the room were simple but seemed reasonably clean. The bathroom had a shower stall of sorts, and Sara immediately set the water to running while she dug out her blue jeans and a t-shirt.

"I'm here! Now I can be just me and wear real clothes!"

Revived by the shower, and feeling refreshed in her change of clothing, Sara set out to find the café. The hotel clerk looked up and smiled at Sara's transformation as she passed her desk. Sara lifted a hand in a little salute and returned the smile. *Tomorrow I'll find Uncle Ross. Tonight I dine, relax, catch up on my Bible reading and sleep—all stretched out straight on a flat, soft, comfortable bed!*

Morning found Sara refreshed and raring to go. A big breakfast of eggs and pancakes with a fruity sauce filled her up. The French menu was readable for Sara, but she still appreciated the English subtitles of the entrees. Eager to begin her search, she ate quickly and headed for the front desk.

"I am looking for the field offices of Tarbell Construction. Could you direct me to that location?"

"Certainly, Mademoiselle, workers from Tarbell often stay here. You could even walk the distance if you're up for some exercise this morning." The forthcoming map was easy to follow and Sara made her way outside.

"Now the skies are clear!" Sara shook her head and lifted her arms as if in surrender. "Where were you yesterday when I wanted to see the world from the sky?"

Five minutes of brisk walking got Sara's heart pumping, and her legs began to ache. *I had no idea I was so out of shape,* she complained to herself. The heat and humidity began working against her and she slowed her pace, mopping perspiration from her forehead. Walking at the slower pace, she began to enjoy the scenery about her. Colorful flowers were tucked into or overrunning the lush greenery that was everywhere. Blue-black skinned Africans walking along the street paused to flash a white grin at her. One child couldn't resist the urge to reach out and touch the long braid that Sara had pulled over her shoulder to the front. Her excitement and wonder was amusing to Sara, and she laughed with the child over her embarrassment, then continued on her quest.

The office was open when she finally arrived, and she was ready to enjoy the cool interior it offered. The scarcity of office furnishings was a bit of a shock. The office equipment sat in full view of the door. There was no effort to cover the air-conditioner rattling in the window or beautify the room in any way. *This office is for men only,* Sara mused to herself, and cleared her throat to get the attention of the clerk at the desk.

"Oh, I'm sorry, miss. May I help you?" The man jumped up and circled the desk to stand in front of Sara.

"Yes, I hope so. I'm looking for my uncle. He's working for Tarbell on a construction project here in Cameroon. His name is Ross Mann." To herself Sara mused, *so there is at least one other white person in Douala besides me!*

"Ross Mann? Yes, he was just in here yesterday. He's on a two-week break." Concern crossed the clerk's face. "Did he know you were coming, Miss?"

"No, he wasn't expecting me. I, uh, wanted to surprise him." Sara didn't want to tell this man the real reason for her sudden arrival. That information should go to Uncle Ross first.

"Excuse my manners, my name is Clark. I know your uncle. I fear you just missed him. He usually spends his time-off at Kama, visiting with ol' Doc Vinton. He's on his way there now. It'll be a couple of weeks before he returns." Clark paused a moment to think. "Ross just left yesterday. He'll probably spend a couple of days at a missionary guest house in Bukavu while gathering supplies to take inland to Kama. If you can track his movements, you should be able to catch up with him, if that's what . . . you would be wanting to do. . . ." his voice trailed off as he looked more intently at Sara. "How old are you, miss?"

Sara decided to take her cue from the boy at the airport. "Old enough to track my Uncle's movements. Thanks for your help, Clark." Sara turned to leave, but paused for one last question. "Do you know how far Kama is from Bukavu?"

"No, I know it's deep in the jungles of the Democratic Republic of the Congo. Neither is really a good place to be going right now with the war and all. Perhaps it would be better if you waited for your uncle here."

"Thanks." Sara closed the door behind her and stared out into the park. *I've got to think!* she chided. *Why didn't I call before I rushed out here like this? Talk is cheap, but how am I going to find Uncle Ross now?* A knot was forming in Sara's throat, and she swallowed hard to try to stop its influence on her tear ducts. Disappointment overruled her defenses and tears trickled down her cheeks. "What am I going to do now?"

Chapter Thirteen

Mrs. Schaffer found life at Calhoun House disheartening without the beloved Calhouns.

As greatly as she missed David and Beth, she came to miss Sara even more. Pastor Evans had his hands full trying to locate new directors with the same love of God and compassion for people that Beth and David had exhibited. Good people willing to live in that neighborhood were hard to come by!

Two days passed without any e-mails from Sara. Chicago wasn't 'that' far away by plane. She wasn't ready to throw the panic switch yet, but her nerves were mighty unsettled.

"Mrs. Schaffer," Pastor Evans' head poked around the kitchen door. "There's a lady here from Social Services looking for our Sara. I told her I didn't know her exact whereabouts. Perhaps you could have a word with her." The pastor gave Mrs. Schaffer a look that shouted *'don't tell her anything!'* then ushered a dreary looking woman into the kitchen.

"Mrs. Schaffer, my name is Clare. We've had inquires about the whereabouts of Sara Calhoun. Our investigation shows she was orphaned last week and that she's underage. We need to locate her. I understand she lived here with her parents until their death. Can you tell me where she is now?"

Mrs. Schaffer shot a look at Pastor Evans, and then looked back at Clare. She took care to wipe her hands carefully on her apron then stepped closer to tower over the social worker who dared to come after her Sara. "Madame, Miss Sara is gone to live with her uncle in Illinois. You don't need to be worrying none about that chile'. She don't need any state help. She be doing just fine with her family."

"Well, there're papers to file if the uncle wishes to accept responsibility for the minor. Do you have an address for the uncle?" Clare backing away from Mrs. Schaffer put a grin on the pastor's face that he quickly covered in a movement that suggested his chin itched.

For a moment Mrs. Schaffer had the grace to look flustered and confused. "No, I don't have no address for the uncle. Sara knows where she be going. It ain't my business nor yours. You leave Miss Sara alone. She be fine, she don't need yo' meddling!"

"Uh, thank you, Mrs. Schaffer," Pastor Evans quickly interjected. "Thank you for your time. I'll see Ms. Clare to the front door now." He motioned toward the kitchen door and Ms. Clare wasted no time getting herself through it.

Pastor Evans returned shortly and perched himself on one of the kitchen stools.

"You were a little tougher on Ms. Clare than I'd expected, but thanks for not revealing Sara's where-abouts. She's got enough on her plate right now without social services tracking her down. I'll get the necessary papers from the social service offices tomorrow and you can send them off to Sara."

The odd look on Mrs. Schaffer's face did not change, and upon closer inspection Pastor Evans spoke again. "You *do* know where Sara is don't you?"

"I just realized the chile' didn't give me no address, Pastor! She said she'd keep in touch through e-mail, and I never gave it a thought. She said her uncle works in Chicago, I think. No, she said his office in Chicago keeps him busy. It's not like Sara to be so vague with me!"

"Well, I'm sure we have an address on file somewhere. Don't let this upset you, Mrs. Schaffer."

The cook was still muttering to herself and swaying her head back and forth when a well dressed and handsome young man strolled into the kitchen.

"Hello, Mrs. Schaffer, Pastor Evans." He extended his hand to the Pastor and bowed politely to the old cook. "You don't remember me!" he accused, and merriment danced in his eyes. "Well, let's see if I can remember correctly." Boldly Kent Cooper walked around the counter and over to the cupboards. For a moment he paused and looked back at the astonished cook, then dramatically turned and pulled open the second drawer.

"Ha! Some things don't change!" Kent gleefully lifted two chocolate chip cookies from their privileged hiding place, and held them up as proof of his right to be there.

Mrs. Schaffer crackled with indignation. "I don't know who you be, young man, but you shouldn't go exposing secrets in front of Pastor like that!" Her declaration caused Pastor Evans and Kent to lock eyes and stifle their laughter.

"Now what makes you think after all the years I've worked here that I don't already know that secret?" Pastor Evans asked, "and I think I know who this young man is as well. There's only been one youngster through here in the last ten years with nerve enough to pull a trick like that on Cook! How are you, Kent?"

"Just fine, Sir. Sorry about the theatricals. I just couldn't resist."

"How you know my secret cookie place?" Still scowling, Mrs. Schaffer wasn't sure if she should embrace the young man or chase him from her kitchen with a broomstick.

"Ten years ago a delightful 7-year-old thought a couple of your extraspecial chocolate-chip cookies and a big glass of cold milk would cheer up a couple of scared kids. So she invited my sister and me into your kitchen and served us like we were royalty. She said you wouldn't mind."

"Sara!"

"Correct! And that is why I am here. I am so sorry about the Calhouns. I know what a blow this has got to be for all of you. Is Sara OK?" Concern quickly replaced Kent's merriment.

Mrs. Schaffer dropped into a chair, and heaved a heavy sigh. "Sara be fine. She promised! She said God would take care of her, and I know He will!"

"I'm glad to hear that, because I've been unable to make contact with her. You know where she is then?"

"She be gone to live with her uncle." The look in the old cook's eyes was one of hope.

"Ross Mann?"

"That be the one."

"You let her go?" Kent's voice betrayed his alarm, and both Pastor Evans and Mrs. Schaffer's heads snapped up. "Ross Mann is working in the jungles of Cameroon, Africa! I've not been able to contact him either!"

Mrs. Schaffer jumped to her feet and started for the freight elevator, pulling Sara's key from her pocket as she went.

"Where you going?" demanded both men together.

"I'm gonna check for Sara's e-mail again. She promised she keep touch with me by e-mail."

The men quickly fell into step behind the old cook and followed her into the lift. Once in the loft, Mrs. Schaffer went straight to the computer station, switched on the power, and waited for all programs to load onto the screen.

Kent suddenly felt out of place and stood hesitant with his hands in his pockets looking around him. It had been ten years since he'd stood inside this room. Toys had been replaced with electronic devices. The piano held an elegantly framed 8-by-10 photo of Beth and Dave Calhoun seated next to each other, with a radiant auburn haired teen standing just behind them, her hands on their shoulders. Kent could only stare.

"She's grown into quite the beautiful young woman, hasn't she?" Pastor Evan spoke almost reverently at Kent's side.

"I've got mail!" shouted an excited Mrs. Schaffer from the computer terminal, and both men turned their attention to Mrs. Schaffer and hurried over to stand behind her, waiting for the message to present itself.

"HI, MRS. SCHAFFER. IT'S JUST ME. I'VE ARRIVED SAFELY IN PARIS. IT'S BEEN A GOOD TRIP SO FAR. I MET SOME REALLY NICE PEOPLE IN NEW YORK, A TAXI-DRIVER NAMED TED, FOR ONE. BUT I'LL TELL YOU MORE ABOUT HIM AND MY QUICK 8-HOUR TOUR OF NEW YORK WHEN I GET BACK HOME. ON THE PLANE TO PARIS, GOD PROVIDED TWO SMALL CHILDREN TO KEEP ME COMPANY. I COLORED WITH THEM, READ THEM STORIES, GAVE THEM GUM TO HELP POP THEIR EARS, AND JUST BEFORE LIGHTS-OUT, I TOLD THEM THE STORY OF JESUS CALMING THE STORMY SEA. THEY WERE SO SWEET. NOW I'M IN PARIS, AND WILL BE FLYING OUT FOR DOUALA, CAMEROON, AFRICA, SHORTLY.

"I'M SORRY I DECEIVED YOU ABOUT UNCLE ROSS BEING IN CHICAGO, BUT I KNEW IF I TOLD YOU, YOU'D STOP ME FROM COMING. I JUST HAD TO TELL UNCLE ROSS ABOUT MOM AND DAD IN PERSON. PLEASE FORGIVE ME. I LOVE YOU AND MISS YOU ALL SO MUCH. PLEASE GIVE MY

GREETINGS TO PASTOR EVANS AND ALL THE REST OF THE MISSION STAFF. I'LL E-MAIL YOU AGAIN FIRST CHANCE I GET.

"GOD IS TAKING GREAT CARE OF ME JUST AS I PROMISED, SO DON'T WORRY YOURSELF OVER ME. ON THE OTHER HAND, IF THE MOOD SHOULD OVERTAKE YOU TO DO SO, A CARE PACKAGE OF CHOCOLATE CHIP COOKIES, SENT TO UNCLE ROSS'S AFRICAN OFFICE WOULD SURE BE NICE! (THE ADDRESS IS IN THE TOP LEFT DRAWER OF THIS DESK.)

"TILL NEXT TIME, LOVE YA. SARA"

Silence reigned in the room until Kent cleared his throat.

"Let's just stop, here and now, and commit Sara's safety to the only one who can grant it," Pastor Evans spoke quietly. Bowing their heads the cook and pastor went to the Throne of God with their requests for Sara's safety and well-being.

Kent watched them in silence, wondering how they could be so calm.

Chapter Fourteen

Sara stood outside the Tarbell Construction office for several minutes before gaining enough composure to make her way across the street into the small park. She sat down on a bench nestled beneath the branches of a tall shady tree.

I've really messed up, God. Uncle Ross is already gone, and I don't know how to find him.

She sat in silence for a while, trying to quiet her emotions. Gradually she became aware of the birds chirping merrily in the branches above her and tilted her head back to watch as flashes of brilliant color fluttered from limb to limb.

Your creations are so varied and beautiful! How did you think up so many different shapes and sizes and colors and varieties of everything? I know, I know, You're God, but still, it just boggles my mind!

The peace and tranquility surrounding the park bench held Sara captive. Gradually the tension eased out of her muscles, and she began to relax. After an hour or so of sitting quietly, accepting God's comfort, Sara's emotional state was such that her mind began working on a strategy to find Uncle Ross.

Kama Station, Republic of Democratic Congo. I'll have to study my maps. If they don't show me a clear route to take, I'll have to practice my detective skills. Mr. Clark said Uncle Ross gathered supplies in Bukavu before going on to the Kama Station. I wonder what kind of supplies?

Without realizing she was doing so, Sara got up and headed back towards the hotel at a brisk walk. She did not notice the heat of the midday sun or the ache in her out of shape muscles. Her body had to hurry to keep pace with the workings of her mind.

At the hotel, she went directly to the front desk. "Hi. Yesterday you mentioned that several Tarbell Construction men stayed here at this hotel. Do you know if Ross Mann ever stayed here?"

"Oh, Mademoiselle. Mr. Mann stayed here many times. He just left yesterday morning, as a matter of fact," the desk clerk volunteered, and Sara cringed at the reminder of having missed her uncle.

"Do you know where he went?"

"I'm not certain. He left in a big hurry - quicker than usual. I know he usually spends his free time visiting a Dr. Sam Vinton over in the Congo. He's quite taken with the old fellow. I figured he'd located last minute transportation inland, and had to hurry or miss it. Is Monsier Mann your father?"

Sara steeled herself against reacting to the clerk's question. It was a fair enough question for she had no way of knowing Sara's father had just been killed.

"No, he's my uncle. I wanted to surprise him, but it seems I missed him by just hours! I'd like to catch up with him. Did he say anything at all about how he was going to travel inland?

"Oh there's really only one way, Mademoiselle, and that would be by air! Few roads are passable in the Congo. All flights in or out of the Congo have been canceled though. Political unrest, you know."

Sara didn't know, but felt she had gleaned all she could from the clerk.

"Thank you for your help. Would you please let me know if you learn anything new?"

"Most certainly, Mademoiselle."

"Thank you." Sara proceeded to her room to check her maps. Hunger told her it was time to eat again. This time she wanted room service, so she could be alone with her thoughts and pore over the maps while she ate. However, calling up room service proved difficult, since there was no phone or menu in her room.

"I guess I'll eat in the dining room," she muttered to herself, heading in that direction without her maps.

The main course was a meat stew and Sara decided to go with a pasta salad instead, and a bottled soft drink to avoid the questionable water. Chocolate ice cream was offered for dessert, and Sara requested two. Once lunch was out of the way, she returned to her room to pore over the maps.

"Well," she spoke out loud to herself, "at least we're on the same continent now!" The Republic of Congo was easy to find, but Kama was not listed anywhere. Bukavu was located on the far eastern border next to the tiny country of Rwanda.

"This is getting me nowhere fast and Uncle Ross is getting further away by the moment. Maybe I should just walk over to the airport and ask around there."

It was a short distance back to the airport, and the little map she'd gotten from the courtesy desk the day before came in handy.

Joe appeared at her side as soon as she entered the terminal, "You have more bags for me to carry, Mademoiselle?"

"No, Joe. Not yet. Perhaps later." Sara smiled at the young boy's eagerness to work, and wondered what kind of family life he had, and where he lived, if he attended school or not, but she resisted the temptation to pry.

Behind the courtesy desk sat the same man as the day before. "Good morning, American Miss," he greeted her warmly, "I trust you found the Banyon Hotel satisfactory."

"Yes, thank you. I'm hoping you can help me once again. My Uncle has gone to Bukavu and I want to join him there. I need some information. Normally I'd check my options out on the internet, but I don't have a phone hookup in my room, or a phone either, of course." Realizing it must sound like she was whining about her accommodations, Sara quickly tried to cover by adding, "so I've found a good excuse to get my exercise today," and she smiled as warmly as she could manage.

"Bukavu, let me think, I believe that is in the Republic of Congo, right next to Rwanda?"

"Yes it is. Which airline flies there?"

"Miss, no airline flies in there now. Air travel has been shut down inside the Congo Republic. That government is in turmoil again. You can't go there!"

"But that is where my uncle is. He only has a two week break, and I must spend it with him. Surely there must be a way. Uncle Ross left yesterday. I just missed him by hours. I must catch up with him in Bukavu."

"You say he's got a one day head start?"

"Yes, Sir."

"Well, it's possible to fly Air Rwanda into Kigali, but then you'd have a day's travel by bus through the mountains to Bukavu, a days travel *if* the roads are open, and *if* the bus can get through. I still say very bad idea. You'd do better to stay here and wait for him to return."

"Are there any private pilots for hire around?"

"I wouldn't be knowing about that, Mademoiselle.

Please give up this idea and wait for your uncle to return here." Concern filled the man's voice.

Sara could see he wasn't going to budge or help her get to Bukavu. She smiled at him and muttered a polite, "Thank you," then turned away from the desk and began looking for any indication of private airline booths.

"You have trouble, Mademoiselle?" It was Joe again.

"Joe, do you know any small plane pilots, pilots for hire?" Sara whispered hopefully.

"Sure, Mademoiselle."

"Would you take me to one?"

Joe glanced furtively over his shoulder. "Meet me outside in ten minutes, I can take you to a bush pilot or two."

Sara wondered if Joe had a scheduled break in ten minutes, or just didn't want the man at the courtesy desk knowing he was helping her. She really didn't care, because time was wasting and she needed to catch Uncle Ross at the mission guest house before he moved even further into the interior, into the jungles.

"Okay, ten minutes, thanks Joe." The young boy shuffled away under the questioning frown of the courtesy desk clerk. Sara shook her head and walked slowly towards the terminal entrance. Once outside she found a bench in an out-of-the-way shady spot, and sat down to wait. The minutes dragged by but finally Joe appeared at her side.

"Follow me." he said.

Sara stood and followed Joe around the side of the building and down a path, away from the main terminal towards a row of small airplane hangars. The first one they came to was closed up tight. A mechanic working on a small plane in the next hangar looked up as the two entered.

"American Miss looking for pilot to fly her some-place," Joe stated as introduction.

"Where do you want to fly, American Miss?"

"Bukavu, on the Congo/Rwandan border. I can pay your fee."

"Really." It was a statement, made without judgment or encouragement. "Sorry, Miss. I don't fly my planes into war zones. Why Bukavu?"

"My uncle is there. I need to join him." Sara spoke as confidently as she could muster, but her voice seemed to echo weakly in the expanse of the hangar. Suddenly she wished she had changed into her mother's navy blue travel suit. Perhaps then the pilot would have considered her request more seriously.

"Good luck." The mechanic turned back to his work and that was the end of the interview. Joe shrugged and led Sara on to the next hangar.

At first it looked as if no one was there, even though the door was open. The hangar bay was empty. Joe stuck his head in and called out, "Chappy, you home?"

A man's form lifted from what appeared to be an army cot against the back wall. "Is that you, Joe?"

"It's me. I bring business."

"Well, now. It wouldn't be the first time, would it?" The man chuckled quietly, and made his way to the front of the hangar.

Sara decided to try a more direct approach, and put out her hand in a cordial handshake. "Good morning, Chappy. My name is Sara Calhoun. I need to hire a plane to Bukavu."

For a moment the wiry old man just stared at Sara, then asked, "Why in the world would you want to go to Bukavu?"

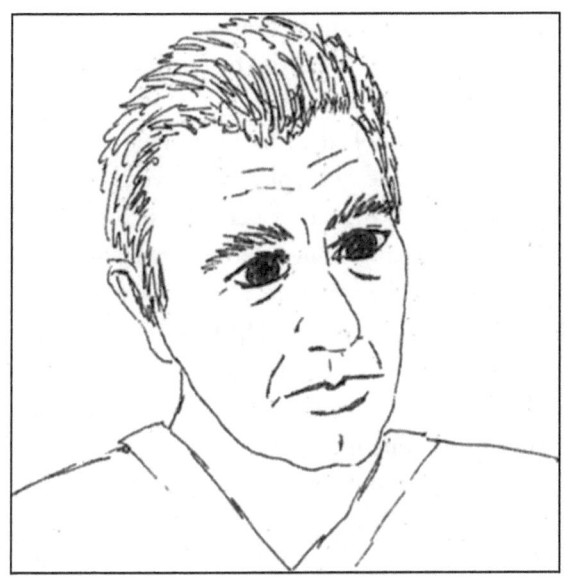

"My uncle is there, and I wish to join him. Can you fly me there? I can pay your fare."

"There isn't enough money in the world to convince me to fly you into Bukavu, Miss. There's a war going on there. Besides it's illegal to fly into that country right now. You don't want to be going there nohow. It's not safe."

"Please, my uncle will only be there a couple of days, and I'm one day behind him now. I need to get there today or he'll go on to Kama without me."

Chappy's pause and open mouthed stare caused Sara to fidget uneasily. Finally he asked, "Is your uncle's name Ross Mann?"

"Yes! Do you know him?" The excitement in Sara's voice put a deep scowl across Bill Chapman's brow, and a growl in his voice.

"I know him. He's a good man. He doesn't know you're follering 'em, does he?"

"No. I meant to surprise him at the Tarbell office, but I just missed him. They said he had already left for Kama. Would you take me to him, please?"

Bill Chapman looked to be an unhappy man, and he refused to answer the girl's pleas for several minutes. "We could get shot out of the air, or I could lose my pilot's license if I'm caught flying into Congo territory. Even if I got you into Bukavu, how would you get to Kama? There's nothing but two hundred miles of jungle and bad roads between the two!"

"Could you fly me into Rwanda, near the border, and let me walk across into Bukavu? I don't want you to lose your license or do anything illegal."

"Where you staying, girl?" The guttural sound was more a groan than a question.

"At the Banyon. I can gather my things and be back here in a half hour."

"Don't rush me!" Bill sat down heavily on a bench against the wall and covered the back of his head with his hands. Slowly he lowered his elbows to rest on his knees.

Sara stood by quietly pleading, *Lord, please make this man help me find Uncle Ross.*

Turmoil churned within Bill Chapman. He hated this task that had fallen to him. *Never in my life have I sidestepped a responsibility and I don't figure it'd be right to start now. Ross would never understand if I refused to get his niece safely to him. Congo's not a safe place, but what place is for a child alone in a strange land and culture. Ohhh, what am I gonna do?*

Finally Bill made his decision. "Go get your stuff. I'll fuel up the Cessna. Don't know that we can get there in time so you'd better radio ahead. If Ross don't know you're coming, he won't know to wait for ya!"

Chapter Fifteen

Radioing ahead was not a familiar task to Sara. How did one radio ahead? By the time she re-entered the hotel, the thought had completely left her mind. Quickly she gathered all her belongings together and transferred as much as she could into the backpack she had brought along for any treks she might make into the interior with Uncle Ross.

I don't imagine I'll need dressy clothing at Kama. I can live two weeks without my computer, but I'll need my Bible, comfortable clothes, water purifier, chocolate bars, . . . and so her thoughts ran ahead of her. Everything else was stuffed into her suitcases and taken to the front desk.

"Do you have a secure place where I can safely store these two suitcases for a couple of weeks while I'm gone with my uncle?" she asked the young woman at the courtesy counter.

"Certainly, Mademoiselle. Does this mean you are checking out?"

"Yes, please." Sara paid the amount due on her room, and paid a little extra for the storage of her suitcases. Then with her backpack slung over her shoulder, she left the hotel and headed directly back to the small plane hangars at the airport. Bill Chapman looked disgruntled when he saw her coming.

"Packed kinda light, didn't cha?" He asked crossly.

"I'm headed into the interior, am I not? I don't figure to need more than I can carry."

Chappy did not respond verbally but the look of surprise in his eye gave Sara hope that she had gained a little credibility in his eyes.

"My stuff's already on board. Our first stop is Bangui, Central African Republic. Let's get going." Taking her backpack from her, Chappy opened the door and motioned for Sara to climb up into the plane. Following close behind, he tossed the pack over the seat into the space behind. "Ever ride in one of these?"

"No. I guess there's a first time for everything."

"I named this plane Joey," Chappy offered, "after baby kangaroos down Australia way. Seeing as how this bird has a ferry tank installed behind us there where seats would normally go, I think of her as having an extra fuel pouch for safety sake. Maybe should'a named her after a camel might've been more appropriate. Anyway, she's a high-wing Cessna 206 with a range of around 600 miles, 700 with the ferry tank. With the extra fuel we should get to Bangula even if we run into headwinds. From Bangula we'll hunt an outpost to land and refuel. I've a couple of ideas on that—out missions with emergency fuel on hand. If nobody else has been sneaking in or out of the country, we should be able to refuel at one or the other. I'll radio 'em when we get close enough. If they aren't overrun with rebels we'll be in business. I reckon that's something you best start praying about."

"I'm trusting you because my uncle's flown with you, and I'm certain you're only doing this because I'm his kin. Thank you, Chappy. I know you're not happy about all this."

Chappy grunted and turned his attention to the task at hand. He'd tried his hand at conversing with this young'un. It hadn't been too bad. She seemed like a right decent enough kid. But now he needed to run through his engine checks, and taxi to the runway. Finally clearance was given for takeoff.

Sara refrained from speaking for several minutes. When she could take the silence no longer, she raised her voice over the drone of the engines and asked, "How long do you think it'll take us?"

"It's gonna take a'while. At least it's a clear day so you can see the countryside. That's the beauty of a high-wing. It don't obstruct your view."

Sara took that as her cue to curb chatter, and contented herself with taking in all the scenery below her. *Small planes are great,* she decided. *I'm flying low enough to really see the forests! The trees look like overgrown broccoli tops, miles of them!* Rivers twisted and bent through the forests and grasslands, with both quiet murky waters that made her think of crocodiles, and sparkling water that coursed over waterfalls. Somehow the strange new views had a healing affect on her. Occasionally a spattering of mud huts and people were visible. *Maybe I'll get lucky and see an elephant herd, hippos or lions. Ooh, another waterfall!* Sara became so engrossed in watching the landscape that she forgot her circumstances and just breathed out prayers of praise for all the beauty passing below her.

Chappy's thoughts were not so upbeat. He hadn't decided yet how he was going to get from Bangui to Kama. Kisangani on the Congo River had an airport, but to think that location wouldn't be overrun with soldiers was like thinking chickens didn't have feathers. The last time he had landed at Kisangani, 2000 soldiers were on hand with all sorts of weapons, including one guy walking around with a grenade launcher that was pointed right at his Cessna as he taxied up to the terminal. He feared at the time that the soldier would shoot first and ask questions later, instead his plane was searched and he was allowed to refuel and fly out of the area on promise he wouldn't be back. That was some kind of miracle. He'd expected them to steal his plane and leave him high and dry inside enemy territory. That had happened to others.

Where to get fuel for the return trip was another major concern. It was very doubtful Kama would have any fuel on hand. Cyangogo, on the Rwandan border had a tiny airport. Perhaps there'd be enough fuel left to slip into Cyangogo to refuel. He'd have to circle around and approach from the east or they would know he'd been flying over the Congo, and he'd have explaining to do.

He'd just have to play it by ear. If any of these plans failed, it was going to be a long treacherous walk home!

Chapter Sixteen

Ross Mann slept soundly on the plane from Paris to New York. It was dark when the Captain announced they would be landing shortly. Ross woke to a growing hunger and realized he still had had nothing to eat. The first order of business in the terminal would have to be finding a hearty meal. It wouldn't help anyone if he passed out from hunger. Checking his tickets, he figured out that he had about a two hour layover. That wasn't too bad. It would give him time to eat and make some phone calls.

Oh, *Sara girl, please be okay. I'm on my way. Surely Pastor Evans and Mrs. Schaffer still work at the mission. Mrs. Schaffer would never allow anything bad to happen to you if she could help it. I should have called Calhoun House before leaving Douala. I might even have saved myself a trip. No, at a time like this, family needs to be together no matter what it takes.*

Wonderful smells wafted from the interior of one of the restaurants. Stepping inside Ross chose a table against the front wall, where he could look out and watch the people passing by. Thoughts of Beth and Dave, and Sara, pressed all others thoughts, except his hunger, from his mind, and he picked up the menu. He was hungry, and a big meal was in order.

At the completion of his meal he found the phone banks, and stood in line for ten minutes before a phone opened up. "In this modern day of cell phones, you'd think waiting lines at phone booths would be extinct," he muttered to himself. *Maybe I should get one of those things. Naw, I doubt they'd even work out in the bush country.*

For an additional fifteen minutes Ross dialed the number to Calhoun House, only to get a busy signal. *Who could be talking so long on the phone? Oh well, now that I've thought on it some, I'm comfortable in the thought that Mrs. Schaffer probably hasn't let Sara out of her sight. So, let's just get on that plane and get there!*

Ross made it to the proper gate for departure just as they began boarding. A few moments longer and he was back on a plane headed for the California Coast.

Chapter Seventeen

Midway through the flight Sara reached for her backpack and pulled out two Power Bars. She handed one to Chappy.

"Sorry I don't have any drink to offer you with this. I never got to a store in Douala."

"Thanks. What is this, some kind of candy bar?"

"Well, sort of, if you use your imagination and don't have too strong a sweet tooth. Actually it's supposed to be sufficient enough in nutrients to replace an entire meal."

"Huh!" Chappy began to turn the thing in his hands as if looking for a way to open it.

Pulling a small Swiss pocket knife from her pocket, Sara folded out the tiny scissors. "Here, let me cut the end off for you. In fact just let me open the whole thing up for you." Feeling the package with her fingers, Sara guided the tiny scissors to cut only foil, and not the food bar. Then she cut the seam fold straight down the length of the package and peeled the foil back, until half the bar was exposed, and handed it back to the pilot. "There, you can peel it like a banana now." Then she began the same process on her own bar.

Gingerly, Bill bit off a chunk and began chewing. "It sort'a tastes like chocolate."

"Yep. Chocolate's the best. It comes in other flavors too, but I'm a chocoholic, so that's my favorite. I wouldn't want to make of steady diet of these things, but they are good in a pinch." Talking with her mouth full was one thing, but talking over the drone of the engines took too much effort, and Sara fell silent again. *Sure am glad I brought these along. This flight doesn't sport food services!*

It was dark when the lights of the Bangui Airstrip came into view. "You up on your prayers, girl?"

"Best as I know how," Sara replied, and thought *I don't know what you expect from prayer, Mr. Chapman, but you can't just ask God for anything you want and expect Him to give it to you on the spot. If that were the case, I'd be in Paris with Mom right now.* A tear formed in the corner of Sara's eye, and she quickly wiped it away.

A taxi pulled up in front of the Calhoun House and Ross Mann paid the driver and stepped out. It had been a while since he'd been here to visit. It appeared that nothing had changed. Drunks still lounged against the building and sat on the curb and steps up to the door. He pulled the door open and stepped into the cool interior. He stood still for a moment, waiting for his eyes to adjust, then walked purposefully to the business office. Pastor Evans sat at Dave's desk, his head on his hands, obviously praying.

Ross waited a few moments, then cleared his throat. Pastor Evan's head jerked up. "Oh, I'm sorry. I didn't hear you come in." Recognition began to grow in his eyes. "Ross, is that you?" Ross nodded and Pastor Evans stood to exchange a firm handshake with him. "Boy am I glad to see you."

"I'm here for Sara. How's she doing?"

"I guess you heard about Dave and Beth. We've been trying to reach you, Ross. Sara's not here. A week after Dave and Beth were killed, she headed for Africa to find you. We thought she was just going to Chicago, and that the change in scenery would do her good. She took it really hard. We didn't know you were out of the States or we would never have let her go."

The impact of his words took a moment to sink in. "Are you telling me Sara has flown off to Africa alone?

"I'm afraid so. We didn't realize it till last night when Kent Cooper showed up. He thought Sara would be here also. He said he'd sent you word from the Chicago office, and not heard back. When he couldn't make contact with you or Sara, he jumped on a plane and flew out here to check on her in person. He's pretty upset. Mrs. Schaffer's a basket case, and I'm not doing so well myself."

"Have you heard from Sara since she left?"

"Yes. After Kent got here, we checked the e-mail again, and she e-mailed Mrs. Schaffer from Paris. She said everything was good and asked our forgiveness for her many half-truths. She planned to meet up with you in Douala. But now you're here . . . without her, and I don't know where she is."

"May I use your phone?"

"Certainly!"

Ross picked up the phone and dialed the number to reach the African Tarbell headquarters. The phone rang several times before Clark picked it up. "Hello Clark. This is Ross Mann. I'm glad I caught you in the office. Has my niece showed up there?"

"Hey Ross. Yes she did. Pretty little thing! She said she'd catch up with you in Bukavu. Hasn't she gotten there yet?"

"Bukavu! I'm in the States!"

"What are you doing in the States? You said you were going to see the 'ol Doc like usual!"

"Well, yes I did, Clark. But one of those office memos you gave me informed me that my sister and her husband had been killed. I'm the only relation my niece has left so I shot out of there to come here and be with her. You say she's trying to follow me to Bukavu?"

"Well, she was just in here yesterday. Maybe she's still at the Banyon."

"Good thought. Thanks Clark. If you can find her, make her stay put. I'm on my way back."

"Sure thing. Good luck."

Ross quickly dialed the Banyon Hotel. "This is Ross Mann. Has a young woman by the name of Sara Calhoun registered there?"

"Yes, Monsieur Mann. She came in just hours after you left. She spent the night, and checked out the next day. She was looking for you."

"She's checked out you say?"

"Yes, she left two suitcases with us to hold till her return."

"Okay, keep those safe for me, and if she should come back in for any reason, please tell her I said to wait for me there. Put a note on hold for her saying just that. Would you do that for me please?"

"I most certainly will, Monsieur Mann."

"And, Peter, did Sara mention how she planned to follow me? Did she arrange transport or anything?"

"No, Monsieur Mann. She just checked out in a hurry."

"Thank you." Ross's face was turning whiter as he talked, and when he hung up the phone he slumped into a chair. "She's trying to catch up with me in the Congo!"

Just then Kent Cooper and Mrs. Schaffer entered the office, and seeing Ross Mann sitting there, they looked confused.

"Ross Mann?" Kent stepped forward to offer his hand. "I'm Kent Cooper, file clerk at Tarbell, Chicago office. You're here!"

"And Sara's there," answered Ross, rising to shake hands with Kent. Turning to Mrs. Schaffer he enveloped the big woman in a warm embrace. "Hello, Mrs. Schaffer. I'm so sorry!" The woman returned the embrace, and tears trickled from her eyes.

"Where's our Sara, Mr. Mann? Where's my little girl?"

"Headed into a war zone, I'm afraid. And we're all too far away to protect her!"

Chapter Eighteen

It was dark when Bill Chapman sighted the runway lights of the Bangui Airport. Permission was given to land and Sara was glad to have her feet back on the ground.

"Can we get a meal here?" Sara asked as Chappy taxied to a stop next to a small plane.

"Yeah, they've got a place to eat here. It's not the greatest, but its et'able."

"Are we staying the night here?"

"Haf'ta. Night flying's one thing, landing on a jungle airstrip with no lights in the black of night is another thing altogether. After we eat, I've gotta stop at the navigation office and pay our landing tax. It may take a while. With luck I'll find somebody willing to chat about conditions south of here. Clerks'r usually friendlier when you're givin'em money, and they like the chance to practice their English on ya. If not, there'll be a pilot or two hangin' out, waiting to file their flight plans. You can stick with me or look around the terminal, such as it is. But be careful. Locals can get pretty aggressive with foreigners.

They're stunned at the sight of a white woman and are known for proposing marriage to total strangers. The last time I transported a single missionary gal out of the Goma airport, she got 5 proposals of marriage in 30 minutes, and she wasn't even a pretty little red-head like you."

"Thanks for the warning, Chappy," Sara smiled, "But I think I can handle it. I grew up around drunks, addicts, the mentally ill, etc., probably good training for this sort of thing. Rejecting marriage proposals won't cause me too much trauma."

"Suit yourself, but be careful, and under no circumstances are you to leave the terminal, such as it is." the pilot instructed and led the way.

The first thing Sara looked for was a restroom. The terminal wasn't that big and finding the restroom was easy. She rejoined Chappy and sat down to a simple meal in the only restaurant offered. Sara wasn't thrilled with the food, but it met her need for nourishment and her hunger was satisfied.

A parade of African women in colorful costumes, complete with matching head dressings, lined the walls inside the terminal. They all had crafts to sell and Sara's heart suddenly ached with the memory of how Mom had loved decorating her home with just such crafts sent by Uncle Ross.

Chappy left her to browse while he took care of his business, and she was aware of the attention she drew as she moved slowly through the wares. Only one male was bold enough to approach and attempt to engage her in conversation. He spoke French and Sara pretended not to understand a word he said.

Chappy appeared suddenly at her side and the man moved away. Chappy's manner was urgent as he touched her elbow and led her toward the exit.

"There's a hotel of sorts close by, Sara," he spoke softly. "I'm told it's not the greatest, but the doors are sturdy and lock well. We'll be leaving at daylight tomorrow. I want to get you settled into a room there, then I'm coming back to refuel Joey and stay with her overnight.

The exterior of the hotel was nondescript by American standards. Once inside Chappy acquired a room and ushered Sara into it.

"Do not open your door to anyone but me, not even hotel staff. I'll collect you at 5:45 a.m., I want to be in the plane ready for takeoff by 6. We'll need the whole day to get you where you want to go."

Chappy's tone brooked no discussion, and Bangui was not someplace Sara wanted to be stranded, so she nodded agreement. The hotel room indeed offered security and close proximity to the airport. Beyond that Sara wasn't favorably impressed. She couldn't *see* any creepy crawlers, but the filth of the room convinced her they must be there and she opted to sleep on top the covers rather than between them. She left the light on in hopes it would draw any flying bugs away from her and discourage any crawly 'bugs' from frolicking over her weary form. She avoided the bathing facilities altogether.

'You've landed in the lap of luxury here, Sara girl," she chided, but to God she said, "thanks for keeping us safe thus far. Please keep the creepy crawlers away from me tonight. In Jesus name, Amen." Only then could she relax enough to sleep.

Five forty-five a.m. found Sara glad to be up and away from the hotel. She had hopes of getting break-fast before boarding the Cessna again. Chappy was sympathetic but nothing was open at such an early hour. Sara took time to freshen up in the terminal restroom, grateful the airport's janitorial crew took cleanliness more seriously than the hotel staff.

By sunrise they were aboard Joey. Chappy was very familiar with the touchy politics of foreign airports and waited diplomatically for clearance before moving towards takeoff.

"Did you learn anything interesting at the navigation office last night?" Sara inquired while digging in her backpack for power bars.

"Yeah. Some. Kisangani is still an unfriendly zone to visitors, but then I already figured that. Last time I landed there, I thought the soldiers were going to blow my plane up with me in it before I even came to a complete stop. Soldiers surrounded my plane, and kept a grenade launcher pointed right at me. I figured my plane would be confiscated for sure, and if allowed to live, I'd be stranded without transportation home. But somebody must'a been watching out for me 'cause they let me refuel and fly out of there on the promise I wouldn't be coming back."

"What are we going to do then? Are there other airports where we can refuel?"

"No other airports . . . Sara, when I left you last night, a man pulled me aside and asked to speak with me. He'd heard I was asking about conditions south of here. Word travels fast! I wasn't sure I could trust him until he told me his mission. He said there were cholera outbreaks everywhere south of here, and medicine was needed to treat it. He wanted to hire me to transport cholera IVs down to the clinic at Kama! Can you believe that?

"I explained I'd need a refueling point between here and there. He said he could supply me with some ideas if I was willing to take the risk. People are dying, Sara, and Cholera's a bad way to go. So I told him to keep talking. He said Jeffrey Stevens was holding out near the Tingi Tingi airstrip, guarding a supply of fuel. He hadn't heard of any other pilots headed that direction, so he thought that supply should still be there. I know Jeffrey, he's an old army buddy. We flew together in Nam.

"I ask him where I was supposed to get the IVs and he said he had 100 cases and was just waiting for someway to transport them. I know Ross is trying to get medicines into Kama by way of Bukavu, so given this chance, I figure we gotta do it."

Chappy finally paused long enough for Sara to get in a word. "How appropriate, it seems we're in the right place at the right time. How do we get the cholera medicine?"

"I figured you'd feel that way. We loaded most of it in the luggage pod last night, and packed what wouldn't fit around the ferry tank behind you."

"Cleared for takeoff" crackled over the plane's speakers and the pilot quickly glanced over his instruments again and began to taxi down the runway. Sara remained silent and waited as they picked up speed and lifted into the ever brightening sky. A whisper of fear and uncertainty unsettled Sara's resolve, but she force herself to ignore both and focused on the sun-rise.

"This airstrip we're headed for is just a wide spot in the road. It's asphalt, part of an old road that was made straight and a little wider for 1000 feet to be used as an airstrip. I'm sorry to take you there, Sara, it's not a happy place. Last time I was there 50,000 refugees (some I knew) were there. It became a mass grave site when soldiers came down from Kisangani and shot as many as possible to make it difficult for the advancing army to get through. I don't know what we'll see when we get there."

Sara had heard rumors of such atrocities on the news but hadn't really believed such things could really happen. Now there was a chance she would see it with her own eyes. It wasn't a comforting thought and she really didn't know how she should feel. One part of her was repulsed by the thought, another side of her was intrigued that she was seeing a part of history in person, no matter how disturbing it might be.

Then the thought occurred to her that they could be stranded in that place.

"Chappy, what will we do if there isn't any fuel when we get there?" Sara could feel her throat tighten and tried to keep all sign of panic out of her voice.

"The Tingi Tingi airstrip *is* within striking distance and we'll be closer to Kama than if we went to Bukavu, which is **not** within striking distance. From Tingi Tingi there's a chance that we could hire a guide with a canoe to transport us a good portion of the way to Kama by river. There is **no** river path from Bukavu to Kama, we'd have to walk the whole way. With luck, we could even beat Ross to Kama and you'd be waiting for him when he got there. I reckon that would surprise him some."

"I reckon." Sara forced herself to smile at the pilot and wondered at the dedication of this man to go to so much trouble to take a young girl half way across the African Continent to deliver her personally into the safe keeping of her uncle. *He must really respect Uncle Ross.*

Chappy was feeling more like an idiot than a hero. Sara's question haunted him. *What if Jeffrey isn't there, and there isn't any fuel available. I'm not much for ground travel anymore, let alone in a countryside that's crawling with rebels, escorting Sara girl who'll stand out like a strobe light! You're an idiot Bill Chapman, plain and simple, an idiot! But you accepted this task, and you're not a quitter. Ross Mann will have your hide for endangering his niece. Ya shouldn't have given in to her pleas. Ya should'a made her stay put in Cameroon. She was safer there than traveling into this war zone! Well, 'ol Chappy, you better figure out how you're going to pull this off!*

If ya 'cud land the plane right at dusk ya might slip in unnoticed. Tingi Tingi requires landing from the west to the east, and that puts the sun directly behind ya. Maybe ya 'cud land the plane as a glider like ya did in Korea that time. If ya timed it right . . . and cut the engine a couple miles out they won't hear ya coming. . . . This high-wing's maneuverable enough, it cud' work.. But ya'll be there around noon, not dusk! No, such a trick would be worse than fool-hearty, it would be just plain insane! Still, a stealthy arrival could possibly give us time to refuel and lift off before the rebels are alerted that we're in the area. Maybe it's worth the risk.

Time passed slowly and the beauty of the landscape sliding beneath the plane lost some of its wonder to Sara. She couldn't get her mind off the mass grave site Chappy described. *How many people died in that massacre? What makes people okay with killing others? They sure don't know and fear God or they wouldn't be doing things like that!* she thought angrily to herself.

"Sara, if we could slip in unnoticed, we'd have a better chance of refueling without drawing the attention of rebels in the area. I'm going to cut the engine a couple miles shy of Tingi Tingi and land this bird like a glider."

Sara could only stare at her pilot, her mouth agape.

"Can you do that?" she finally stammered.

"I did it once in Korea during that war. Well, girl, get to praying!"

Without bowing her head Sara prayed, *We need a miracle here God! Help please!* Suddenly the drone of the engine stopped and the propeller slowed. Only the air passing through kept them spinning at all. Sara's stomach backed up into her throat and her eyes widened to saucers. Her knuckles turned white as she gripped the edges of her seat. *God, please help! Don't let us die!*

Bill Chapman hadn't glided a plane in for a landing in many years, and he hoped it was like riding a bicycle—something you never forget how to do. He hoped the wings or landing gear wouldn't catch on the tree tops as he banked to come into line with the straight section of road. Chappy wasn't a praying man, but he was sure relying on young Sara's prayers. For sure they couldn't hurt anything.

The Cessna barely brushed the treetops and dropped gently to the asphalt with barely a whisper. Bill slowly but firmly applied his brakes and rolled the plane to a stop before the road narrowed and curved out of sight up the hill and into the forest. A deep sigh of relief escaped his lips. "Good praying girl. Good praying!" Opening the cab door, he stepped down, and offered Sara his hand. "Come on, girl, we've got to turn this bird around ready for takeoff and find that stash of fuel fast!"

Deliberately Sara pried her fingers loose from the seat, and smiled weakly at the pilot. "Good Flying, Chappy."

Once on the ground, Bill showed Sara where to hold on the side of the plane and the two began pushing the light-weight plane in a semicircle. A dark form strolled from the shadows of the forest and moved towards them.

"You're crazier than I thought, Chap."

"That you Jeffrey?"

"Yep. Saw the plane, but couldn't hear any engines. You're the only nut I know gutsy enough to try a fool trick like that. Figured it had to be you."

Jeffrey stepped in behind Sara to lend his weight to the task.

"How bad is it here?"

"Bad enough, but I haven't seen too much activity since the massacre. Why you flying in here like this? Must be something awfully important to make you risk your sorry hide!"

"Got a passenger. Meet Miss Sara Calhoun. Niece to Ross Mann, friend of ol' Doc Vinton. She insisted on following Ross to Bukavu and going to Kama with him. Ross is a good friend,

I couldn't just turn my back on his kin. No telling what she'd do if left to her own devices. She's a determined young'n."

"So you brought her into this war zone?" Disbelief colored Jeffery's tone of voice.

"What can I say, I'm an idiot!" Chappy sounded disgusted with himself, and Jeffrey softened. One look at the girl, and he knew his friend could never refuse a request from her. Sensing his friend's understanding Chappy continued, "Then in Bangui we picked up another cargo, cholera medicine, 100 cases of the stuff. I hear its needed bad in these parts; decided to take it and Sara straight on into Kama."

"Well, you're an answer to prayer, Chap. Folks are dying by the dozens. The roads are impassable. Night traffic on the river is the safest, and that's not saying much. Ca'mon, lets get started. I've got a couple fuel drums hidden back here." The men moved away and Sara stepped closer to the plane, trying to blend into its shadow. "I hear the Mai Mai rebels are currently in control at the Kama compound."

"You're just full of good news, aren't ya?"

Then Sara could no longer hear what was being mumbled back and forth between the two men. *Thank you God for getting us down safely. Please help us get to Kama."*

The next thing she knew, Jeffrey and Chappy were back, straining to roll two 55 gallon drums onto the airstrip. A young African boy followed close behind them carrying some hose and a big bucket resembling a watering can with a long spout on one side, a handle on the other.

The stealth of their actions left Sara feeling breathless and nervous, but God had gotten them down out of the sky safely, and these men seemed to know what they were doing. Gradually a sense of peace settled over Sara and her courage returned.

"Seems quiet enough," Chappy murmured to Jeffery. The drums were righted close by the plane and their caps twisted off. Chappy attached the siphon hose to the fuel strainer drain under the plane's engine. Within seconds the hose was filled with fuel and Bill placed his thumb over both ends.

"Bring that jerry can over here." The young boy moved forward and sat the odd can between them. One end of the hose was stuck in the drum, the other end jabbed into the jerry can. Fuel began flowing from one can to the other. Jeffrey followed Chappy's example. With both hoses siphoning fuel the can quickly filled, and the hoses were crimped. Bill handed the crimped end of his hose to Jeffrey and hauled the jerry can over to the wing of the plane and poured it carefully into the fuel tank. The process was repeated with the men taking turns emptying the jerry can into the plane until the first drum was emptied and half the second was transferred to the plane. Both drums were recapped and rolled back into their hiding place.

Hunger tugged at Sara's stomach while she waited and watched. Nowhere could she see any indication of mass grave sites, and she was glad. She hadn't seen much from the air coming in either, but then, she had been praying hard at the time, and on reflection, remembered that her eyes had been tightly closed part of the time. She tried to hear what the men were muttering.

"Should I return here to refuel, Jeffrey? Or would the militia be waiting for me?"

"You're two hours from Kama. Deliver your cargo and get out of there. I'd recommend you skip over the border into Rwanda to refuel. The quicker you're out of the Congo, the better chance you'll have of keeping your bird. You do realize the rebels will assume you're flying in ammunition for the opposite side."

"Yeh, you're probably right about that." Chappy fell silent.

"Besides, we're hightailing it out of here as soon as you've gone," Jeffrey continued quietly. "We don't plan on being here should troops show up to check on a plane sighting."

Chappy grunted knowingly.

Timidly Sara spoke up. "Before we all hightail it out of here, could I beg a potty stop and something to drink?"

Blankly the men looked at one another, then grinned. "Great hosts we make, eh, Chap. Of course, Sara." The refueling was completed, and Jeffrey led the way through the trees. The forest opened up to expose what remained of a huge refugee camp. Litter lay everywhere, and an eerie silence hung in the air, causing Sara to shiver in spite of the midday heat. Motioning Chappy and Sara to follow him, Jeffrey led the way to a makeshift outhouse. The whole structure was only three to four foot tall and boasted no roof or much privacy.

"Sorry the accommodations are so primitive, Sara, but it's the best I have to offer. Chap, you stand guard, I'll get us some water."

Sara nodded her understanding, and decided this was no time for modesty. Entering the outhouse she saw only a deep dark hole in the ground with a foot pad on either side. Flies were buzzing everywhere. She took care of business as quick as possible, and thanked God she at least had the four walls.

When she was done they joined Jeffrey in the camp. He had set out an odd looking chunk of bread, a long green banana, and a small jar of peanut butter, as well as a jug of water. The young boy was nowhere to be seen.

"Would you mind assembling sandwiches for us, Sara?" Jeffrey looked apologetic but grinned mischievously. "I don't get to enjoy the creative touch of a white woman's cooking skills very often."

Sara smiled at the joke, hastily rubbed her hands on her pant legs, and took up the offered knife. She cut the bread in thick slabs, covered each with a layer of peanut butter, and sliced the banana on top. Jeffrey offered three large shiny banana leaves as plates, and she placed one sandwich on each. Before allowing the men to take up their meal, Sara bowed her head and quietly prayed out loud. "Dear God. Thank you for the safe landing on this airstrip and the fuel. Help us get this medicine to the people at Kama. Thanks for this food, and for stationing Jeffrey where we needed him. Amen."

"Amen," both men echoed, and Sara handed each one a sandwich and cup of water.

For the first time Sara took a good look at her surroundings. She noted overturned and broken benches, a pile of empty tin cans, garbage, and scattered papers turned yellow from the rain and sun. A piece of a toy truck stuck up out of the mud. *Were children massacred here too?* Before the horror sunk in, Chappy interrupted her thoughts.

"I think we'd best take off and not press our luck any further." Chappy quickly finishing off his sandwich, and downing the last of his water. "Thanks Jeffery. You were a Godsend."

Jeffrey nodded as he wiped his hands on his pant legs, and his mouth on his sleeve. "That's what I'm here for."

"Are you here alone?" The thought of being in such a haunting place with just the one boy made Sara cringe.

"Oh, no. I have lots of friends close by. You just can't see them. They're standing in as lookouts. You don't think I made that bread myself, do ya?" Jeffrey grinned. Sara just shrugged her shoulders and grinned back. "The Africans here are a bit shy of outsiders. They've been through a lot."

"Understandable. Thanks for being here Jeffrey." Though Sara had known Jeffrey only a short time, she felt like she'd known him her whole life. Impulsively she gave him a big hug, and shook his hand firmly as well. Then she followed Chappy back to the plane. Once there he pulled two boxes of the cholera medicine from behind the seat and handed them to Jeffrey. "Just in case you need some, friend . . . just in case."

Chappy fired up the engine, quickly scanned his instruments, and applied full power, rapidly gaining speed. Then they were airborne and headed for Kama without interference from any military force. Sara looked back at the rapidly shrinking airstrip. It was deserted.

Chapter Nineteen

Kama's dirt airstrip became visible as dusk settled over the forest. At first it appeared as a long pale scar which grew ever larger as they neared, beckoning them to the floor of the dense rain forest surrounding Kama. The setting sun glinted off the occasional tin roof below. Once again Bill cut their speed, then cut the engine and glided down like a big bird.

"This really is fun once you get the knack of it," Chappy grinned, but a sideways glance at Sara's white face and widened eyes decided him on a quick change in tactics. "God *must be* protecting us, Sara. I mean the lack of wind or clouds and all. Gliding in at dusk like this, we won't get a typical Kama welcome, but with the war on . . ." Chappy paused and glanced over at Sara again. Lamely he muttered, "Sure hope the airstrip's clear. You watch out below and warn me of any activity. Okay?"

Shifting in her seat, Sara tried to keep her hands relaxed in her lap. Her eyes were glued to the view below her. The only light she could see was the setting sun reflecting and shimmering in the two winding rivers that merged not far from the fast approaching airstrip. "I don't see any lights down there," she said, licking her lips nervously.

"You won't. Electricity's not common in the jungle. Missionaries have generators, but rarely use them. Fuel's too costly out here, and not easy to get. This airstrip is a testimonial to the people living here. Five hundred volunteer Congolese a' week, ten weeks running, built this airstrip with their bare hands. Men chopped down and dug out the trees. Women and children carried thousands upon thousands of baskets of dirt and sand, balanced on their heads, to fill the slumps, and level the land. It was a formidable project! But there it lies—making access to Kama possible!"

The awe in Chappy's voice touched Sara. While he didn't want to get trapped by warring factions, it was obvious that he greatly respected the spirit of the Congolese people. The plane bumped gently to the ground and Bill allowed it to continue rolling as far down the airstrip as its momentum allowed.

"The closer we are to the end of the airstrip, the shorter the distance those cartons will have to be carried," was all the explanation he offered. Coming to a stop, Chappy popped the door and climbed out. Silently he offered assistance to Sara and she stepped down to the ground. Together they turned the plane around, ready for takeoff, then Chappy lead the way to Baba V's home.

"So far, so good. I want to turn you over to your uncle, tell Baba V about the IV shipment, get it off-loaded, and then I'm out'a here."

Swallowing hard Sara braced herself to see her uncle again. Quietly they made their way across the grassy field flanking the airstrip to a network of paths through manicured grass and flower patches as neat as any city park in America. Evening light filtered down through the trees and danced shadows with a sudden breeze. Palm trees of differing heights stood proudly among a variety of trees Sara did not recognize.

"I guess we should thank God for the clear skies, Sara. We've arrived safely, and still have enough light to find our way to Baba V's door." Chappy spoke quietly in Sara's ear, as he steered her along a walkway to the left and led her onto the porch of a rustic looking brick home. Looking around, Sara saw several buildings of equal stature placed around the park area. *Homes of other missionaries,* she thought.

Bill tapped sharply on the front door, and they waited, listening for responding sounds inside the home. Nothing happened for several minutes, and Chappy rapped again, a little louder. A thump and then scurrying sounds came from inside, but no one came to the door.

"May I help you?" The speaker appeared at the corner of the house. He was of medium height by American standards, and slender. Distinguishing age or features, other than the white of his eyes, was impossible as he stood in the shadow of the house.

"We're looking for Ross Mann. Is he staying here with Baba V?"

"No Ross Mann here. Baba V not here. You need medicine? Come back in morning."

"Well, Ross is coming. I have his niece here and she needs housing tonight—here with Baba V. We've brought medicine in a plane for Baba V's work. It needs to be moved to the pharmacy before it is discovered and stolen. Could'ya round us up some muscle?"

"You wait here." The shadowy figure vanished so quietly Sara wondered if anyone had actually been there or if her imagination was playing tricks on her. It seemed like forever before he reappeared, but he had several young men in tow.

Chappy led the way back to the plane. The cargo bay was opened, and as quickly as possible the plane was emptied of all cartons. Just as quickly silent dark forms carried the cartons away to a brick building off the end of the airstrip. Chappy pumped the hand of each helper in gratitude, then spoke softly to the man in charge. Turning to Sara he said, "Kilongo's wife will get you settled in for the night. You're in good hands. Good luck to you, Miss Sara. Ross will be proud of you." He embraced her in an uncharacteristic hug, climbed into the cab of the plane and handed down her backpack. "Look me up when you get back to Douala."

Before Sara could dig out her money to pay him, Chappy fired his engine and taxied down the airstrip, gaining speed and a clean liftoff before the dark of night could ground him at Kama.

Dumbfounded, Sara raised her hand to wave and watched till the plane was out of sight. Kilongo touched her lightly on the shoulder, and stood waiting for her to follow him. She hesitated, staring up as the stars began to show themselves. The night air suddenly felt cold, sending shivers down her arms and spine. *Lord, what have I gotten myself into? What if Uncle Ross doesn't come?*

Fighting the panic that threatened to overwhelm her, Sara forced herself into practical thoughts. *Well, I'm here now, God. You got me here safe, now I've just got to trust you'll continue to take care of me. Please help me trust!* Turning her back to the airstrip, Sara surrendered to Kilongo's lead.

Back at Baba V's house, Kilongo's wife led the way into a small bedroom off the entryway. She carefully stepped over two small forms that lay sleeping on a blanket bathed in crisscrossed moonlight shining through the latticed window and motioned Sara to the single bed. "You sleep here, Miss. Tomorrow Baba V return."

"Thank you for putting me up. I hope I haven't put these children out of their bed."

"They young. They not care. Sleep well, Miss Sara. Mornings come early in Kama." Sara turned to thank her hostess only to find she had gone as quietly as her husband.

Sara laid her backpack aside and pulled off her shoes. She lay staring at the ceiling and swatting at mosquitoes a long time before she drifted off to sleep.

When the activities along the airstrip were completed, and it again lay naked in the moonlight, a man's form separated from a tree and walked swiftly away from the compound.

Chapter Twenty

Morning did come swiftly. A strangely beautiful chorus of exotic birdcalls, humming insects, crowing roosters, and bleating goats filtered through Sara's subconscious. A perception of people moving softly about soon joined the strangeness of her dream. Giggles erupted close by when she stretched and moaned in protest of her grogginess.

Growing awareness turned to panic sending adrenaline pumping into her veins. Suddenly her eyes popped open and she bolted upright coming face to face with two small black faces, bright eyed and curious. Again giggles erupted as Sara blinked in disbelief for a moment or two before memory came flooding back. *I'm at Kama! These are the children I displaced last night.* Forcing herself to relax, Sara smiled at her roommates. "Good morning. Is it time to wake up?"

One child nodded enthusiastically and the other just stared at her with curious eyes and a shy smile.

"Amu can't hear you. She don't talk. Baba say she a deaf mute," offered the boy. "I talk English. Baba teach me. You live here now?"

"I don't know. I haven't talked with Baba V yet," Sara answered honestly and swung her legs over the side of the bed. "Does Baba V know I'm here?"

"Baba know. Apol say come eat."

"Okay. My name's Sara. What are your names?" Sara looked from the first child to the second, and reached out her hand to take the little girl's hand, squeezing it gently.

"I'm Vincent, she Bi-Amu. We call her Amu. Apol make chakula. You come eat."

Sara's gaze swept from coarse, short cropped black hair, curled tightly against the heads of both children to the bare feet and toes sturdily hugging the wood floor. Amu's faded checkered cotton frock looked like a hand-me-down from a thrift store on skid row. Vincent wore tan shorts and a blue shirt, both were stained. *They seem healthy enough*, flashed through Sara's mind. She gathered up her knapsack, pulled out a brush and hair clips, and set about grooming herself for the day.

The children watched in fascination, and rewarded her with grins when she let them feel her soft auburn hair. In turn Sara felt their coarse black curls and they all giggled. Finally combed and feeling somewhat presentable, Sara followed Amu and Vincent through the house to the kitchen. Two cooked eggs and a flat bread cake set on the table. Apol gestured for Sara to sit down and help herself.

"Good morning. I hope you were able to get back to sleep last night. Thank you again for your help." Sara recognized the women as the same who had helped her the night before.

"I not sleep hard, Kama under rebel control. I must sleep light."

"Where is Baba V?"

"Baba on medical safari to dispense dawa—ah, what you call medicine. People need him, come long way for help. Sometimes Baba goes to people. He be back today."

"Oh."

"You eat now. You see Baba later." Disappointment must have shown on Sara's face, for the cook touched her lightly on the arm and said, "There's much time to see Baba. You eat now and put on dress. Then you walk around Kama. Maybe go to market."

Sara wondered why Apol wanted her in a dress, but hesitated to ask. "Is it safe for me to wander around alone?" Immediately Sara regretted asking such a tactless question. *I'm not 'safe' wandering around my own hometown in America, why should I expect better here?* But Apol did not seem to take offense at her question.

"Ngalia go with you. She speak fair English. She need hear you speak, learn more." Apol nodded her head in determination, communicating to Sara that she was expected to help Ngalia as much as Ngalia helped her. It seemed a fair deal.

"I didn't bring any dresses." Sara watched Apol's reaction to her confession. "Is that a problem?"

"In Kama women wear dresses. Men wear pants. Ngalia will find you a dress." Apol began chattering excitedly to Vincent in Swahili, and he disappeared outside.

The bread looked odd to Sara, but she did not want to offend. *Please help me like this food, God. I can't get squeamish now!* Looking up Sara saw Apol was waiting for her reaction to the food, so she picked up the bread, dipped it in an egg yolk, and bit off a piece. To her surprise, it tasted pretty good, and she finished with enthusiasm. Apol seemed satisfied, and set a mug of white foamy liquid before her.

"Goat milk," Apol supplied. "Baba V must have milk. You have milk too."

"Thank you." Sara smiled. She had never tasted goat's milk, or any other milk fresh from the udder, still warm and frothy. Swallowing hard, she put the mug to her lips and sipped the white liquid, letting the rich creamy flavor rest on her tongue, comparing it to the 2% grocery store milk she knew.

Both were white. Both were liquid. But the comparison ended there. *This is good! I could get used to this.*

By the time Sara finished savoring her milk, Vincent returned with a folded garment in his hands. He handed it to Apol and scampered off, grinning over his shoulder at Sara.

Apol handed the small bundle to Sara. "Please put on dress. Then Ngalia can show you Kama."

Reluctantly Sara complied with the command. *Dresses. Who'da thought it?* The dress was much too big for her, and not at all a complimentary color or pattern. To ease her discomfort, Sara pulled a pair of shorts on under the dress —thankful that no one from home could see her.

Apol made no comment, but led Sara outside to where Ngalia was busy weaving a small basket. A tiny child played in the dirt at Ngalia's side, and looked up to study Sara with curious eyes. Something very familiar struck Sara as she looked at the child, and when she turned her attention to the girl, her suspicions were confirmed.

"You made my basket! Uncle Ross sent me your picture with the basket! I love it! You do beautiful work!"

Ngalia accepted Sara's outburst with humor. "You muss belong to Baba's friend Ross Mann. He have flame hair too." Ngalia set the half-finished basket aside and stood, scooping her young son into her arms. She offered her hand to Sara, and when Sara responded in like manner, Ngalia pumped her hand enthusiastically. "Karibu, uh—welcome. We hope you enjoy your stay," and she grinned.

"You show Miss Sara around Kama now, Ngalia."

"It be my honor." Ngalia's son continued to stare at Sara, even as Ngalia settled him into a sling of cloth on her back. The toddler's stare was so intense Sara got the giggles.

"He doesn't know what to make of me, does he?"

"Baba V only white people Paipi know," Ngalia grinned. "Other missionaries gone since war. Soldiers say white people spys. Paipi know Ross Mann. He pull on Ross Mann's wooly red face. He like you soon. What you see first?"

"Oh, everything!" Sara blurted. "I've seen nothing in the daylight. Uncle Ross comes here to visit Baba V, and he's sent me gifts from your market. Could we go there first?"

"Good. Maybe you find dress you like better." Amazed at Ngalia's discernment, Sara's appreciation of her new friend grew. "I show you to people at market, so they know you friend."

"Okay," Sara chuckled. "Let's go see the market. Maybe I'll find a smaller dress."

Ngalia nodded approval and led the way. She was fully as tall as Sara with curly hair cropped about shoulder length. Sara guessed her to be somewhere between fifteen and twenty years old.

People turned to stare as Sara passed them. *I'd better minimize my hair,* Sara thought self-consciously. *Perhaps really tight braids rolled into a tiny bun, or maybe Ngalia'll make me hundreds of tiny braids tight against my head that I can pull together at the neck. I've seen that back home. My pale complexion and auburn hair sure stand out against the native black!*

Sara pulled away from her thoughts to hear Ngalia saying, "The *marche'* is open Saturdays. You come at good time. No rain today, maybe."

They had traveled less than 100 yards from Baba V's home. Already a milling sea of villagers were on hand to view the displays.

Just like flea markets back home, one's got to get up early to beat the crowds. New smells assaulted Sara's nose. The smell of unwashed bodies seemed to intensify at every turn. *I'm guessing African huts don't have showers.* Sara fought the urge to wrinkle her nose.

Everyone seemed excited about Sara's presence, and Ngalia introduced Sara to all the merchants she knew. Sara could follow some of the French chatter, but nothing in Swahili. Ngalia supplied, in English, a lively account of any item that caught Sara's interest. Small whitened eggplants, mangoes, manioc—looking to Sara like sweet potatoes. Lenga lenga looked like hog greens or spinach; chickens ran about underfoot. Sara saw chili peppers, curry, and a spice Ngalia called manzame, dried and powdered. She explained they were used for seasoning. Large, handmade wooden ladles and bowls, with beautiful designs burned or carved into the handles were available, along with a few baskets, and salt stored in various size jars.

"See big leaves?" Ngalia said, pointing to a stack of large leaves beside one of the women. "Watch how used to wrap things for carrying home. Men and boys fish the river, women dry fish to sell at market. See dried fish there? Here is soap. It's made from palm oil and lye. Since planes stopped coming its hard to bring things from big city. No more big bundles clothes from America, our supply run low since war started. War ruins everything."

"Do you get any outside merchandise now?"

"Not many. People from Mari have a ream with

Mai Mai. They cross over the river to path through jungles to Shabunda. From Shabunda they go by river and foot to Bukavu for supplies. They buy goods and return same way unless soldiers in area. If soldiers, they go different way home."

"Ugh," was all Sara could think to say. She didn't understand what Ngalia meant by a 'ream', but she understood the general drift of her explanation, enough to know her knowledge of the soldiers and geography of the Congo needed much improvement before she would understand any better. Wisely she let the subject drop.

A small roped off area with a makeshift leaf shelter appeared to be serving as an outdoor restaurant. A few villagers already sat under its shade to eat from their early morning purchases.

Sara saw several kinds of flour. Ngalia explained these were ground from rice, manioc, and cassava. "Cassava flour best mixed with ground corn, it not taste good by itself." Sara tucked the warning away in her memory.

In the tall grass several yards away, several men were deeply engrossed in something. Their backs were turned to the main thoroughfare.

"They're butchering a goat." Ngalia pointed, and laughed as Sara scrunched her nose when she caught the smell on the breeze.

They came to the area with locks and keys, shoe polish, thread, mothballs, razor blades, small tape recorder/radio unit, batteries, hard candy, needles, thong sandals, nylon cord, and a few odd pieces of used clothing . . . nothing that interested Sara.

"Are the soldiers dangerous, Ngalia?" Sara asked after two gun carrying stern-faced men in tattered shorts brushed past them staring at Sara with sullen faces.

"Shhhh. Pretend they not here and stay ready to run hide in forest. Not all mean. Most angry. They not get paid often, so they steal and demand bribes from us. If you anger them, they burn your crops and house," Ngalia whispered, her head low and close to Sara's.

Sara shuddered at the menace she saw in the eyes of one soldier. He seemed to be following them at a distance, never taking his eyes off Ngalia. Every time Sara looked his way, he was staring at them. Ngalia was so careful not to look in the man's direction that Sara knew she was very aware of him.

"Do you know him?" she asked quietly.

"Yes. He always watching, always angry. There's no cloth today, we go to clinic now."

Sara was fascinated with all the wares on display, or lack thereof, but the stares of the soldier following them unsettled her nerves and she did not argue with Ngalia.

"Paipi has competition in the staring department!" Sara tried to laugh lightly, and reached out her hand to touch the baby's cheek. When she did, Paipi grabbed her finger and tried to put it in his mouth. "Someone is getting hungry."

"Paipi always hungry. No more food for baby till night." Sara's heart went out to the darling baby and young mother.

Perhaps Apol could suggest someone to return to the market and make some purchases for her. Maybe she would be allowed to thank Ngalia for her hospitality with food.

Ngalia led the way to the clinic swiftly, and Sara matched her steps. The staring soldier did not follow them, but Sara could feel his angry eyes following them till they disappeared behind the pharmacy.

The crowd of people lined up in front of the clinic entrance caused Sara dismay. Men stationed among the people seemed to be preaching from the scriptures to those who waited. Sara saw open wounds, crying children, and tottering older Africans looking as if on their last leg. She wondered if any had the cholera and would receive IVs from the shipment they brought in the night before. Ngalia walked a wide berth around the line and headed back towards home.

"Baba V very busy now. Many people come on Saturdays, stay for church on Sunday. Baba will take time out for lunch soon. You see him then."

Ross Mann and Kent Cooper stayed at the mission in Los Angeles for two more days, waiting, hoping and praying that some word would come from Sara.

On Saturday morning Ross determined it was time to return to Douala. "My contacts in the government have heard nothing about an American girl on her own in Africa. The missionaries in Bukavu haven't heard anything yet. I can do nothing further from here."

"I'm sorry you made this long trip for nothing, Ross," Pastor Dave sympathized. "I'll continue to pray for God's protection over all concerned. If you hear anything, anything at all, please, keep us posted."

"You know I will." Ross enveloped Mrs. Schaffer in a final hug and shook hands with Dave. Kent then did the same. The two caught a cab to the Los Angeles International Airport and flew out together. Ross tended to some business at Tarbell Headquarters in Chicago before Kent dropped him off at the airport for his return flight to Douala.

Twice Ross made contact with the guest house in Bukavu and spoke with the missionaries there, but no one had heard of Sara, and little was known of what was happening in the interior of the country. Sara had seemingly just vanished off the face of the earth.

"Well, Lord, You know Sara's whereabouts. When the time is right would you cut me in? I hate not knowing, it makes me feel so helpless. But You know, and You are not helpless. Please keep our girl safe, please, Lord."

The prayer was uttered out loud, but others on the plane didn't seem to notice.

Chapter Twenty One

True to Ngalia's prediction, Baba V broke away from the clinic at noon. When he arrived home Sara was there to meet him.

The horseshoe of feathery white hair crowning his head was all that revealed the man's multitude of years. His tall pear shaped torso was strikingly energetic and unstooped for a man in his nineties. Despite the strong chin and heavy dark rimmed glasses that straddled the bridge of his long straight nose, his gaunt face conveyed kindness.

Sitting down at the head of the table, Baba addressed Sara. "Jambo sana, Miss Sara. So, you are niece to my friend Ross Mann, are you?" He spoke rapidly and with a heavy accent, probably caused by speaking Swahili and French so many decades. Sara's eyes became glued to his huge bony hands and sensitive fingers, which he waved expressively as he talked.

"Yes Sir. He is my uncle."

"What brings you to Kama?"

"My parents are gone. Uncle Ross is my only living relative. I tried to catch him in Cameroon, but missed him by half a day. It's my understanding that he's on his way here with medical supplies."

"I see. So you bring us a planeload of medical supplies as well. It seems God is at work providing our needs in miraculous ways as usual. Let's thank Him. Dear God," the old man began with head bowed, "thank you for bringing Sara to us safely. Please watch over my dear friend Ross, and bless the work here with your wonderful people. Thank you for this daily supply of food and the hands that prepared it. Thank you for the church Services we will enjoy tomorrow, here and at the colony, and in all the villages. Prepare now the hearts of your people to hear your words. Give me strength and wisdom to do the work you have given me. Amen."

"Amen," Sara echoed and Apol began serving a simple lunch complete with more goat's milk. Sara drank the warm milk, but silently missed having a cold soda with her noon meal.

"Well, girl," Baba V spoke around a mouthful of food, "what do you intend to do while you are here?"

"I don't know. Is there some way I could help?"

"Of course. How much schooling have you had?"

"I just finished high school. I've had a couple years of French." Sara spoke tentatively.

"Good! We'll put you to work teaching English in the high school. Proper pronunciation and use of English is very important. You will be a great help to the students." His huge hands flailed about expressively. "Our school system is quite extensive. We have 18 hundred teachers for 20 thousand students in 300 schools throughout the province. In order to graduate high school or go on to higher education, students must understand and speak good French and English. Their final exam is given in English, both oral and written. By high school graduation our students speak four languages; their tribal dialect, the trade language of Swahili, the official language of French, and English." Fatherly pride flavored the doctor's speech.

Sara stared at the aged doctor. He expected her to jump right in and teach school? "Of course, I'll help any way I can." Sara muttered quickly, and felt her stomach begin to tie in knots. *I've never taught school. I'm barely out of school myself!*

"Good. Consider yourself hired for the duration of your visit. You start Monday."

Satisfied that the matter was settled, the doctor focused on finishing his meal, and pushed back from the table. "Enjoy your Saturday at Kama, Sara." At the door, Amu appeared as if she had been waiting for him. She took his hand and led him away.

Sara sat staring at his retreating back. *My word, no wasted time or resources here! Now I'm an English teacher and still have only one dress to wear!*

Apol appeared to clear away the dishes, and Sara seized the moment. "Apol, could someone go to the market for me. There are several things I wanted, but thought it best not to make a show of money my first time out."

"You show wisdom, Sara. The children would show no mercy from begging and the adults would cut you no deals. Very wise. What you want? I go. I get best prices." Apol flashed her very white teeth at Sara, who couldn't help grinning back.

"Thank you, Apol. I should have another dress if I'm to be teaching school, but I didn't see any at the market today. I'd like to thank Ngalia for her kindness with a basket of food. Is that OK? I mean, would I offend if I gave her food?"

"Ngalia's proud, not foolish. She need food."

"Good. You'd know so much better than me what to get. I want something fun for the baby too, and a little gift for Amu and Vincent for sharing their room with me. How many franc will you need to do all that?"

"Can't use francs anymore, Sara. Government says we must use zaires, but I can get your money changed. You pay for transaction."

Apol stood figuring in her head for a moment, then suggested an amount and Sara added a little extra to it. "Please add to Baba V's pantry for me too. I can't just drop in on him like this and expect him to feed me all the time I'm here."

"You are kind Sara. I speak with Ngalia. She find you a dress. Vincent go to watch for you."

"Thank you."

The cook nodded and turned to carry the dishes out to the yard for cleaning.

Ngalia and Paipi joined Sara at the table before she had finished her lunch. "Apol say you need two dresses."

"Baba V hired me to teach school, Ngalia. Surely I'll need more than one dress."

"Africa poor country. One dress okay, but two better. One to wear while you wash other. I take you to my hiding place. You pick out a dress."

"You hide dresses?"

"Not mine, belong to missionary ladies. When soldiers break into one empty missionary house and steal everything, I ran to house of single lady missionaries who teach school. They gone because of war. I grabbed all clothes and ran into the forest to hide them for when they come back. They not mind you wear them."

"Do you think any of them will fit better than this one?" Sara grinned pulling the waist of the dress away from her body.

"We try," Ngalia giggled. "I not see you before going to secret place this morning! We take baskets and fill with kuni," Ngalia said pointing to the shrinking wood stack next to the fireplace. "Vincent follow and give warning if anyone follow."

Paipi broke away from Ngalia and tottered over to Sara. Sara looked at Ngalia with questioning eyes, and with only a slight hesitation the young mother gave her permission to let the baby have the last of her milk. Sara was prepared to hold the cup tightly and keep the baby from spilling more than he drank. But Paipi was very careful not to spill any of the special treat and Sara's heart hurt that this one so small instinctively knew the value of nourishment.

Paipi looked at her with such gratitude in his big brown eyes that Sara scooped the baby into her arms and hugged him.

"You really know how to keep those treats coming don't you," she crooned to the squirming toddler, "You are one adorable little boy." After one more hug she released him to totter back to his Momma, and the two girls, with Vincent trailing a discreet distance behind, set out to shop at Ngalia's secret hiding place.

Ngalia carried her basket gracefully on her head, her baby on her back. Sara tried to balance her basket on top her head a few times, but quickly gave up and carried it the American way—under one arm braced against the hip. Vincent and Ngalia both giggled at her attempts and failures.

"Another day I teach you," Ngalia promised. "Amu seems very devoted to Baba V," Sara commented as they walked along. "She met him at the door and took his hand to walk with him back to the clinic. She must miss him very much during the day."

Ngalia looked at Sara sideways. "Amu loves Baba V, yes. But she walk beside him to guide him. Baba almost blind. He sees only from sides of his eyes. Baba very old."

Sara was silent for a several minutes, thinking about what Ngalia had said. It made sense. Subconsciously she had noticed that the doctor hadn't looked at her straight on, but seemed to look just past her across the room. Now she knew why.

"How does he treat patients if he can't see clearly?"

"Baba been doctor longer than most people live. He knows what questions to ask. People trust him, they tell him what he needs to know. And he has helpers he train. Baba's been delivering babies 70 years—he delivered most his patients, their parents and grandparents. Besides he can feel a broken bone or fevered skin with his fingers."

Ngalia paused a moment, then continued almost defensively. "If someone come and need more help than he know, he send them to government hospital. But people want Baba. He treat people with dignity and not steal from them. He train others to be his eyes and help him. They clean and bind wounds and give medicines he says. The babies are hardest. They not like bad tasting medicines. Sometimes the men have hard time getting medicine down inside baby."

"I could help with that." Sara thought of the times she had assisted her mother in doctoring sick children who came in off the streets with their homeless mothers. How many times had she shampooed and fine-tooth-combed small heads infested with lice? Remembering caused the pain of losing her parents to flood over her again. She walked on in silence, picking up bits of wood here and there, until Ngalia dodged behind a tall clump of giant-leafed plants, pulling Sara off the trail with her.

Ngalia knelt down and pushed aside dirt and leaves revealing the lid of a large Tupperware box buried in the forest floor. She lifted the lid and leaned it against the tree trunk, revealing half a dozen dresses, neatly folded and laid inside. Tucked in around them laid brushes and mirrors, and other personal effects that Ngalia had considered important to the women from America.

"What color you want?" she asked simply.

"Blue is a good color on me, or green."

Ngalia lifted a light-green dress from the middle of the stack and stood up. She shook it out and held it up against Sara. "I think it fit you with a little needlework." The dress had a simple shape, short sleeved top with v-neck collar, and a full skirt. Not really something Sara wanted to tackle with thread and needle, but it had possibilities.

"It's beautiful Ngalia. Thank you." Sara took the dress from Ngalia and began studying its seams and basic construction. "Ngalia, why do the women here only wear dresses?"

"Because we are women. Man step behind tree to relieve himself. Not so easy for us. We need to squat. Dress give privacy."

"Ohhh," was all Sara could manage in response, her eyes widening in comprehension. Come to think of it, she hadn't noticed any outhouses.

Kneeling again, Ngalia pulled all the dresses aside to reveal a blue one on the bottom of the box. "This one blue?"

Grinning, Sara responded, "Yes, that one is blue. You do well with your English Ngalia." Paipi was becoming unsettled with all the ups and downs his mother was putting him through, and began to wail. Sara reached out to him, and he held his arms up to her. Sara snuggled the baby close, comforting him, and herself. *Babies,* she thought, *are the same the world over. They need comfort and help, yet always give more than they demanded in the bargain.*

Ngalia sealed the lid back onto the box and pushed dirt over it. Rising, she sprinkled leaves and other forest matter over the top to match the surrounding area. Moving swiftly she folded the two dresses together and rolled them up in a large leaf, and stacked it along with several chunks of firewood in the bottom of Sara's basket. She gathered several chunks of wood for her own basket and reclaimed her son. Swinging Paipi onto her back, her basket onto her head, Ngalia motioned Sara to get her basket and follow her back to the trail. Obediently Sara lifted her assigned basket to her hip and followed.

"My neck hurts just watching you do that!" Sara exclaimed.

"Kuni is heavy," Ngalia acknowledged. "We go back on trail now and hunt more kuni. Vincent is close. Would you like to see river?" Sara nodded and Ngalia led the way. "Watch for good kuni. Everyone gathers close to home. We'll find more as we get farther away."

Sara nodded and marveled that Ngalia could so easily carry such a weight on her head, a baby on her back, and still bend and pick up heavy firewood. "Ngalia, is Paipi your own baby, or is he your brother or cousin?"

Ngalia froze in her tracks and stared at Sara. "You do not know?"

"No, I really don't. I just wondered." Sara lifted one shoulder subconsciously and twisted her mouth questioningly at Ngalia. She realized she had been insensitive in her question and wished she could take it back. "I'm sorry, that was a bad question, please just forget I ever asked."

"No. It is fair question. Paipi is my own baby, but I have no husband."

"Ngalia, I'm so sorry. I didn't mean to pry. This is none of my business." Sara's cheeks flamed red and she lowered her eyes to the path at her feet and wished she'd kept her mouth shut.

"No. You are friend," Ngalia said, placing her hand on Sara's arm. "You should know. God very good to me. Soldiers come to my village, everyone run. I not run fast enough. I was young and scared. Soldiers did bad things to me, Sara. They used me in a very bad way. I wanted to die. But God said no Ngalia, you not die. I give you beautiful baby that will be all your own. No one can take him away from you."

"They raped you?" Sara was astounded and couldn't keep from staring directly into Ngalia's soft brown eyes.

"Many soldiers," Ngalia whispered, her gaze lowered momentarily, but then she lifted her head high and proud. "But God better than soldiers. Soldiers only shame and hurt me. God take away my sorrow and gave me Paipi."

"Do you live with your parents?"

"No. I live with Apol and Kilongo. My family ashamed for me. In Africa children belong to father and father's family. If father die, children go back to father's family for raising. Mother must go back to her family and hope another man chose her to wife and mother children for him. But no one can say who father of Paipi is, so Paipi is mine only."

"Ngalia, was that soldier in the market this morning one of those soldiers?" Sara asked softly.

"Yes, he one of them. He thinks baby his, but everybody know he can't prove Paipi his. I live, and Paipi mine alone."

"In America children belong to both parents. If one parent dies, the children can stay with the other parent. I can't even imagine how awful it would be to lose your husband, then have all your children taken from you on top of it." The girls walked on in silence until Sara sighed. "Ngalia, God was good to you! If I had a baby, I can't imagine giving it up, no matter what the customs were. I'm sorry for your pain, but glad you're free from such a harsh custom."

The glimmer of water sparkled through the trees and Ngalia lifted the basket from her head and sat it against a large tree trunk back away from the river bank. Sara lowered her basket beside it. Vincent caught up with them and grinned as he sauntered to the water's edge.

"Can I go out in the water, Ngalia?" He asked. "You watch for crocs and stay very close to shore."

"Okay." Vincent quickly stripped down to his underwear and after peering into the water several minutes, he let out a yelp and jumped feet first into the water. Ngalia and Sara stood close by watching for any sign of crocodiles, and let the boy have his reward for guarding their privacy. He didn't swim long, and was quickly back on the shore pulling his clothes on over his dark wet body.

"Thank you, Ngalia. That was very good!" With that the boy shouldered Sara's kuni basket and set off for Kama ahead of them.

Ngalia lifted her basket of wood onto her head and motioned Sara to follow. Sara pulled herself away but couldn't help glancing back at the murky water wondering if indeed there were crocodiles in there or if they were just teasing her because she didn't know one way or the other.

Evening came swiftly, and Baba V came home to shower and dress in his pajamas. Apol built a small fire in the fireplace to chase the cool night air away.

Baba V sat at the ham radio and made connection with Tom and Michelle Sanchez at the Mission House in Bukavu.

"Hello, dear friends," Baba's voice boomed over the scratchy static of the radio currents. "I have a house guest here. Her name is Sara Calhoun. She's the niece of Ross Mann. Has he arrived there in Bukavu yet?"

Goose bumps prickled over Sara's arms as she waited for a response to come back.

"Hello, Baba V. Hello Sara. No, Ross is not here. But we have heard from him."

"Where is he?" Sara snapped and flinched at the tone she heard in her own voice. What right did she have to make demands of Uncle Ross. He hadn't messed up. She had.

Gracious chuckles cracked across the air waves and Sara felt her face flush. Would she ever learn to show restraint? Her embarrassment turned to horror when Tom said, "He's in Los Angeles, Sara, looking for you."

Uncle Ross in Los Angeles? That just couldn't be! Shock nearly rendered Sara speechless, but she squeaked out, "Los Angeles? He said he was coming here!"

Baba V took back the conversation. "Can you make contact with Ross to let him know Sara is here at Kama?"

"We'll try now that we know where she is. He already spoke with his contacts in Duoala. "They told him she was in Africa looking for him. He's headed back this way."

"Get word to him that Sara has landed safely at Kama. She came in last night on a plane carrying cholera medicine. I've put her to work teaching English in the high school. Ross can retrieve her whenever he's able, but assure him her time here will be well spent."

Apol called Sara to get her shower, and she jumped at the distraction. *How can you get yourself in so much trouble, Sara Calhoun?* She fumed, *You'll be lucky if Uncle Ross even wants to come get you now! You can't blame him if he decides to just leave you here till you learn your lesson.*

"Now, watch for crawlies in shower, Sara," Apol's warning tone cut through Sara's thoughts. "Sometimes spiders or snakes come in. It not happen often, but you should be aware. Be quick. Water's limited. Vincent carry extra water from the Village well for you today, but only two jugs."

Thoughts of spiders and snakes sharing her bathing space filled Sara with apprehension and she had a hard time focusing on the mechanics of starting and stopping the water as Apol demonstrated. "Is the water cold?"

"No, Sara. Baba has a 50 gallon water drum heated by fireoven under it. We used to pump water from a well to the water tower, but the pump is old and we can't get parts to fix it. Now Vincent carry water to pay his keep. I show you tomorrow."

"Thank you Apol." It seemed like a month, not three days, since Sara had benefited from a shower at the hotel in Cameroon and she had no intentions of missing this one. Thoughts of spiders or snakes intruding upon her space so rushed her that there was water to spare when she stepped out to dry off, feeling foolish she forced herself to get back in and rinse the soap out of her hair.

"Baba V showers here every day and he's survived to be in his nineties, Sara," she scolded herself. "Don't be such a baby."

When Sara joined the rest of the family in the parlor, the sun was setting over the distant mountain range and cast a warm orange glow over the land. Vincent pushed a chair up close to the fireplace for her to sit and dry her long hair. Amu shyly took the towel away from Sara and carefully pushed it against her hair. Sara smiled at the little girl and allowed her to play at drying and styling her hair. It would seem children were the same the world over.

It was peaceful and quiet in the room. Apol had gone home to her family. Ngalia sat in the light of the fire weaving her basket. Baba V sat rocking gently in a well-worn rocker that Sara thought must have rocked all the Vinton babies, children, grandchildren, great-grandchildren, and countless African babies as well. Paipi lay sleeping in his arms.

God's love permeated the room. It was a familiar feeling and Sara felt she had come home. *If only Uncle Ross were here with us it would be perfect,* Sara sighed. *If only.*

Chapter Twenty Two

Six hundred Africans crowded into the tin roofed church building Sunday morning. Sara looked around at the mud brick walls and arched lattice windows that cast a checkerboard shadow on the dirt floor. *I bet rain thundering on this tin roof would drown out even the loudest preacher,* she thought to herself.

Except for the half dozen chairs lined up on the platform for the speakers, folks sat on row upon row of long, well-worn, split log benches. Sara was amazed that people seemed happy to sit on hard rough-hewn benches without complaint. She hoped she could do the same.

Pigs, goats and chickens wandered past the side door, looking in as if interested in what was taking place inside those walls. It was all Sara could do to keep from giggling.

Baba V rose from his chair on the platform and stepped forward to a crude pulpit.

"Many of you have already met our new friend, Sara Calhoun." He spoke in Swahili, and Ngalia translated the words in Sara's ears. "God sent her to us in the plane that brought us medicine." A cheer rose from the crowd and the people clapped their hands. Sara felt overwhelmed and embarrassed, but it was hard not to feel enthused. The people seemed to accept her presence with gladness. The thought that Baba felt God had sent her to them sent shivers down her spine.

As Baba V sat down, a tall lanky man stood and began to sing in a strong voice. Magnificent, untrained African voices burst into harmony all around Sara. It was beautiful to hear, not like anything she had ever experienced before. Ngalia whispered in her ear, "That is Pastor Andre." Sara nodded her head that she had heard.

At the end of several songs, the Pastor sat down and several ensembles, following in rapid succession, added their beautiful melodies to the stirring service. As they sang, their bodies swayed in unison, and they clapped together in rhythm. As the end of their song approached, they began to sing more quietly until only a whisper could be heard, all the while descending slowly to their seats. By the time each group finished, the next group was in place on the platform ready to start their singing.

Ngalia tried to keep Sara informed about each of the songs. Some were Bible stories set to music. Some Sara recognized as old hymns and smiled as she followed the tune with English words in her mind. She loved hearing the songs in Swahili. It was a fascinating language.

Finally it was time for the message and Baba V again rose and strode to the podium. His bright-colored, flowered sport shirt and plain slacks seemed appropriate for the setting. The group grew quiet as every ear strained to hear what Baba V had to say on this occasion.

After quoting Second Corinthians 5:17 from his Swahili Bible, the missionary-preacher dramatically called on those who had Bibles to open them and read the passage with him: "Therefore, if any man be in Christ, he is a new creation; old things are passed away; behold, all things are become new."

The 45-minute sermon that followed was punctuated with appropriate gestures and hearty amens from the listeners. Sara marveled at the respect shown the aging missionary as the people hung on every word. Never had Sara experienced such a worship service. Two hours later Sara was glad to stand and stretch as best she could in the crowd milling towards the exits.

Apol appeared at their side as soon as the service was over. "Please hurry home for dinner, Sara. Baba V wants you to join us in the services at the colony after dinner."

Sara arrived home to find the table set with dishes of fish, rice, mangos, and bread thinly spread with peanut butter. By the look in Vincent and Amu's eyes when they saw the peanut butter, Sara determined it must be a special treat.

Powdered milk replaced goat milk. *Apol must ration goat's milk to Baba V because of his age, and me just 'cause I'm his guest,* Sara decided. *With more people at the table we're stuck with the Klim.* Sara grinned at the facetious brand name when she saw it. The makers of the product knew its limitations, and spelled it backwards, just as she suspected it would taste.

Ngalia and Paipi, Apol and Kilongo joined the mix-matched family at the table.

"Let's pray," Baba V stated standing tall at the head of the table. Ngalia kicked Sara under the table in time for her to look up and see hands offered to her on either side. She readily grasped the hands offered to complete the circle around the table.

"Thank You God for the worship service today and for those around this table. Bless the work of our hands and hearts as we continue in your service this day. Thank you for your bounty. Bless it to our health. Amen." Baba finished his prayer and sat down.

The food rapidly disappeared and Kilongo, Baba V and Vincent wasted no time in excusing themselves from the table. "We're going to the government hospital to get the supplies needed," Baba V explained. "We'll be back before you miss us."

Apol and Ngalia began clearing the table and Sara jumped up to help. Amu ran to get a cloth to wash Paipi's hands and face, then gathered the baby in her arms and half carried, half dragged him into the other room to play while waiting for the adults to be ready to leave.

It didn't take long for the three women to wash the dishes and put them away. When the chore was completed, Sara followed Apol and Ngalia to chairs on the front porch to wait for the men. Soon women Sara recognized from the morning service began arriving, and baskets of food collected on the porch floor. Apol laughed and chatted excitedly with each one.

Noting the puzzled look on Sara's face, Ngalia spoke softly for her ears only. "We take prepared food with us for the lepers. This frees them from cooking chores for the day, and allows them to come to the service."

*Lepers! It's a **leper** colony?* For a moment Sara just stared at Ngalia as the impact of what she said registered. Shivers ran up and down her spine in spite of the moist heat clinging to her skin.

Ngalia did not miss the reaction or flash of panic in Sara's eyes. Squeezing her arm gently she ask, "Have you never seen a leper, Sara?"

"No," Sara managed, moistening her lower lip. "Leprosy doesn't exist in North America any more, its controlled with medications."

"Lepers be God's children too."

"I know. I'm okay. I just didn't realize . . ." Sara's voice trailed off, and she forced herself to smile. "You take Paipi there?"

"I take Paipi everywhere I go."

"Of course. Can't we get leprosy from contact with lepers? Is it safe?"

"All God's children need to hear His Word," Ngalia quietly insisted. "We're careful. The lepers have a nurse who lives with them and keeps them on their medicine." Sara was not much comforted by Ngalia's words.

Baba V, Kilongo and Vincent arrived, bringing several men, including Pastor Andre, with them. Some carried packages Sara assumed held medicines.

Amu disappeared into the house and returned carrying Baba V's worn Bible. Ngalia swung Paipi into the sling on her back and the whole group set off walking down the dirt road through the Kama compound. It was a beautiful sight to see all the women swaying gently in rhythm, baskets of food carried gracefully on their heads. Their brightly colored clothing contrasted against the dirt road and the thatch-roofed mud houses they passed.

"How far is it? Isn't there a truck to carry Baba?" Sara whispered to Ngalia.

"Rebels steal Baba's lorrie (truck). But we have no petrol to feed it anyway. The roads are bad. You will see. It's only 6 1/2 kilometers (4 miles). We will be there in an hour and a half. Paipi will sleep. He'll be ready to play when we get there."

Sara fell silent but her thoughts continued to tumble. *First a refugee camp, now a camp of lepers. Please, God help me. I need the courage and strength not to offend your dear children. Please.*

Leaning against the pharmacy wall, unnoticed by either girl, was the soldier who thought himself responsible for fathering Paipi. He watched with a curious expression on his face as the group set out on their quest. What made these people go to the leper camp and take food and medicine? Such kindness or utter stupidity was beyond his understanding. He was still pondering this question long after the group disappeared from sight.

Apol started singing Amazing Grace in Swahili and one by one the others joined in. As they passed through the African village women came out of their homes with gifts of food to add to the bounty already gathered. It appeared to Sara that no one had much to give, but the small offerings added together made for a goodly feast. She hoped Apol had bought something for her at the market yesterday to add to this bounty. Children left playing to run alongside the singers until their mothers called them back. The festivity of the occasion heightened Sara's awareness and perception of her surroundings.

"Ngalia, the Village is so clean."

"Of course." Ngalia's response left Sara feeling silly to have said something so obvious. Her eyes rested momentarily on a stooped grandmother leaning on a homemade and well-worn broom. The woman paused to watch the parade go by and for a moment she joined in the singing. The hard packed earth around her was spotless even though chickens ran free, pecking at worms in the grass in her side yard.

I wonder if the inside of the huts are as perfectly kept as the outside. I guess poverty is no excuse for poor housekeeping in Africa. Sara kept these thoughts to herself not wanting to feel foolish twice in one day.

"Ngalia, tell me about these homes. I see several buildings in each yard. Are families grouped together?"

"Sometimes. Each building has purpose. The front houses have three rooms—a common room with a sleep room on each side. The back house also has several rooms, one for food storage, one for kuni, and one for everything else. The side buildings may have a kitchen area, and more sleep rooms. We do most of our work in the courtyard, like pounding roots into flour or thrashing rice. Unless it rains we cook outside. The racks in the yards are for drying dishes. Not everyone has drying cloths."

Curiosity satisfied for the moment, Sara joined in the singing, quietly humming the tunes she knew, or just listening to all others.

Kama soon disappeared from their view. The singing stopped as they approached a sinkhole in the road.

"Wow, you could hide a boxcar in that pothole," Sara spoke out loud to no one in particular. Either end of the hole had been caved in to form a ramp of sorts. A man in the lead started telling a story. He acted out his words, jumping about and leaning forward and back, making all the others laugh, just watching his antics and excitement made Sara grin.

Ngalia paused in her mirth to fill Sara in on the joke. "Fundisali is telling us of a time when he rode a truck through this pothole on a medical safari with the missionaries."

I'm thinking that's not possible, Sara thought. *A truck would have to drive down into the hole, cross it, and drive up the other side. With all that muck in the bottom, even with four-wheel drive, I can't imagine getting out without a real battle. I think I'm glad to be on foot!* The group spread out, circling into the trees and joining back together on the far side of the sinkhole.

Long logs, laid side by side, bridged the rivers they had to cross. Once again Sara marveled. *It's challenge enough just to walk across these unmilled logs. I'd be terrified to try to drive across in a big 'ol lumbering truck. Man!* Edging near the side of the bridge Sara peered at the murky water below. She wondered if a crocodile lived under the bridge, or if a truck had ever gone over the side.

"Did you really drive across these bridges when you had a truck?" she asked Ngalia.

"Of course. Baba V don't drive anymore, but he taught others. One man is signal man and guides the driver with hand motions and much yelling. It takes much time because logs sometimes shift. It very hard to get lorries out of the water when logs give way or move. Everybody but the driver has to walk across anyway, carrying all cargo. Once lorries over safely, everyone piles on the cargo and climbs on, and away we go 'til next time. If not enough logs, we wait while men cut down a tree and trim it for bridge. It takes many men to put log over river. Takes much time."

"Amazing," was all Sara could think to say.

Ngalia seemed to take such inconveniences in stride.

I guess one does what one must.

Ngalia grinned at Sara. "It was fun to ride in back of truck with all the people and cargo."

Sara knew they were nearing their destination when children ran out to welcome them, yelling greetings to Baba V and all the others. The visitors broke into song as they made their way into the camp.

They all funneled towards a building that served as the church.

"These children don't look sick," Sara whispered to Ngalia.

"No, some are here only because their parents are lepers. Healthy children live in separate houses from their parents, but they get to see them every day, and can help by gathering firewood and bringing water from the river. Sometimes lepers are cured by the medicines and can return to their own villages."

Again, in typical African fashion, the guests were escorted to the front row of the church and the benches behind them quickly filled with people from the settlement. It made sense that the time of the service depended solely on when the visiting participants arrived. The food they brought was set along the front of the church against the wall.

Again the observer, Sara noted burned brick walls, bamboo slatted arched windows and a swamp-leaf roof. The building overflowed its capacity and the doorways were jammed with would-be worshippers. Others peered through the bamboo covering in the window openings.

Pastor Andre immediately greeted the audience. The singers followed swiftly leading the congregation in spirited songs. Once again their swaying added a dramatic touch to the musical interludes, and their volume decreased slowly as they exited the stage making room for the next group coming up to sing.

"I could get used to African music," Sara whispered to Ngalia taking Paipi from his mother's back. The baby was wide awake and making eyes at everyone behind them.

Baba V rose and walked carefully to the crude pulpit provided. "See the food we have brought you?" A murmur of appreciation swept over the listeners. "We don't bring you raw food. We bring cooked food. What do you do with food? You eat it. What do we do with God's word? We nourish our souls by feeding on the Word of God. Let's do so together. Listen and hear what Pastor Andre has for us today."

Pastor Andre spoke to the people for a full hour. At one point the people all cheered, and Ngalia grinned at Sara. "He just reminded them that if they have accepted Jesus as their Savior, they will all have new bodies in Heaven." Sara was doing her best not to stare, but already she had seen people with fingers, toes, noses, ears, hands or feet missing.

Finally the singers moved onto the stage again and began singing. One by one, fourteen lepers came forward to place an egg in the offering plate.

"The eggs are a gift offering to us as a token of love and appreciation," Ngalia whispered to Sara.

All was quiet in the audience except for the occasional crying baby. Even that distraction was quickly carried out of the assembly. There was no piano, no organ, not even a guitar.

Yet the singers managed to coax amazing music out of the rattles they used to keep tempo.

I could make a rattle like that, Sara determined halfway through the first musical package. *They're nothing more than dried gourds with rice inside.*

How hard could it be? Thinking about crafting a rattle offered some distraction to the misery Sara witnessed all about her.

Baba V once again walked to the pulpit. "We have a visitor with us today. She has come a long way to greet you. Her name is Sara. She will be teaching English in our schools. You have met her uncle, the big American with a bushy red beard." Baba V grinned as a rustle of laughter spread through the congregation. "Sara came to us on a plane filled with medicines for our people. We praise God for her." Baba V paused and motioned for Sara to stand.

Slowly Sara stood and turned to smile at the congregation. Her eyes were filled with tears. She could not see clearly and she thanked God. There was only so much misery her heart could look on in one day. Paipi saved the moment by waving at everyone, a big grin across his face, and everyone laughed. Sara turned back and sat down on the bench grateful for babies.

Pastor Andre took the pulpit again and the second portion of the service began. When he paused, two young men from the settlement came forward to sing a duet. The song must have been a favorite of the congregation, because everyone hummed along. Ngalia translated the words into English for Sara:

"When this tabernacle passes away, we have a new building in heaven, not made with hands. We will have a new body." The duet was followed by a trio of two men and a woman. They sang:

Many things make people wonder today, but the greatest wonder of all is that God loves even me. In the body of Christ are many members. The church is the Body of Christ. We all work toward one end in Christ. Christ, help me, guide me, I don't want to be an invalid, a babe in Christ. We pray and the Lord is working for us. When we welcome Visitors, we are welcoming the Lord.

The singing ended and an elder of the church came forward with several announcements. Ngalia again interpreted for Sara. "Pastor," he said, "you can't accomplish much if you don't work. We also must work. Today the women of the church will work pulling weeds in the old garden. Men will plant a new garden right here at the church. The harvest from this new rice garden will be turned over to the church for the Lord."

People stood to go and Sara turned to see one leper helping another, supplying what they could to make up for what another could not. Again her eyes filled with tears. Baba V put out his arm for her and gathered her to his side as he walked out of the church. She tried to guide him gently as she'd watched Amu do, but her tears blurred her vision.

"You are brave to come with us today, Sara. God will bless this. In the early years of the leper settlement, the population here included nearly 300 patients and more than 500 family members. You should have seen them. For the most part pagans and dressed like them—fierce looking. They came, but not willingly, preferring to die in their own villages among their own people. But the government realized they must be isolated and made them come.

"We sent out teachers, but they weren't welcome. The lepers said they had their own religion and they didn't need any interference from the mission.

"But a woman came into the settlement from another mission station and began, in her own humble way, serving and singing in her home. A few women began gathering to hear her sing and give her testimony. This went on for some time until one day one of the head men sent word to ask what was the matter with the Kama station; why weren't they sending out someone to teach them? We just said, 'Praise the Lord,' and began to come out to the leper settlement and hold services with them. That was the beginning, and slowly the Word of God took root in hearts and one by one there were believers among them.

"We were fortunate in getting a reclaimed back-slider as a 'caretaker and shepherd' of the flock here. Bernard Mulenda had a real ministry among them. He wasn't a leper, but lived here with his family and became a real spiritual leader. Others have come over the years to continue the work. The new sulphatrone drugs have been producing marvels. They're very expensive, but the government has been giving them to us and many are encouraged.

"I know it's hard to see mutilated people suffering so, but just to see them come to meetings is something, and then to have others hold the communion cups for them . . . praise the Lord, they are whole in spirit."

Baba V fell silent. Sara continued to walk beside him, her arm around his waist, gently guiding his steps. His words helped her to hold her head high and smile as they waved goodbye to the leper congregation and set off for home.

Dusk was falling when the weary band of travelers arrived back in Kama. Sara still walked beside Baba V but as they neared the park area, she motioned Amu to her and motioned for the child to walk with Baba V back to the house.

"I'd like to have a few moments alone to think about my day," she explained to the aged missionary. He nodded understanding and allowed the child to lead him on home.

Sara wasn't far off the end of the airstrip and could see both the pharmacy and Baba V's house from where she stood. Everyone else had gone to their homes. Even Ngalia and Paipi had dropped out of the troupe as soon as they neared Apol and Kilongo's home.

The cool evening air felt good against her skin. *I wonder if I'll get a bath tonight? Vincent hasn't had time to haul water for us.* Her mind bolted from bathing to parents and a sudden loneliness settled over her, isolating her from the calming jungle noises surrounding her. *What would her parents think of all she'd been through in the past few days. Uncle Ross, where are you? Are you coming?*

The fatigue in Sara's muscles forced its way into her awareness and she began looking for a place to sit down. Just ahead was a small patch of flowers, carefully placed and fenced in with a pretty stone border. Freshly trimmed grass bordered the area and seemed to welcome Sara to rest there. She accepted the unspoken invitation, lowered herself to the ground and put her hand out to touch the stones so carefully placed around the flowers. Somehow the place reminded her of her parent's grave and for her time stood still.

An hour later, in the darkness of night, a tall lanky form sank down next to her on the grass. "I see you found my mate." Baba V said simply.

"Your mate?" Sara was so lost in her own world that she was unaware of Baba V's approach and his presence pulled her back from far away. She was unaware too that tears had streaked her face. "How did you get here alone?"

"Oh, I need no help in coming here. I've been coming here too many years now." The man was quiet for a few moments then continued.

"Mama V is buried here," he spoke so quietly that Sara wasn't sure she heard him correctly.

"Mama V?"

"Yes. Marie. She was my mate and helper for fifty-one years before she passed on. When I get to Heaven, I'm going to ask God if He didn't make a mistake in taking my Marie so soon. Oh, not from me, but from His people here. They still need her. No one has replaced her. I wanted to bury her in the churchyard with all the others, but the Africans said 'No. Mama V will be buried in a special place in the center of the compound.' So here she lies. Someday I will lay here beside her, God willing."

Sara was touched by the simplicity of his statements, and out of her mouth tumbled the words, "God took my parents from me."

Baba V did not argue the statement Sara made, but simply asked, "When was that, child?"

"Two weeks ago. They were killed in a drive-by shooting. A carload of thugs drove down the street with guns, shooting into buildings and at the youth center. My parents, and a little child died, others were hospitalized. Why do people do things like that? What is wrong with them?"

The privacy of the night had loosened Sara's thoughts and tongue. Tears again trickled down her face making new paths in the dust that powdered her cheeks. Baba V was careful in the wording of his next question.

"Is this why you ran away from home and came in search of your uncle?" The kindness in his voice let Sara know he was not condemning or judging her.

"I just couldn't stand to be there anymore. I am so angry with the cowards who did this that I just can't face them. In my heart I want to hurt them back, but I know that is wrong."

"Time will sort all this out for you, Sara. You don't have to have all the answers at once. God is sufficient to the task of teaching you the answers to your questions in His timing. We don't always like the answers He gives us, but they are always right nonetheless.

The heavy brogue in which the old man spoke made it necessary for Sara to sit in silence as her brain comprehended what had been said. The night maintained its coolness. The moon played hide and seek behind clouds casting shadows over a landscape that went unnoticed by Sara. The murmur of village life and jungle noises were at a minimum. To be silent seemed right for the moment, but other worries pushed their way to the surface.

"What if Uncle Ross doesn't come?"

"Well, I guess you'll learn to be a first-rate English teacher."

Sara sniffed and tried to chuckle but the sound was strained. Baba V reached out to her and wrapped his arm around her shoulder. "Sara Calhoun, it's very late now. You have a big job ahead of you tomorrow. Let's go in now."

Sara did not resist the suggestion. Someone must have carried water for their needs in Vincent's place because there was water enough for her to shower off the day's grime before retiring for the night. She found Vincent and Amu both sound asleep on the bedroom floor. Once again light from the window cast wispy shadows over their sleeping forms.

Apol had added mosquito netting over Sara's bed. Sara wondered where she found the time to tack the netting to the wall above the bed and drape it so nicely. It seemed a hundred years had passed since she got all those immunizations to protect her from the diseases mosquitoes spread. The mosquito netting should prevent the vampire insects from snacking on her all night and she was grateful for Apol's thoughtfulness and provision.

Sara parted the netting, crawled under the sheet and pulled the netting closed. She was instantly asleep.

Chapter Twenty Three

Amu tugged on Sara's arm, pulling her from dreams about Paris and all the wonders to be seen there. The crowing of roosters outside the window quickly drew her back to reality.

I'm a school teacher today. Full realization hit and Sara bounded out of bed. She had presence of mind to catch the startled Amu in her arms and hug her. A shy smile turned up the corners of Amu's eyes, warming Sara's heart. The child was already dressed and stood waiting patiently for Sara to do the same. Instead Sara searched through her bag for a pretty hair ornament to fasten in the child's curls. She found a springy butterfly clip, and fastened it upon Amu's curls, then held out a mirror so the child could see herself. White teeth flashed and Amu was out the door to show her treasure to anyone who would pause to look, leaving Sara to enjoy the privacy of dressing alone on her first day as teacher.

Sara slipped into the green dress and wished she had taken time to tailor it for a better fit. She pulled the belt from her blue jeans and fastened it comfortably around her waist—then carefully smoothed pleats in the excess fabric of the dress, securing the pleats by tightening the belt one more notch.

"You need to look like a teacher, Sara girl," she spoke quietly to herself. "Brush out your hair and braid it into your most crowning achievement. It worked well enough to get you safely out of America and into Africa, so maybe it'll get you past posing as a teacher to kids your own age."

Apol had breakfast waiting. Goat milk and bread no longer seemed strange. Baba V came to the table and nodded towards Sara. Nothing was mentioned about the exchange of heartache the night before.

"Slow down, Vincent," Apol scolded the eight-year-old. Vincent ignored the command, and squirmed about in the chair as he wolfed down his meager meal. "He's washed behind both ears, Sara, and even combed his hair. He plans to walk you to the school this morning. He is a proud boy to be living in the same house as the new teacher." Apol's tone expressed both amusement and dismay at the boy's attitude.

"I will appreciate the escort, Vincent, but we don't need to rush. Listen to Apol and do as she says." Deliberately Sara slowed her own worried pace. Vincent finished his food and sat watching her so intently that she finally gave in.

"Okay. Let's go."

Vincent sprang to his feet and offered his elbow. Sara winked at Apol and then at the doctor, even though she knew he could not see it.

"Please pray for me, Baba, I've never taught school before. I'm a bit nervous."

"You will do just fine, Sara. The students need to hear you speak the English. It's hard to learn a language you seldom hear. You're a Godsend for them. God will direct you. You'll do fine." He emphasized his last words by pounding both hands down on the table. Hoping such conviction was contagious; Sara squared her shoulders, sent a desperate little prayer heavenward and placed her hand in the crook of Vincent's arm.

"We'll be off then." It was only then that Sara realized she didn't even know in which school she was to teach.

Baba must have sensed her sudden hesitation, for he waved his arms towards them. "Vincent knows what school to direct you to. Go with God!" Vincent marched out, his chest puffed out and head high. Amu shyly stepped to Sara's left and took her hand, smiling sweetly up at her. Her eyes sparkled with excitement and she patted the butterfly ornament nestled in her black curls. *Simple things means so much to these children.* The thought stayed with her as Vincent and Amu lead her across the airstrip toward a U-shaped building complex. Students were making their way towards the school from every direction. Sara noticed the church building stood off to the right, set back further off the dirt road.

As they approached, a tall thin African man advanced towards them with arms opened wide in welcome. A dignified smile graced his face.

"Miss Sara, I am so pleased that you have agreed to come and share your English with our students." Enveloping Sara's exceedingly white hand in both his extremely black hands, he pumped it with typical African enthusiasm and warmth. He continued speaking as he led them on to the school.

"I am Madua, acting school administrator in place of Steve Vinton, grandson to Baba V. He is gone back to America now. This war has pushed many of us into awkward roles, Miss Sara, but God is faithful to strengthen one as needed." Madua grinned and looked proudly humble, if that's possible. Sara wasn't sure if he was talking about himself or her. "The students are lining up. I've assigned myself to help you on your first day. I've brought you the textbook Miss Beverly used before she returned to America. It will help you teach the students."

Sara grasped the book as if grabbing a life jacket offered a drowning man in choppy water. "You don't know how much I appreciate this book! I'll take good care of it."

As they neared the school Sara could see it was actually three buildings situated in the shape of a U with a walk space between the structures. Inside the U, the buildings each boasted overhangs that rested on brick columns every ten feet or so and shaded the windows from direct sunlight. The side buildings seemed to house three classrooms. At least each wing had three doors, and six windows with vertical slats. *So, are the slats to keep students in or out,* Sara wondered.

The end building was longer than either side building, and Sara quickly counted enough doors to house an additional six classrooms with several offices in the center.

Lining up quickly, students filed into six parallel paths divided by lush green grass. All wore white tops with either green or blue pants or skirts accordingly. The difference in color seemed to match line assignments.

Vincent and Amu squeezed Sara's hands, wished her good luck and turned to go.

"Where are you guys going?" Sara fought to keep panic out of her voice.

"Our school's the other side of Kama. We'll be late if we don't hurry," Vincent quiped.

"Oh, of course. Well, good luck. Have a good day." Of course there had to be another school. All the students before her were junior and senior high age.

Suddenly the air was filled with the rhythmic beating of big drums and the students began to sing and clap rhythm. No one seemed shy. They all sang with gusto just as the church folks had done. Madua motioned Sara to move forward with him to stand next to the official in front who seemed to be in charge of the school.

"Kantamba is our principal," Madua whispered to Sara. "He will be making announcements and assigning discipline to students in trouble." Sara nodded that she'd heard.

The singing continued for a good twenty minutes, song after song. Then, to Sara's delight, the principal began speaking in French. Sara understood French.

"We have a new teacher with us today. She has come from America and will be teaching English in the upper forms. It is uncertain how long Miss Sara will be with us, so let's not waste this opportunity to learn from her." A few other announcements were made and then Kantamba called several young men by name. There was considerable shuffling of feet and heads hung low but the young men stepped forward.

"We need not discuss here the misdeeds that have landed you in discipline." Relief showed on some of the faces. "You will spend your day with the building crew. You will knock down a brick wall and clean up the mess. If you serve your punishment well you may return to classes tomorrow. You are dismissed."

Sara wanted to ask Madua what the students had done that got them in trouble, but she didn't speak up quickly enough. An older man stepped forward and motioned the singled-out students to follow him.

As they marched away beating of the drums signaled students to sing their final anthem and a flag slowly ascended the flagpole. Immediately afterward the students filed into their respective classrooms.

Teaching students this well managed may not be so bad, Sara thought. Madua tapped her on the shoulder and moved off across the courtyard. Sara followed.

"The Principal's office, teacher's lounge, store-room, and library are there in the middle of the central building," Madua informed Sara, waving his hand towards the rooms as they passed them.

Sara noted clay brick walls, corrugated tin roofs, and slatted window openings that provided ventilation for breezes to flow through stuffy rooms.

Madua slowed and pointed to a piece of paper inside the front cover of the book he had given Sara.

"I made you a chart of your students. They sit in the same place every day. You will have three classrooms of students with a ten minute break between. There are about forty students in each class. The students go home midday to help with family chores. Those that can often stay after school to see if they can't get a soccer or volleyball game going, we have many of the best soccer players on God's earth right here in Kama!" The words were spoken with pride. Sara wondered how he came to that conclusion but managed to keep the thought to herself.

Madua entered a classroom situated off the inside courtyard in the left-hand wing, motioning for Sara to enter ahead of him. He spoke first in French, then repeated his words in English.

"As Principal Kamtamba said, Miss Sara has come from America to help you with your English. We are most fortunate to have her with us. We don't know how long she will be able to stay, so make the time we have count."

Whether it was Madua's words, the cooler interior of the room, or the unspoken responsibility heaped on her, Sara didn't know, but a chill slid down her spine stiffening her back.

Three rows of very black students sat on crude benches staring at Sara. She counted three students to a bench, five benches to a row. Taller benches, no deeper than the seat bench, stood in front of each bench to serve as a desktop. At her back were two blackboards. One piece of chalk lay on the rim of one board's frame. There was no teacher's desk, but a stool sat off to one side of the blackboard. There were no charts on the walls, and if the students had ever had paper and pencils, their supply was now gone and they sat empty-handed. "Good morning." The voice Sara heard didn't sound like her own.

"Good morning, Teacher," responded the class in unison.

Before Sara could move to the stool and perch herself on it, the class broke into song. Madua nodded approvingly and assured Sara that each class would welcome her in the same way. It was beautiful and she warmed towards those she would be teaching. When the song was over, she opened the textbook but quickly snapped it shut again.

"I would like to open every class in a word of prayer."

Some of the students grinned at her, and others continued to stare at her without understanding. A girl stood and spoke to the class in French. Everyone bowed their heads and closed their eyes.

"Thank you," Sara flashed a smile at the girl, then began her prayer. "Dear Heavenly Father, we are here to learn together. Please help me to be a good teacher, and help these students to be quick learners. Amen."

"Amen," echoed across the room. Madua bowed to Sara, saluted the students and marched smartly out of the room and back to his office.

Again Sara opened her textbook, scanning the contents quickly. *At least this book is user friendly,* she thought. Within moments Sara became a teacher of English.

The morning passed quickly, too quickly. Madua appeared each time the old tire rim clanged, and escorted Sara to the next classroom. She was a little shocked to learn it was the teachers who moved to the next classroom at the "bell" clanging, not the students. But it was a lot less hectic to move a dozen teachers than to move five hundred plus students around. It made good sense.

Each class greeted her with, "Good morning, Teacher," and thrilled her with a song. The students harmonized beautifully—except for that occasional student that could be heard singing off-key, yet with enthusiasm. Each classroom looked similar to the one before.

Sara opened each class with prayer. A few students squirmed in their seats, but no one showed disrespect. Most of the students took the prayer in stride as the most natural thing to expect. One classroom boasted a wall plaque that read "I can do all things through Christ who strengthens me" in French. I'd like to see that on every classroom in America, Sara thought. Ngalia and Paipi were in her second class. As happy as she was to see familiar faces, Sara was careful not to show favoritism.

At one point in the morning a low rumble rolled beneath their feet. Subconsciously Sara noted the tremor to be about a 3.0, but she was too focused on her teaching to give it much thought. Neither did the students.

After three classes Vincent and Amu found her and led her to the grassy area between the school and the airstrip to watch a soccer game. The competition between the teams was fierce and Sara was instantly caught up in the excitement of the game. Time sped by and the game was over all too quickly. Sara found herself hoarse from yelling encouragement to both sides and from her mornings teaching responsibilities.

Somehow she felt more accepted and less different after the soccer game. She no longer questioned the pride Madua had in these kids. They were superb players. Sara had not seen better anywhere.

When the excitement was over, the three headed for home and lunch. Sara was very aware that many of the students would not have anything to eat till evening and it broke her heart.

Chapter Twenty Four

The midday meal was under preparation when the trio arrived home. Sara put her book on the fireplace mantel and joined Apol in the kitchen. "Uncle Ross isn't coming is he?" Sara's abrupt comment sounded more like a statement but Apol answered her anyway.

"How could I know something like that, Sara?"

"I don't know. I guess I'm just thinking out loud and you're the only one here to listen."

"Many things could keep your uncle away, Kama not easy to get to. Just remember, wherever Ross is, God is there too, just like He is here with you and me. You did not warn him you were coming to Africa to visit him." Apol's scolding reminded Sara of Mrs. Schaffer. "Now, make yourself helpful and bring me the rice from the cupboard." Every day it was easier for Sara to understand Apol's English.

She did as Apol requested while mentally comparing the whole situation to Mrs. Schaffer's spacious well equipped kitchen, close proximity to supermarkets and the pantry filled with every supply she might possibly need. She thought of the drawer that always yielded plump freshly baked chocolate chip cookies. Life wasn't fair. Yet, Apol managed.

"How you like teaching?" Apol threw the question over her shoulder as she pounded manioc roots into flour.

"The students are so quick to learn, Apol. They learn English easier than I'm learning Swahili." Apol beamed with pride at Sara's praise of her people.

"Did the rolling earth scare you today?"

"No. I'm used to it. My city is built over many earthquake faults. At least here I don't have to wonder whether or not the whole city is going to break off into the ocean and float away." A wry smile twisted Sara's face as she spoke.

"Your home is near an ocean?" Apol looked puzzled and Sara realized there was little chance Apol had seen a lake, let alone a big ocean.

"Yes. It's beautiful there. When you stand on the edge of the land, and look out over the ocean, all you see is water as far as your eye can see. Sometimes you see a big boat, or big fish, and clouds of course. At night the sun falls all the way down to the water and makes the sky full of bright orange and pink light. We call that a sunset, just like here. Then the sun drops out of sight and its night.

"But it's beautiful here too. I love all the trees and the rivers, with the mountains off in the distance. Rivers in Los Angeles, the name of my city, usually have no water in them. They are lined with cement or rocks so that when the rain comes, it won't wash away the land around the rivers. We don't get rain very often, but when it comes, it just pours out of the sky and tries to wash us out to the ocean."

It was the longest speech Sara had made to Apol, and the woman stared at her with wonder in her eyes. Then she shook her head a little, and went back to pounding her roots.

"Would you buy things at the Saturday market for me, Apol?" Back on familiar topics seemed to put the woman at ease, and she grinned at Sara.

"What you want now?"

"I need to add to Baba V's food supply again. It seems I may be here a while." As Sara went to her backpack for the needed francs she marveled that she could say those words without panic or severe home-sickness, especially after the long speech she made to Apol about the ocean. Not even the ocean could tempt her back to a place where thugs roamed the streets at will, shooting anything they took a mind to shoot. Of course, soldiers roamed the streets of Kama too, but so far Sara hadn't seen any shooting.

The afternoon was spent studying her English text. Apol kept Amu busy, and Vincent made his water runs. Sara studied in peace.

Baba V came home for supper and Sara helped Apol set the table and serve up dried fish and mango sauce. When Apol left for home to care for Kilongo and the rest of her family, Sara pressed several francs into her hand, and promised to clean up after supper.

Sara stood to clear the table just as a loud banging on the front door disrupted the peace of the evening. Baba V excused himself and made his way to the door. A conversation in clipped polite tones caught Sara's attention and she asked Vincent what was being said. The boy had moved to the door frame and with eyes wide he translated for Sara.

"Baba V, I've come to get you."

"What do you want with me?"

"I want to take you."

"Well, where do you want to take me?"

"To the General."

"I have a letter from the General of the Mai Mai saying you must not do anything to disrupt my work here, and not to touch me. Your General was a student of mine 40 years ago. He knows what I do here. Why do you want to take me to the General?"

"I know all this is truth, Baba V. But a plane landed on your airstrip. Somebody sent a letter to the general saying while you sit up there at your place Baba V down here receives a plane load of shells and ammunitions. He is sending it to our enemies across the river."

"A plane did come, that is truth. But it only brought us medicine. I send only medicine to the sick across the river."

Curiosity moved Sara to the doorway beside Vincent. A gasp escaped her lips when she saw soldiers standing on the porch pointing guns at Baba V. Vincent continued to translate what was said.

"I must do what the General now commands, Baba V. I have 18 men and orders. Go to Kama, get Baba V and bring him here. Go to the airstrip and destroy it, go to the grave of his wife, dig it up and take all the guns out of the grave, go to the house, and get all the shells and ammunitions and bring them all here."

"Do you have a car, or motorcycle or some way to transport me?"

"No, we'll walk."

"I don't think I can walk that far north. That's 200 kilometers. I am an old man."

"We'll carry you if you can't walk. I'm to go through all your houses here and take out all the ammunition."

"Fine. Start right here in my house."

"No, Baba V, I'll come tomorrow." The officer looked at the floor in embarrassment. "Baba, I know you are an honored member of the "Order of the Leopard", and that's the highest honor our Congolese government can bestow on anyone. And you have immunity to government interference. I do not want to offend you."

"I am not offended, friend. But if you leave now without making an inspection, and find nothing when your company comes back tomorrow," Baba paused and lifted his hands expressively, "take my word, someone will say Baba V had people carry off all the ammunition and hide it in the jungle. They'll say I bought you off for time to hide the ammunition. You must start your search right now."

Sara's heart nearly stopped beating when Baba V calmly stepped aside and insisted the officer enter. Five soldiers followed and began searching the house. . . front room, bedrooms, bathroom, kitchen and pantry. Then they inspected the yard.

Sara pressed herself tight up against the kitchen wall and pulled Amu to her side. "Let's just stay out of their way, Amu. I'm sure Baba knows what he's doing." The deaf child couldn't hear Sara, but it made Sara feel better to hear herself. Quietly she prayed for safety. The soldiers ignored them and in a short time they returned to the living room and reported to the officer.

"Sir, we found nothing."

"There's nothing to find," Baba V said with assertion. "I deal only in medicine and the truth of God's Word."

"I must search the house next door," the officer answered apologetically.

"Alright, let's go next door."

"Thank goodness Baba isn't entertaining the soldiers in his pajamas." Sara whispered nervously to Vincent, recalling how quickly Baba V usually donned his pajamas. He grinned in response.

Sara and Amu moved to the bedroom window and watched as the soldiers searched through the next house just as they had done at Baba V's. Sara strained her ears to hear even though she couldn't understand Swahili. Vincent seemed to know his place was to watch over the girls, for he stayed by Sara and Amu's side and kept Sara informed.

"This young fellow says you're hiding the ammunition in the old pharmacy up there."

"Alright, let's go."

Baba V reached out to take the officer's arm as if to lead him to the pharmacy. Sara realized he trusted the man's integrity to spare him further humiliation.

His trust was well placed. The officer led his men toward the pharmacy with Baba V in tow. Vincent scurried after them, and Sara and Amu followed to see what would happen next. Chickens and a goat scattered out of the path of the marching troupe. The sun had retired and a sliver of moon did it's best to shed light on the activity below.

The pharmacy's big double window was thrown open. A crowd began to gather as word spread through the village that soldiers had come to arrest Baba V. Everyone wanted to see what was happening.

"Pick a company of five men," Baba V said loud enough for all to hear. "Bring them inside the pharmacy. Let each man pick a carton and bring it here to the window."

Murmurs spread throughout the gathering throng. Ngalia slipped in beside Sara and Amu. Paipi rubbed his sleepy eyes with the back of his hand.

"Ngalia, you're here. What are people saying?" Sara whispered to her friend.

"Some say Baba V is in trouble because he has done something wrong. Others defend him."

Sara licked her dry lips and fought her compulsion to stare at the soldier's guns. *You're not going to let it happen again, God. You just can't!*

Five men selected cartons from the shelves and carried them to the distribution ledge at the window. Baba V fumbled in a drawer for scissors to cut the tape that sealed the serum boxes. As each carton was opened, Baba motioned for the soldiers to pull out the contents. Each box yielded only serum.

The murmurs running through the crowd changed from "Baba V is in trouble. He hid ammunition, how will he ever get out of this?" to "Baba V is going to win this battle, he's going to win!"

"Officer," Baba V spoke so all could hear him. "Someone made a mistake. Only medicine for the sick came on that plane. I am here to teach about God. You know I do not take sides in your wars."

"Baba, since we find no ammunition here we won't dig up Mama's grave. We won't dig up the airstrip." The officer turned to the murmuring crowd. "We are not arresting Baba V. It's clear this informant is a liar. Please forgive me Baba. You send a man and I'll send one of my men on a bike, or motorcycle if you have one, to the general with my report."

Sara gasped, and realized she had been holding her breath as she clung to Ngalia's arm. "What'd he say Ngalia?"

"He say man was a liar who accused Baba V. He say Baba OK. He will report so to the general."

"Praise God!" escaped Sara's lips and she pressed forward with Amu to get closer to Baba V. Pharmacy workers stepped forward to lock up the pharmacy again and the officer once again took Baba V's arm and marched back to the old doctor's house in the center of the compound. Sara lost sight of Ngalia and Paipi in the milling crowd as people began to filter back to their homes.

Vincent appeared at her side and pulled her and Amu towards a shortcut to the back of the house. They entered as quietly as possible, and began clearing the kitchen table.

Baba V and the officer came in the front way and Baba called out, "Vincent, please get my typewriter for this officer, and some paper."

Vincent ran for the typewriter and carried it to the officer who in turn handed it to one of the soldiers. He nodded politely to Baba and left. Sara rushed to Baba's side.

"Well, young Sara. Have you had enough excitement for one day?" The old missionary eased himself down into his rocker.

"Yes sir. I think I've enough excitement for my entire stay in Africa!"

"We were never in more danger than God can handle, Sara. God is always in control. Nothing will happen He doesn't allow." His words did not bring a comfort she would accept.

Even though the danger appeared to be over, Sara's legs felt weak. *The man was only doing his job.* She told herself. *He did not hurt Baba V. He was even gracious and respectful to him. I've got to keep focused here, Lord.*

Gathering her nerve, Sara shooed Amu and Vincent out of the kitchen and off to prepare for bed. When sleep finally came to Sara, she dreamed of rockets exploding in the night.

True to his word the officer arrived early the next morning with a typed report in hand. Baba V's motorcycle was commandeered to transport a soldier back to the general with the report.

"Will we ever see your motorcycle again, Baba?" Sara asked after the officer had left.

"No, I suppose not. I wanted to keep it around for our pastors to ride to outlying villages for Sunday Services. But God knows what we need here. It's His motorcycle. He can send it off with anyone He wishes. It's not for me to question."

Baba settled on a porch chair. As soon as the general's officer was out of sight, the officer in charge of Kama slipped onto the porch and took the chair nearest him.

"That fellow going there is going to get me in trouble."

"Oh? How's that?" Baba responded.

"He's going to tell the General that I exploded a rocket, a launch rocket!"

"Is that what I heard last night?"

"Yes, Baba. One of my young recruits took my launch rocket, and the gun to shoot it. He was fooling around with it when the thing exploded. Now there's a hole in the floor, ceiling and roof. That rocket went up into the sky a red ball, turned over and came down on the front porch where I was sitting with four others. It landed in the dirt of the flower bed, right between the bricks and didn't explode"

"You're a fortunate man, Kyassa." Baba spoke kindly.

"Yes, Baba. Had it exploded on impact I would not be here talking with you. Your God protected me, Baba. I am grateful."

"God has been good to you, Kyassa. He loves you and died in your place for your sins. Don't you think it's time to ask His forgiveness and accept Him as your Savior?"

Kyassa flushed at the direct question and squirmed in his seat. "Let's wait to see if the General sends someone to replace me, Baba. I don't know yet what the general is going to do to me."

"Ah, Kyassa. God is more patient with you than I. Please excuse me, I have work to do at the maternity center.

"Let me walk you there, Baba."

The old missionary did not argue but accepted the offer graciously.

"Ha, some day you'll have today, Baba, huh? I bet you handle over 100 women today. Ha, Ha. I should be so lucky," the officer jeered.

"You will be a changed man when God gets a'hold of your life, Kyassa. God will change your heart and you will not think such evil thoughts. I will pray for you, friend. I will pray for you."

Kama's head officer had the grace to hang his head and keep his mouth shut the remainder of the trip down the road to the maternity center and all the mothers-to-be who waited patiently for their weekly progress exams and injections of prenatal vitamins.

Ah, how many babies now live who never had a chance before you brought medicine to Kama, God? Gradually the spring in Baba's step returned and energy flowed through his veins. Babies now lived to grow up and become students, pastors and doctors. Progress was being made. Now was not the time to get discouraged. God was still in control. *You do not forget your people, Father. You are faithful to call workers to come and help. Oh, that the war would be over, and the missionaries come back. It is hard and weary work. Strengthen me today, Father, strengthen me and fill me with your joy. Help young Sara, Father. Thank you for bringing her to us. Keep her safe, teach her much, and we will praise You, God. We will praise You!* ***Keep working on Kyassa, God. He's weakening***, Baba prayed.

Chapter Twenty Five

"Apol, I think I'm getting the hang of teaching school," Sara confided to the cook over her lunch.

"Getting the hang? What you mean?" Apol frowned.

"I'm more comfortable with it, less nervous. Today I taught that in America a 'lorrie' is called a 'truck'. And we studied the difference between 'wonderful' and 'horrible'. We made up sentences using each correctly. Like . . . 'Talking parrots are wonderful, but spiders and snakes are horrible.'"

"Each has its place. God made them all."

"True, but I'd take a talking bird over snakes or spiders any day." Sara finished off the last of her milk and stood to clear away her dishes. "Where's Baba V? Why isn't he home for lunch?"

"Been and gone already. Today he's working at maternity clinic. He said you come help him when done with lunch."

"Really? You don't mind?"

Apol shooed Sara away from the cleanup. "Baba says you come, so off you go. Amu will show the way. The maternity house is at the far edge of Kama, as far as possible from the houses," Apol said apologetically. "Men not want to hear women birthing,"

"How exciting, I love babies!" Sara was out the door before Apol finished, and failed to hear all she had said. She slowed down enough to rinse her hands at the water tap and dried them on her dress. Knowing Apol beat the laundry clean beside crocodile infested rivers kept Sara from resenting the lack of a clean towel. Air drying hands and faces weren't so bad.

It didn't take long to reach the clinic. Sara could hear the chatter and laughter of the women before she turned the bend in the path that allowed her to see the line of thirty-some women, all in varying stages of their pregnancies, waiting patiently outside a small square mud-brick house.

"Ms. Sara's iko hapa," yelled a chorus of those waiting in line, and the front door swung open to reveal a woman in nurse-white waving Sara to "come on in."

Shy smiles or friendly pats on the shoulder ushered Sara forward to the head of the line and inside the door. A registration table sat just inside the door. As each patient entered, they were signed in and handed their chart to hold till it was their turn to be seen. Benches lined the wall, every inch filled with pregnant women, many with restless toddlers in tow.

Sara was ushered through an interior door. There she noted an examination table (complete with patient), a makeshift desk, two wooden chairs, a cabinet, and Baba V, intent on probing the expanding abdomen of his patient.

"Ha ha, this one is active today. He kicks at my hands. He is progressing well. Lizzie, you are doing fine." The doctor patted the baby-filled mound affectionately. "Sara, come greet Lizzie. This is her third child."

Lizzie grinned wide at Sara, revealing uneven teeth that needed cleaning. "I have two daughters," she spoke in French. "Baba tells me this is a boy. I'll wait to see for myself."

"Ha ha, she doesn't believe me," Baba chuckled. "You'll see, you'll see. Sara, put your hand here. Feel him kick. Lizzie's girls never kicked like this. It must be a boy.

"Help her up, Sara. Lizzie, get your vitamin shot from Paul. This baby should be coming soon. Stay close by if you can. Come back next week."

Sara helped the woman down from the exam table and watched her waddle to the next room and hand her chart to the man sitting at the table by the back door. She eased herself down into a chair beside the desk and fearlessly leaned her upper arm toward the male nurse. Sara cringed as a seemingly huge needle slid under Lizzie's skin injecting a milky white substance into her blood stream.

The next patient used Sara's shoulder to steady herself up the two steps onto the table providing a welcomed distraction. And so the afternoon flew, patient after patient, until excited screaming outside shattered the calm progression of the day. An older woman who looked full-term to Sara was carried into the room. Her dress and feet were wet. Pain filled eyes begged for relief and mercy.

"Lay her here," barked Baba V in Swahili. Sara knew what he said by his hand movements and backed out of the way, pressing herself against a wall. Fear snatched her breath.

"Sara, get back here. Hold Mupenda's head and shoulders. Remind her to breathe." Baba reverted to French.

"I can't speak Swahili."

"Say 'pamuzi, pamuzi.'"

One of the aides mopped mud and blood from Mupenda's feet and slid them into bands of fabric sewn crudely onto the end of the table's cushion.

The woman who had scrambled off the table to make room for Mupenda stepped forward to help secure a foot in it's band.

Frightened moans escaped Mupenda's thick lips until at last a tiny lifeless form slid from her body into Baba V's waiting hands. A male nurse stepped forward to clamp the umbilical cord. Gently Baba V turned the infant upside down and swatted his tiny bottom. No cry sounded. Again Baba swatted the infant, and everyone held their breath, waiting for a cry that would not come.

Sobs shook the shoulders Sara held against the cushion. Gently Baba laid the tiny form in his mother's arms.

"This one didn't make it, Mupenda. He's too small. His lungs can't pull in the breath of life. I'm so sorry." Sara didn't need to know Swahili to understood the firm compassionate words of comfort given the bereaved mother. Delivery of the afterbirth was a blur thru Sara's tear-filled eyes. The baby was gently removed from his mother's arms, cleaned, and wrapped in a tiny blue receiving cloth.

"There is not enough food." Baba muttered angrily. "Mupenda has been hiding in the forest. She came too far to deliver. She is too old for this."

Taking the tiny baby in his hands once again, Baba prayed loud and earnestly over him and his mother, then laid him gently in his mother's arms and helped her slide off the table. An aide stepped forward to gently guide the woman out of the building where others waited to surround her with caring, sympathy and comfort.

Sara watched as Mupenda slowly worked her way through the crowd and off into the trees of the forest, carrying her infant back to her family for burial.

The rest of the afternoon progressed with less joviality as each mother-to-be ached for the pain of a woman too old and feeble to birth a healthy child.

Sara was comforted and thanked by each mother who used her shoulder to steady themselves up the steps onto the birthing/examining table. Still her tears fell.

The sun was setting when Amu appeared to lead them home to supper.

"How many of these mothers live outside Kama?" Sara queried as they walked towards home.

"Many. People fear the soldiers. Whole families hide in the forest, coming into Kama only for emergency care, marketing, or to attend church. We don't know when a different army will come charging in here with bigger guns to take control of Kama. When they come there'll be shooting, looting, and panic. Innocents will be injured. There's no safety but to take what they can and hide. You can't blame them."

"Why don't you have a gun, Baba V?"

"Two reasons. One, I'm not here to fight anyone except in spiritual warfare. Two, it's illegal for me to have a gun. If I had one, I would be dead. We almost lost some missionaries years ago because their child had a toy gun. Soldiers surrounded their house and made them all come out to be shot. When the toy was proven to be just that, a toy, they were released unharmed, but it was touch and go there for a while. The toy was taken, of course. Missionaries do not have guns. No one has a gun here unless they are in the military. If I had a gun, I'd have to judge who was worthy to be shot. I'm here to serve and love these people, not to punish those with whom I disagree."

"With so many in hiding, who lives in the mud houses now?"

"Ah, peoples from the Mai Mai army that controls Kama now. They've been here many months. They'll flee when these soldiers flee in face of a stronger army. Then the others will come back."

"What about Kilongo and Apol, Ngalia, the pastors, teachers and medical staff?"

"Ah, these brave folks have stayed because they are committed to the work. They stand ever ready to run, but fear God more than man. Think of the opportunity we have to reach all these new people. God brings them here, we serve them, and teach them about Him."

"I guess that's one way to look at it," Sara searched Baba's face for bitterness, but saw none. "What was it like when you first came to Africa, Baba?"

"Ah girl, when I came to Africa there were no roads. We came by railroad as far as we could, then we walked into the jungle for ten days. Every village had a little shed there, huh? With a roof, there were bones there, wooden dishes there. And I noticed that.

"Well, the third day, when we were sitting around our campfire at night with the village elders, I asked, 'What are those little sheds out there at the entrance of your village?' They looked at each other for a while and finally an elder stood up and said, 'That is where I go to pray.' 'Oh, you pray? Who do you pray to?' 'To our ancestors, our great spirit.'

"'What do you do?' I asked, so he told me. 'When there is sickness in the village, I take a white rooster, with no spots on it, and I take it out to that shrine, and I hold that rooster up and I call out to the great spirit. The evil spirits are killing our people, we're dying, you are the great spirit. Drive out those evil spirits. Here is the sacrifice I bring. I take that rooster, tie it up, put it down there and cut his head off and make the sacrifice.'

"I said, 'Do you know that I'm out here because of the Great Spirit? My Great Spirit is different than yours. Mine is greater than yours.' 'Oh, that's not possible.' 'Yes it is.' And I said, 'Where did your forest come from?' 'We don't know.' 'I know.

Where'd you come from?' 'We don't know.' 'I do. The Great Spirit. That's what I'm here to tell you about. He's the Spirit that put the forest there, that put the animals in the forest, that put your streams, the water, put the people, He did all that.' 'Well, tell us about Him.'

"I said, 'I'd be glad to tell you about Him. He loves us.' 'What?' 'He loves us.'" And that was my opening. I began to teach out here. Today there isn't one shrine, I don't care where you go in our whole area, not one shrine left.

"Ah, that was long ago. Your question calls for a long answer, Sara girl. We must be nearing home. Ask again when I have time to give you a proper answer."

Baba V's house came into view and Amu skipped ahead to warn Apol that they were coming.

What had Kama been like 70 plus years ago, before missionaries? Had there been elephants, witch doctors, lions, naked or clothed natives? Sara promised herself she wouldn't wait long before asking again.

Baba V and Sara washed at the water drum, and dried in the slight breeze. Sara splashed water on her face in an effort to remove all signs of her crying. Apol had started a fire under the drum to heat water for the night's showers, but the water was still tepid, not hot, yet not cool and refreshing either. Supper awaited them and they ate their usual fare of bread, fish and bananas quietly.

"I'm sorry your first day at the clinic was visited with such sadness." Apol spoke softly as Sara helped her clear off the table and rinse the dishes before stacking them to dry.

News travels even in Kama, Sara thought but she appreciated Apol's compassion. Vincent, Amu and Baba V took turns showering. It was quickly Sara's turn. Since she determined it unnecessary to wash her hair, her shower was equally short.

Vincent had a nice fire burning in the fireplace when she joined the others in the front room.

Baba V's life held fascinating mysteries for Sara, and she determined to pry all she could out of him. But he sat once again at the short wave radio, talking with the Sanchezes at Bukavu.

"Report, Tom. Have you reached Ross yet?"

"Greetings, Baba V. Not yet. He should be back

in Douala soon. He'll contact us then. We got word to the mission in L.A. that Sara's with you. They were relieved to hear she's okay."

"Ah, thank you, Tom. How's the medical clinic in Bukavu? Has anyone interfered with your work?"

"So far we're stable. Our numbers are down, people are hesitant to move about any more than they have to. But that allows us to give greater attention to those hurting enough to brave coming in to the clinic for care. We heard gunfire from the guest house last night. We were warned by the embassy to stay inside and away from the windows. We haven't heard of any casualties yet."

"We had a bit of excitement here last evening."

"What happened?"

Baba V gave a short account of the soldiers' intent, the search, the outcome, and after warning them to stay alert and be careful, he blessed them and signed off the air. Sara was ready with questions as soon as he relaxed into his rocker.

"When were you born, Baba V?"

"Ha, Ha, a very long time ago, child."

"Come on, Baba, how old are you really? How long have you been here in Africa? How did you meet Mama V?

"We'll be up all night if I answer all these questions."

"Please."

"Ah, well, let's see. I was born in Pennsylvania on a farm, December 3rd, 1907, so I guess that makes me about 91 ½ years old. Pretty old by African standards, huh?" Baba chuckled softly and winked at Vincent whose face showed disbelief that anyone could live that long.

My folks were good Christian people. There were ten children in my family, though number ten came along after I left for Africa. The Stewart family lived just down from us. They housed their horses in our barn. Jimmy Stewart went to my school. Sara, have you seen the movie "It's a Wonderful Life" starring Jimmy Stewart? Well, I haf'ta tell ya gal, God gave *me* the wonderful life!"

"You grew up with Jimmy Stewart?" Sara's question fell on deaf ears. Baba's faded eyes softened with memories as he continued.

"I was raised Methodist. Missionaries came through our church, and I felt God's call to go to Africa. I was 19 years old, and attending Pittsburg Bible Institute. So I went to our pastor. I said, 'You need a preacher there in Wemboniama.' 'Well,' I said, 'I don't know if I want to go to Wemboniama or not, but I want to go to Africa.' So he said I should get prepared. He said, 'You're not yet 20 years old, you should go to college. Then God will call you.' I said, 'No, I don't want to go to college, I just want to go to Africa.' So he sent me to the bishop, who said the same thing.

"Then Dad, my Dad, decided to help me out. He took me to the family physician who said, 'You want to go out to Africa and start a medical work. Great, but, let me send you to medical school. I'll pay all your expenses. You get your degree as a doctor, I'll supply you with medicine and then you go out.' I said, 'That will take me five, six, seven years.' He said, 'Congo will still be there seven years from now, and there probably still won't be any missionary there.'

"I said, 'Ah, I can't wait seven years, but thanks for the offer. There's something in my heart says GO.' So I went down to this little mission group there and told them, 'I have to get to Africa.' They said 'You're too young, we can't take you.' I said, 'You don't have to send me. Just let me go with your people who are going out there. I'll come again in two days, ask the Lord if He made a mistake by calling me.' Ah, in a few days time they called me out and said, 'Smile, we'll let you go out.'"

"How did you meet Mama V?" Sara prompted when Baba paused.

"Ah, Bible conference in America. Two years we wrote back and forth. Then I told her I was going to Africa. She came to our farm. 'What are we going to do in Africa?' she wants to know. So I told her. I said, 'I can't take you now, I can't make a commitment. I don't know what it's like over there. I don't know whether we can get married legally over there. I'll go and find out.' So, she said, 'I'm your Ruth. I'll wait for you.'

"So I came to Africa. A year and a half we are separated. Finally I sent her word that I'd built a mud house for her, to come on.

"She was working at a beauty parlor the day she got that letter. She walked into that beauty parlor, and the owner, the lady that owned that parlor said, 'Marie, what is it?' She said, 'I just got a letter from my fiancée, he's called me, I'm going.'

"So she got on the telephone, called the mission, and the mission said, 'There are two things. First, you can't go by yourself to Africa. Secondly, right now in the blocks for missions, there's no money to send anybody out.'"

Ngalia leaned close to Sara and whispered, "What's a telephone?"

Sara tore her attention away from Baba's story to whisper back, "It's like a ham radio."

"Oh."

Baba continued, "So Marie goes back over to the owner of the beauty shop, and the boss saw the tears in her eyes and the long face. She said, 'You'd better go on a vacation for a day or two, you'll get the hair all messed up here,'" Baba chuckled.

"So she went home. Fourteen or sixteen days after, her father said, "Marie, since the day you told us your fiancée was waiting for ya, I couldn't quit thinking about it. I've figured out that our tithe right now, if we give it to you for the rest of the year, will pay your way out there.' Then she was up to the sky, huh?

"Marie goes right away over to the telephone, 'God's opened the way, I've got the money,' she tells the mission board. The missionary society said, 'God's opened another way, we have a professor here, Miss Burke, who wants to go to Africa to study the language. She needs somebody to go with her. There you are. You've got your money. We've got your way. You can go.'"

"So were you married here in Africa?"

"Ah, we tried to get married here in Congo. We got all the papers needed except one. The administrator for America said 'I can't marry you. You've got to have a letter of permission from your Ambassador at the Congo Embassy in Kinshasa. It's closed.' It was during the great depression, so they closed it up. It seemed impossible.

"By then I was in Belgium, in school, medical school . . . Ah, but that's another whole story in itself. Once here, I learned how wise my physician back home had been, but it was too late to take him up on his offer. The need was so great I went to Belgium to the government's special one-year tropical medicine school. When I finished my studies, I ask the medical authorities to give me a good hospital for my internship, someplace where I could really practice and learn doctoring.

"They sent me to the hospital at Albertville, right across from Tanzania. The first thing when I got there, I talked to the people. I didn't know where I was going to live, and I didn't have any money. But I went to a hotel there, 'Have you got a room? I'm here and I'm going to be here for three months.'

"I asked, 'You know English?' They spoke French there. The clerk said, 'No. I don't.' 'Well, you want to learn English?' 'You bet I do.' 'Okay, I'll be your teacher. All I need is a room and a place to study.'" Baba slapped his huge hand down on his knee. "He gave it to me! For three months I taught him. I had a beautiful apartment on the first floor, overlooking the lake and everything. I went over to the English territory and told them I wanted to get married, what were the rules? They said you both have to live here one week.

"So, I called Marie, come on girl, it's all set. She came and I signed her up in a hotel and with the English authorities. Then I went back to school, and studied. She stayed there at the hotel that week. The next week I went back, got there on Sunday morning. On Monday morning we went to the Justice of the Peace. No missionaries there, no church there, no pastor there. We went to the Justice of the Peace and I married her."

"You had a good marriage, didn't you, Baba?" Sara asked softly.

"Ah, Marie was a good wife. She worked alongside me till the day God took her home. We had four children you know, raised them all right here. Three boys and a girl."

"Were your children born here at Kama?"

"Ah, no, girl. When Sam Jr. was to be born, the Africans carried Marie in a chair for ten days to Kindu. In Kindu we got on the train and went to Kibombo. That took another day. Then at Kibombo, we met a missionary from Tunda. One hundred thirty kilometer we came. He took us then, in his car. We drove around a curve and in the middle of the road there stood a big water buffalo. Poor Mama, she said, 'What are we going to do?' I said, 'Be quiet, Mama, it's going to be alright.' That buffalo charged us, hit the fender on driver's side so hard he keeled over. We had to get out and raise the fender up before we could proceed." Again the old man chuckled.

"We got back in that Ford and drove on to the hospital. Of course, it was just a mud room. Doctor Lewis, she got Mama over to the delivery table. I had to get out of there, they wouldn't let me in." The man's focus was far away as if he were seeing that mud hospital room again. "And Sam was born. We raised him and three more right here at Kama you know.

"After attending Bible College in America, Sam Jr. brought his wife Becky home to Africa. They worked here with me as missionaries for many, many years. Sam's back in America heading up Grace Ministries International now you know. He served as President of Grace Bible College in Grand Rapids, Michigan, for several years before moving on to head up the mission. His son was born here, my grandson, Bill. Bill and his wife Sue and my great grandchildren were working here with me until this war broke out again." Wistfulness pulled Baba's voice down to a whisper. His gaze was focused unseeing on a spot outside the window. The room was quiet for a moment before the old man continued.

"You know, we planted a palm tree for each of our children and grandchildren, and now our great-grandchildren. When I first came to Kama there were no palm trees, just ordinary forest trees everywhere. Now we have mahogany trees for building lumber. We have orange, tangerine, grapefruit, guava, lemon, avocado and papaya trees. The people need a variety of fruits in their diet. The land grows strong trees, but they had to be planted." Again the room was quiet.

Amu's head rested peacefully in Sara's lap where she had been fingering the child's tight curls. Her soft snores alerted

Sara to the time, and she used the pause in Baba's story to lift the child into her arms and move her to the bedroom. Vincent stirred from his place, and sleepily stumbled after them as if pulled by an invisible rope.

"Ah, it's late." Baba confirmed. "Tomorrow is another day. I'll take myself off to bed now too. Good night, Sara, good night children." Using his arms to push himself up out of the rocker, the aged missionary strode off to his room. Sara turned her head to watch him go and shook her head.

"Nobody that old should have such energy. It's just not natural," she muttered admiringly. "I guess what they say is true. God supplies whatever you need to accomplish the work He gives you to do."

Chapter Twenty Six

Ross Mann's steps were purposeful as he hiked across Douala to the Tarbell offices. He hoped there would be word from the Sanchezes at the Bukavu mission guest house. Birds chattered in the trees, and brilliantly colored flowers along the way soaked in the sun's not rays. He focused only on reaching his destination.

"Hey Clark. I'm back, I gave this number to the Sanchezes, those friends in Bukavu, to contact me here, have you heard anything yet?" Clark had risen to his feet and reached across the desk to complete a firm handshake with the man before him.

"Sure have. They're waiting to hear you're back on the continent. She did it, Ross, somehow that little girl got herself clear to Kama. She's at that ol' missionary's place in the Congo. I tried to convince her to wait for ya, but I guess you can't tell the young what to do now a'days. She sure was determined. Make your calls. Hope you don't mind me eavesdropping, but call Bukavu first, then you'll know more what to tell 'em back home."

Bill Chapman was restless but doing his best to relax on the cot at the back of his Douala Airport hangar when Ross strolled up to him.

"Hey, Chappy, what's a raspy ol'codger like your self doing lolly-gagging about on a fine cool day as this?"

Chappy's restless form stiffened, his eyes popped opened and fixed on Ross before he bolted off the cot. Ross stepped back.

"What in blazes are you doing here?" he demanded.

"Saying hello to an old friend and looking for a ride?"

"NO! You're supposed to be at Kama looking after your niece!" Chappy persisted as if saying it would make it so. When that didn't work he demanded, "Why aren't you at Kama?!"

"Ahhh," Ross pointed at Chappy, "you're the missing piece of the puzzle. I wondered how she could up and disappear so fast."

"You said you were going to Kama!" When Ross reached out to clasp his shoulder, Chappy pulled away. "If you're here, she's alone there!" The older man sagged back onto the cot. "I'm an idiot! Just shoot me now."

"So you're the guy that delivered Sara right to Baba V's front door. You refused to do that for me! She must have really gotten to ya." Ross stepped over to the cot and sat down beside the distraught pilot. When Chappy refused to look up, Ross kept talking. "She's okay, Chappy. She's with Baba V, she couldn't be in better company, she's gonna come through this just fine. We've got to believe that or we'll drive ourselves nuts. How'd you get mixed up in all this?"

Chappy was silent for a minute or two, shrugged his shoulders and lifted his hands as if the words just wouldn't come. Finally he began.

"She just showed up here at the hangar. Joey brought her over. He's a good kid, brings me business when he can. He's my eyes and ears over in the terminal. Anyway, Sara tells me she missed you by half a day, and she's got to catch up to you. I tried to talk her into waiting for ya here, but she was so danged determined. I could see she was going to follow ya one way or another." Chappy rubbed his forehead, and sighed.

"I figured she'd be safer with me than some of the other characters around here, so I agreed to fly her to Bukavu. At the Bangui Airport I was approached about an urgent shipment of cholera medicine needing a ride to Kama. Word was we could refuel at the Tingi Tingi airstrip; Jeffery, an old military buddy of mine, would be there to refuel the Cessna. And he was. Its just two hours on to Kama, Sara got her wish, the medicine got there. The change in plans just happened. We slipped into Kama at dusk. I dropped off Sara and the medicine with Kilongo and Apol and hightailed it out of there before the rebels could hijack my plane. Baba was gone on safari."

"How'd you 'slip' in anywhere? Those Cessna's are noisy birds!"

"Ol' trick I learned in Nam. When I got close to the landing strips, I cut the engine and glided in, took care of business, powered up and split." Chappy sat with his hands pulling down the back of his head, his elbows resting on his knees, but as the silence in the hangar penetrated, he lifted his head to look sideways at Ross. He was shocked to see his friend slowly shaking his head back and forth and grinning from ear to ear. "What's so funny?" he demanded.

"Do you have any idea how tough an act you're going to be to follow? After stunts like that, my niece will think I'm boring!"

"How can you be so so…so…" Chappy stammered, "Sara's stuck out there all alone in the middle of a war zone!" he exploded.

"Well, first off, she's not there alone, she's with Baba V, my Bukavu contacts have been in radio contact with him and she's doing fine. Baba has her teaching English in the high school!" Ross took a deep breath. "Chappy, Sara came to Africa to escape."

"Escape! From what?" Chappy demanded. "Her folks were both killed week before last. I'm the only family she's got left."

"Oh, Ross, I'm so sorry." Chappy was quiet for a few minutes. "How were they killed?"

"Drive-by shooting; random target practice for gang initiation or some such idiocy."

"Hell, no wonder charg'n a war zone didn't faze her! She'd been living with it in America already!" Again Chappy paused, finally he asked, "You really think she'll be okay?"

"Yeah, I think so."

"Okay." Both men kept to their own thoughts for several minutes before Chappy spoke again. "Could I get ya something to drink?"

"No, I'm good. Thanks for offering."

"Ross, can I ask ya something?"

"Shoot."

"I, ah, well I relied on that little girl's faith and prayers to get us out of the mess I got us into. I'd tell her to pray, and she would. Now she's there, and I'm here, and. . . ."

"and, you don't know how to pray for her now?" Ross completed Chappy's thought.

"Yeah. I guess that's it. I know there's gotta be a God. How else did we get here; hell, how else did the whole cottinpickin' planet get here? Every culture acknowledges some kind'a higher power, human nature I guess, just the way we're wired. But that niece of yours, even when grieving, she had a confidence and strength that baffles me."

Again quiet settled over the hangar, a question hung heavy in the air, and Ross knew to wait for it. Finally Chappy whispered, "How does one know God like that?"

"Well," Ross paused, "first of all, you're right. There is a God, the one true God of Abraham, Isaac, and Jacob. He desired companions that could willingly return his love, and He did 'wire' into us a void only He can fill. But to ***willingly*** love someone, requires the freedom to reject them, so God gave us a free will to choose."

"What about Satan, how does he fit into all this?" Chappy asked.

"Satan provides that balance of influence. He wants us to reject God. His failed attempt to over-throw God drives him to get revenge. God created us and deserves our love, but Satan does everything he can to make us hate God, or at the very least be indifferent to him. The Bible says our battle's not with flesh and blood, but against evil rulers and authorities of the unseen world, and against evil spirits in the heavenly places."

"I ain't never heard anything like that before," Chappy interrupted, "but it sure explains a lot of the crap I've seen. I know mankind can be murderous, but there's just no makin' sense to things I've seen…."

Chappy's voice faded away. He leaned back against the wall and closed his eyes. "So how'r we suppose to get on the right side of this invisible war?"

"God made us a way. In his perfection, God can't look on sin, and Satan uses that to his advantage. He pushes us into sin to drive a wedge between God and us, or like you've seen, he'll just drive man to kill one another off." Ross paused to pick his words carefully.

"Chappy, God sent His Beloved Son, Jesus Christ, to pay the death penalty for all mankind's sin. Sin causes spiritual death and eternal separation from God. So Jesus came to earth, lived a sinless life, and then allowed Satan to crucify him on the cross of Calvary. Satan thought he'd won, but all he'd done was play right into God's plan." Again Ross stopped and weighed his words carefully.

"Since Jesus lived a sinless life here on earth, then paid the death penalty with his own life, God can apply Jesus death to anyone who asks for it. And since Jesus was sinless, death couldn't hold him. He laid down his life and took it up again."

"If we accept the Son and His payment for our sin, we're accepted by God for all eternity. It's a pretty sweet deal unless you reject it and end up bunking with Satan, eternally separated from God." Ross paused.

"Why can't we pay for our own mess ups?" Chappy wanted to know.

"Because we're not sinless." Ross shrugged his shoulders. "It's only through the filter of His sinless Son that God can even look on us and we can fellowship with Him."

"Huh, that's intense!"

"Tell me about it. But making the choice to accept what Jesus did for me at the cross of Calvary, was the best decision I ever made, and I know making that same choice is what gives Sara courage to race ahead like she does."

"How come you never told me about this before?" Chappy demanded.

"I don't know, Chappy. I guess the time just wasn't right. Is it right now?"

"I reckon it must be."

"So, why are you telling me? I can't do anything but point the way. Tell it to God. He's the one who has to hear it."

"Just like that?"

"Yeah."

"Okay." Chappy closed his eyes, as if to focus on things he couldn't see. "Count me in, God. I need saving from my sin. I need your forgiveness and the peace Sara and Ross have.

I accept your provision for my sin and ask your forgiveness. I want to join You when I leave this earth. Uh, Thanks."

Again silence enveloped the hangar. Both men sat quiet in the stillness of that sacred moment, till Chappy looked over at Ross and saw an ear to ear grin that belied the tears streaming down his cheeks. "I feel better."

Ross laughed out loud and hard. "I bet you do, you ol' sinner. If Sara's trip into a war zone is what it took to get you through heaven's gates, she and I both rejoice that we could oblige you!"

"Back on that topic, where have you been?!" Ross suddenly sobered. "The day after I left you,

I went by Tarbell offices to check in and get my mail. In with it was a fax of my sister and brother-in-law's obituary from the LA Times. I hit the road running to Sara. You know the rest. We probably crossed paths in Paris.

"It's funny how God works things out. Now you're right with God. Baba V still got medicine. Sara's teaching English at Kama, and learning about life and death there with Baba. Who better could help her through this? I would never have chosen such a plan, but God allowed it. And, we can always bombard God with our concerns! Ya with me?"

"I'm with ya." Chappy grinned.

Chapter Twenty Seven

Supper was interrupted the next evening when Tom Sanchez's voice crackled through the ham radio.

"I've had contact with Ross Mann. Come back if you're there, Baba."

Everyone deserted their dinners except Amu and Vincent. Amu looked puzzled at the sudden burst of energy from the adults. Vincent just looked longingly at the last bit of fish left on Sara's plate.

"Ross Mann you say?" Baba boomed into the microphone."

"Is he there with you?"

"No. But he's back in Douala, Cameroon. Now he knows Sara got a flight to Kama, and that you've put her to work teaching English in the school."

"What's the plan? Is Ross still coming?"

"Not yet. He's looking for ground transportation. He needs government cooperation for a military escort since he's coming in after Sara. I suggested he use that pilot friend of his, but the airspace over Congo is still restricted and refuel stations are a problem."

"Understood."

"He said to tell you 'Thank you' for caring for Sara and that he owes you. He also said, 'Work Sara's tail off - for disappearing on us like she did.'" Tom chuckled good-naturedly, but Sara doubted Uncle Ross had chuckled at all.

He may leave me here for months. Her thoughts were interrupted when Baba asked, "Do you wish to send a message back to your uncle?"

"Yes. Please let him know I'm sorry about the mix-up, and I'll make myself useful. I look forward to seeing him again but there's no rush." Her clipped tone depicted a chin held high.

"Did you get all that, Tom?"

"Ten four. I'll pass the word along."

Baba and Tom continued to converse and Sara returned to her supper. Her plate was empty so she must have been done eating when the call came in. Good thing too. She'd lost her appetite. So preoccupied was she with her own thoughts that she missed Amu's glaring look at Vincent who was wearing his best angel look.

"It's time for your shower Amu," Sara motioned to the child and Amu slinked off to comply, looking unusually sour. Vincent followed, all too eager to be away from the kitchen and feeling blessed that Amu couldn't rat on him and that Sara was now happy to have heard from her uncle. Surely God would forgive him this once. He'd never do it again. Not right away at least.

Saturday arrived quicker than Sara dreamed possible. Now that Uncle Ross was definitely not arriving anytime soon, Sara poured herself into her role as teacher. So many students were chronically hungry; she wondered how they could learn anything at all.

"Baba V," she inquired at breakfast, "how can I help my students get more food? Surely they'd learn better if their stomachs weren't so empty."

"Ah. Age-old problem. Well, the missionaries used to find jobs the students could perform, and they'd hire them for pay."

"Could I do that? What wage should I pay per hour?"

"Per hour? Oh, no child. Pay workers per job completed, and pay what the job is worth."

"What kind of work could I hire students for?"

"Let's see. Jeff used to hire students to machete grass on the game field or around the mission houses. That employed several young men and was great sport for others to watch."

"Okay, that's a start. I'll work on that. Thanks Baba."

Apol was enlisted to change Sara's francs into Zairian coin and she advised Sara on how much wage would be needed to purchase one day's food staples for a family of six.

Ngalia and Paipi arrived and the three headed for the market. Sara discussed her plan with Ngalia. "Any ideas, Ngalia, on who to hire?"

"Kyanga, Yakobo, and Abedy are worthy students. They are good workers too. Shindano, Alimasi and Mukula come from big families too, they are Mai Mai but they don't be pushy at others. Can you hire six?"

"I think that's all I dare try today. I've never been a boss before. I don't know anything about machetes. Will these guys have their own?"

"Everyone have machete."

"Okay. How do we go about rounding them up?"

Ngalia grinned and chattered away in Swahili to the first group of young boys they met. The boys scattered.

"Yakobo's brother's in that group. He'll spread the word. The boys will find us. We can wait here."

"Clever girl. Thanks." Sara and Ngalia settled on a log to watch the marketers coming and going. Paipi explored the activity under a small rock.

Sara turned her attention to the variety of parrots fluttering about a nearby tree. "Do any of those birds talk?"

"African Gray parrots best talkers in the world. They smart too. We give baby parrots to many missionaries as special gift. Now lots of African Gray parrots live in America with missionaries."

"I had a friend once whose parents bought her an African Gray parrot from a pet store. They cost a lot of money! Her parrot talked a little bit, but not a lot."

"Maybe it was a boy parrot. I think the girl parrots talk best."

"How can you tell which is which?"

"Simple. Girl parrots lay eggs, boy parrots don't."

Sara laughed, and pretended to push Ngalia away. "Seriously, why doesn't someone sell parrots at the market?"

"If someone wants parrot, they go to tree when babies are old enough to leave mother and get their own. Who has money for such nonsense?"

"Okay, second silly question."

Sara's work crew of six arrived leading several others who seemed free to just hang out and watch the activity. Sara addressed them in English.

"I want to hire you to cut the grass on the game field. I can pay you six Zaires each when the job is done to my satisfaction. Do you want the job?"

Nods and grins accompanied the show of cutting tools and the whole group set off for the game field. It was obvious to Sara that her crew had done this chore before. They commenced cutting next to the airstrip and headed toward the tree line. The six youth spaced themselves at six foot intervals and swung their machetes with precision back and forth, always in the same direction, left then right. A carpet of long flattened grass lay behind them.

Sara was amazed at how quickly the work progressed. Ngalia whispered to her, "They showing off for pretty red haired teacher," and grinned at her wickedly.

"No they're not," Sara quickly denied, but her face suddenly flamed red.

The cutters stopped short of the trees and repositioned themselves to cut another swath back towards the airstrip. School chums that came to watch cheered the workers on, chanting in rhythm, then bursting into song.

Teamwork is a beautiful thing, Sara thought. "You chose good workers, Ngalia. Thanks for your input." Ngalia's teasing was forgiven and Sara waded out into the high grass to assess how far the cutters should mow for their six Zaires.

"Sara!" Ngalia screamed behind her.

Sara stopped and looked back at Ngalia. Ngalia began screaming in Swahili, waving her arms and screeching. Sara caught movement in her peripheral vision and looked back to see her work crew charging right at her, their machetes raised as if to strike her down. When they reached her they sped right past. She followed their motion in confusion. *What in the world?* . . . . . . five feet from Sara stood the largest cobra she had ever seen. It swung its eyes from her to the others that surrounded it, uncertain where to strike. Sara froze.

Yelling, screaming, and dancing about to confuse the snake and draw its attention away from Sara, the barefooted students in one accord made a sudden dash into the snake's range. Machetes flashed sunlight until the snake lay writhing in death, hacked into multiple pieces.

"Did it strike you, Ms Sara? Did it strike you?" they all asked at once.

Suddenly Sara wanted nothing more than to wretch up her guts and cry, but teachers mustn't react so in front of their students.

"No, no, I'm okay. Thank you. You saved my life. I, I didn't see it." Sara stepped back from the chopped remains of the great snake. Surely it was dead, but it still looked menacing. She swallowed nervously.

"You go back by Ngalia," Kyanga ordered kindly. "We clean up this mess then finish our job."

Nodding numbly, Sara carefully retraced her steps to Ngalia and the crew divided the snake remains and wrapped them in huge leaves and laid them on the airstrip. Would they be cooked and eaten? Just the thought made Sara weak in the knees.

The cutters returned to the field and took up their mowing, making four more swaths before considering the job complete and lining up in front of Sara for their wages.

"Thank you," she repeated to each student as she paid each one. Someone produced a soccer ball and teams were quickly chosen. Sara watched in disbelief. What if there was another snake out there? How could she just stand there and watch them play ball like nothing had happened?

Ngalia pressed close to her side reassuringly. Paipi played at their feet. And there they stood, quiet observers, till the game was over and winners were declared.

Chapter Twenty Eight

"I've seen cobras in the zoo, sleeping behind safety glass, but never so up close and personal. Its head was raised above the tall grass, and it looked me right in the eye." Sara nervously recounted her near death experience to everyone at supper. "The guys charged right past me and killed it with their machetes. I've never been so frightened in my whole life!"

"One must be as careful in Africa as in any other place on this world, Sara. You can't just barge into the vegetation and expect everything there to be gone. You have to make noise and give creatures time to escape. The cobra was probably moving away from the cutters when you surprised it. It's usually safer to stay on the paths and roadways."

"Oh, I know that now."

"Can I see the cobra, Sara, please, please," Vincent begged in typical boy style.

"The guys split up the pieces, Vincent. I think they took it home to eat. What other surprises should I know about, Baba?"

"If I told you, you wouldn't be surprised now would you?" Baba countered teasingly.

"I don't want any more surprises of that nature, thank you. I'd rather be informed."

"Then learn to watch yourself—be aware of your surroundings and potential dangers."

"Okay. But what kinds of things am I watching for?"

"Crocodilesnearwater,snakesorspidersanyplace. Mrs. Bayler found a tiny, but most poisonous snake in her sewing cabinet drawer once. Snakes also like rafters in cool places. Mostly just be aware of your surroundings, Sara, pause to listen to your instincts. God gives them to us for a reason."

"Are there elephants anywhere close by?"

"Not for many years now. We had elephants when I first came to Kama. One elephant could feed the whole Village. There was great excitement when a hunter came back with news of an elephant kill."

"You killed and ate them?" Sara stared at the man open-mouthed.

"Oh yes. Elephants were not considered friends. They trampled crops and crushed huts, killing people in angry charges. The elephants have slowly been pushed further and further back into the jungles. We don't see them anymore. They've moved to areas where there are fewer men." Baba didn't seem saddened by the loss of the mighty animals.

"Tell Sara about our gorillas, Baba," Vincent squirmed in his seat, mischief dancing in his dark eyes.

"Vincent," Baba kindly scolded. "We're not trying to scare Sara, just educate her. In America you have a movie called 'Gorillas in the Mist.' Do you not?"

"Yes. I've seen it several times on TV."

"What's TV?" Vincent jumped into the conversation again.

"Never mind that now, boy. Sara can explain that to you later. That whole movie was filmed not far from Bukavu. Those are our gorillas." Baba sounded proud but wary. "We see large families of gorillas every now and then, moving through the area. Not often mind you. They prefer to avoid people—unlike those mischievous, thieving monkeys that plague us from time to time. We eat those too by the way."

Sara looked up from her plate to read the expression on Baba V's face. Was he kidding her again or were the people really that desperate for meat? He didn't seem to be teasing and she realized she already knew the answer to her question. If they'd eat cobra, they'd surely eat monkeys if they could catch them. Any meat would be better than none.

"I hope I get to see a family of gorillas," she stated sincerely. "That would be awesome."

"It would also be dangerous. But right now there are so many folks hiding in the jungle I doubt we'll need to worry about it."

"Oh." Disappointment sounded in Sara's voice and Baba reached over to pat her arm kindly.

"Surely you saw enough raw nature with that cobra to last you awhile, huh?"

"Yes. I think so. Thanks for the reminder."

Night came early as thunderstorms rolled in overhead. Shutters were latched against the sudden winds and heavy rain. Lightning clashed overhead illuminating the darkened skies with jagged bursts of light.

Sara lay listening from her net covered bed. One couldn't read or study by lightning flashes and Baba said it was best to save kerosene lamp light for emergencies. In spite of the drama that played itself out around her, Sara soon slept, lulled by the beating of raindrops on the tin roof.

Vincent paced excitedly back and forth from the kitchen to the bedroom. Such news as Apol brought with her this morning couldn't wait much longer or he'd burst.

"I'm sorry I told you, Vincent," Apol scolded, "you surely will wake the whole household before I ever get breakfast on the table."

"Can I be the one to tell Baba V and Sara?" the boy begged.

"Only if you sit down and stop pacing. Such energy could irritate the dead, and for sure annoys me."

Vincent worked at sitting quietly till Apol finished her breakfast preparations.

"Okay, I hear Baba V stirring. You may go wake Sara and Amu."

Vincent shot out of the kitchen before Apol finished her words.

"Sara, Sara, the wind blew the roof off the school building last night. Wake up now. The school's roofless."

Some of Vincent's words, and the urgency of his voice, awakened Sara—pulling her back from dreams of home, emergency sirens, screeching trains and honking automobiles.

"Sara, Sara, wake up. The roof blew off your school last night!"

It was difficult to shift continents so suddenly, but Sara blinked and sat up, pulling her legs into a knot in front of her for balance.

"Good morning, Vincent." Sara stretched and yawned. "Now, what's wrong?"

Exasperation marked the boy's movements. "The school, it lost its roof in the storm last night." The boy danced from one foot to the other and watched for signs of understanding to widen Sara's eyes. Satisfied that she finally got it, he rushed off to spread the news to Baba V.

"Oh my," Sara yawned again. "What day is this?" She tried to rub the sleep from her eyes and focus her mind. "Yesterday... cobra. Saturday. Okay. It's Sunday. No school today."

Amu slid onto the bed next to Sara and copied her leg knot. Sara smiled at the child and hugged her warmly.

"It's time to get up, Amu," she sighed. "Today's Sunday." The child looked so solemnly at Sara, she couldn't resist raising her hands and fingers in the tickle bug tradition and descending slowly, teasingly, towards the child's ribcage—grinning all the while.

Amu's eyes widened in glee, but she didn't move till Sara's fingers tickled up and down her boney ribcage making her squeal and squirm off the bed, giggling all the way.

Sara followed, quickly donning her green dress, still baggy at best. She located her hairbrush and began working on the numerous tangles that had invaded her hair during the night. The smell of damp earth and humid air filtered thru the closed shutters carrying with it the muffled sounds of chickens scratching and a far off rooster greeting the day.

Did Vincent say the school blew down? No. Bricks don't blow down in a thunderstorm. Better get to breakfast and find out what all the excitement is about, she thought.

Baba V and Vincent were already at the table when Sara and Amu joined them.

"What is Vincent so excited about this morning," Sara asked, sliding into her chair.

"The roof blew off the school last night," Apol answered.

"Really? Where did it land?"

"Part in trees, part on the ground - upside down, trusses skyward like ribcage of big animal picked clean by vultures and sun bleached."

"Wow! Will we still hold school, Baba?"

"No child. Repairs will have to be made. We have to dismantle the roof and rebuild it. That will take time."

"What'll happen then?"

"Well, after church today the students will come and start the dismantling and carry the parts back to the school building. Parents will help if they can.

Then they'll rebuild the roof as best they can from what they have salvaged."

"We take so much for granted in America."

"Yes, that's true. But you have storms of your own that deliver damage to property and people. Fires, hurricanes, tornados, earthquakes, floods, even volcanoes. God allows all mankind to be humbled and strengthened by nature's forces."

"I guess so. Will we go to the leper colony today?"

"Ah, only the men will go today. The road will be a nasty challenge after the rain last night. There will be plenty of work to do right here in Kama."

"But first church?"

"Yes. First church." Baba confirmed.

Apol cleared the breakfast away while Sara wound her hair up in the tightest knot she could manage. Amu watched, admiration shining in her tiny black eyes.

Church first. The damage from the storm would not prevent Sara from participating in African worship once again. Today she had special thanks to give. Only the cobra had died because of her folly. It was something for which to be truly grateful.

As she prepared herself, she prayed for Mupenda, whose baby was stillborn, and for Uncle Ross, Chappy, and those so far away at the Calhoun Mission back home. Mrs. Shaffer must be beside herself with worry. By now, Uncle Ross would have told everyone back home where she was, yet there was comfort in knowing they would surely all be praying for her.

Baba V and the men left for the leper colony as quickly as church and dinner were over. Sara saw an opportunity for an afternoon of leisure, and dug in her backpack for a sketch pad and drawing pencils. She'd originally bought these art supplies for use in Paris. Packing them had stirred up painful memories, yet something inside her wouldn't allow her to leave them behind. Now she was glad. She wanted to spend her free day sketching the students at work dismantling the roof. If there was time, it would be fun to capture her memories of the cobra scene from yesterday on paper as well.

Sara found an out-of-the-way spot where she could observe all the activity. She cast about, "noisily," for a rock or log upon which to sit. At first she was alone, sketching quietly, but as the scene before her began to take shape on the paper, the younger kids began to gather behind and around her, their eyes wide with fascination as Sara's hand added detail after detail to the sketch. Faces took on form and recognition of family members brought squeals of delight. Sara's focus was broken by this one and that one who would run to an older working sibling and shout at Sara, pointing to the brother or sister, then her sketch book, pleading in their voice and eyes. Few of the younger kids knew any English yet, but Sara got the message.

Ngalia and Paipi soon found their way to where Sara sat, but seeing the crowd around her, Ngalia chose to sit a short distance off. The temptation was too great for Sara. She set the sketch of the roof repair aside, and began sketching her dearest friend and baby.

Quickly the sketch took on form, then detail. As soon as she finished one, Sara began the second sketch just like it . . . Ngalia seated gracefully on a stump adoring her baby, Paipi leaning against her knee watching the work beyond them, with fascination beautifully captured in his expression.

Shyly Sara called to Ngalia and offered her the choice between the two sketches.

"One is for you to keep Ngalia. Which one do you prefer? I'm keeping the other one for myself so I'll never forget how you both looked today."

"Oh Sara, how did you do this?" Ngalia whispered in awe. "Oh, what a wonderful gift. I want this one. Is it really mine to keep?" Wonderment softened Ngalia's face and Sara hugged her.

"Yes, it's really all yours. Do you really like it?"

"It's, it's, oh it's just wonderful." Ngalia giggled as all the children began begging for Sara to draw them.

The afternoon sped by as Sara divided her paper into quarters and sketched quick caricatures of a single child or a group of siblings. Her audience dwindled as each sketch was carried away by the subjects pictured to show to parents and neighbors.

Ngalia stayed near Sara, fascinated with the process of sketching form to paper with simple, or so it seemed, strokes of a pencil.

Noticing the commotion, Principal Kantamba left the supervision of the roof dismantling in Madua's control and slid in behind Sara. He stood quietly, watching as sketch after sketch was penciled and carried away by the delighted recipients. Madua left the work momentarily to stand beside Kantamba and observe the sketching. After he and Kantamba exchanged meaningful glances, he returned to the roof, confident Sara would soon be teaching art if she were willing.

The work was called to a halt before dusk with plans to finish the dismantling the next day. Reconstruction would begin as soon as lumber was carried back to the school site.

Sara gathered her art supplies and sent the remaining children home with promises that perhaps she could sketch them another day. Ngalia translated for her and the kids reluctantly disbursed for home.

Kantamba stepped up beside Sara making his presence known.

"You have more to teach us than just English, Miss Sara."

"Oh, Principal Kantamba," red crept into Sara's cheeks, "You saw?"

"Oh yes, I saw." Dark eyes crinkled with delight. He placed his hand on Sara's shoulder, "You teach others how to do this, yes?"

"I don't know. I suppose I could try. Mrs. Schaffer taught me, but she started when I was too small to even remember it. I could teach the basics perhaps—" Sara ended lamely. What had she gotten herself into?

"We don't have paper or pencils right now, but perhaps we could figure something out. I will talk with Baba V about this." The man bowed toward Sara, still grinning and backed away, turned abruptly and strode away, head bent down as if determined to solve the problem at hand.

"Oh Sara," Ngalia squealed, squeezing Sara's arms. "An art teacher, right here in Kama, and it's YOU!"

"I don't know how I can teach without supplies Ngalia, students would need to practice—and I already teach English all available school hours."

"Kantamba looks awfully determined."

"I noticed."

Together the girls made their way toward the mission house. Supper awaited them. Apol was delighted with Sara's sketch of Ngalia and Paipi.

"You are full of surprises, girl," she scolded as if Sara had deliberately withheld valuable information about herself, but Sara knew she was proud of her. Mrs. Schaffer would be proud of her too, especially if she could transfer Mrs. Schaffer's talent to others in this part of the world.

Baba V returned home late. The muddy road had made progress slow and difficult. Apol served him a late supper and shooed him off to a hot shower and waiting bed.

I wonder what Baba will say to Kantamba about my taking on more teaching. Sara wondered from her bed. *I bet he'll say*

"Oh, child, God brought you here to teach, so teach all you know. God will provide the supplies you need." That's what he'll say.

Weary but happy, Sara slept knowing she had brought delight to many that day, and that her drawings were probably featured on many mud walls throughout Kama that night.

Chapter Twenty Nine

Sara woke to the muffled echo of pounding hammers. It took her several moments to orient herself to being in Africa. The mosquito netting canopy over her bed shrouded her world in a misty fog until full awareness stabilized her thinking. *They've already begun work on the school roof,* she thought scrambling out of bed, careful not to wake Vincent and Amu. *This is a first. I wonder if Apol has started breakfast.*

The house was quiet when Sara slipped into the bathroom and still quiet when she emerged a few moments later. She peeked into Baba V's room as she passed, and paused only slightly as he was kneeling beside his bed, hands folded in prayer. Thankful for the reminder, Sara sank to her own knees beside Baba's rocker.

I need your guidance God. I'm here at Kama till Uncle Ross comes for me. Help me be useful and not a burden on anyone. Help me be a good teacher and please protect us all from harm. Amen.

With pad and pencil in hand, Sara slipped out the kitchen door, grabbing a banana on her way. She wouldn't stay gone long. She just wanted to capture the early bird workers in the early morning light. It was one thing to get up early to go to market, but rising so early to work on the school roof took dedication.

Sara was careful to stay on cleared ground or pathways, and avoided tall grass; one encounter with a big snake was one too many in her book. Few people were stirring, mostly chickens pecking at the ground for seed and worms. The early morning light held Kama in a surreal light that reminded her of the first night in Kama when Chappy had led her from the airstrip to Baba's house. She had been anxious that night, everything was new and strange. Not so anymore, Sara was learning her way around Kama. She had friends here, good friends.

As Sara neared the airstrip, the slumped figure of a soldier stiffened into alertness. His eyes followed Sara's progress. Reluctantly he bent to retrieve his rifle from the ground, and walked into the trees, careful to keep Sara in his sight. When she settled on the same log she'd used the day before, and began sketching, he stationed himself behind her. Anyone looking her way would note his presence and be wary of approaching her.

Quietly Sara added details to her sketch of the roof project. She went unnoticed by the workers for several moments. Even at this close range the hammers sounded strangely muffled. Sara focused on her sketch. The crew worked in silence. No one cajoled or taunted another, no one sang. To work and not sing was unusual for these people, and Sara pondered the consideration of the workers for those still sleeping in the compound. A worker looked up from prying nails from a board, and uttered a startled cry.

All work stopped and the men stared at Sara, then beyond her. The encounter with Saturday's cobra caused Sara to turn her head slowly to see what behind her drew the attention of the workers. A lone soldier stood between her and the trees, his feet apart, his rifle cradled across his arms, but there were no cobras. Sara turned back to the workers and goose bumps raised on the back of her neck. They had all vanished. She was alone with the soldier.

Clutching her pencils and sketch pad, Sara scrambled to her feet and ran for her life back to Baba's house. But no footsteps pounded after her and when she looked back, no one followed.

What's going on? Why did the workers vanish? Were those hammers muffled for stealth? Why in the world don't I think before getting myself into such messes?

Sara was breathing hard when she let herself into the house through the kitchen door and slid into Baba's rocker. That is where Apol found her when she came to prepare breakfast. Sara was quick to tell Apol what she'd seen.

"What was going on Apol?" she finished. "Sounds like you scared off thieves to me."

"They just vanished. And that soldier. He just stood there looking at me."

"You lucky, Miss Sara. Remember Ngalia's troubles and be more careful after this. Wild creatures of nature include mankind. You're old enough to know this."

"I thought the students had gotten an early start, that's all. I didn't expect to be alone out there."

"God protect you this time, child. Be thankful and go on. Be more careful next time. We not want any harm come to you, child."

"Do we have to mention this to Baba V? I don't want to worry him with my foolishness."

"No, I not tell. You learn from mistakes and not do them again. That's what I say."

"Thank you Apol. I won't forget."

"Eat breakfast now, our workers will soon be pounding away, and Ngalia will be coming for you."

Vincent made his appearance. "There you are, Sara, why you up so early? You don't have school today."

"Don't be fussing at Miss Sara, Vincent. Is Amu awake? Is she coming? You two do have school today. Tell her to hurry along now. You're going to be late."

Sara noted Vincent's eyes rolling towards the ceiling as he turned about to fetch Amu.

"Thanks, Apol."

Baba V joined Sara at the table and settled into the chair at the head of the table.

"How are you planning to use your time today, Miss Sara? Seems you have a holiday."

"Ngalia's coming to keep Miss Sara company, Baba," Apol spoke as if revealing a great confidence. "Perhaps she can teach Sara how to weave a basket today, or better yet how to balance one on her head."

"That would be a first," Baba chuckled. "Our American women don't start young enough. Now my granddaughters, they're young. They could learn early and develop strong neck muscles. But it's probably too late for you, Miss Sara. Don't let Ngalia push you too hard."

"Perhaps today I'll teach Ngalia something about drawing." Sara suggested looking sideways at Apol to catch her reaction.

"You draw?" Baba and Apol asked together. "Yes." To prove herself, Sara fetched her sketching tablet from Baba's rocker, and pulled out her sketch of Ngalia, then opened the pad to reveal the sketch of the roof work in progress. Baba turned his head till he could see the drawings in his peripheral vision.

"Very nice, Sara, very nice indeed. Yes, teach Ngalia well. Perhaps she can be the art teacher when you have left us. That would be splendid, splendid indeed."

Two hours later Sara and Ngalia sat side-by-side in the work yard at Apol's house.

"Promise me you'll never go out alone again, Sara. You could have been hurt very bad!"

"You'd think I'd learn, wouldn't you. I scared myself this morning. I won't be making that mistake again, or any other, I hope. Promise me you won't mention this to anyone. Please."

"I promise. Did you recognize the soldier?"

"No. Maybe. It could have been Paipi's father." Ngalia gasped at Sara's words.

"I don't know that for sure, Ngalia. But he stood kind of like he does. Whoever it was, I don't think he meant me harm. He may even have been protecting me. That's it, Ngalia, God put him there to protect me from the thieves."

"I don't want to think about it anymore," Ngalia shuddered. "Teach me to make pictures like you do, Sara."

"Okay, let's get started." Sara had left her art supplies at Baba's. After Sunday's experience, she feared drawing a crowd if seen with the sketch pad. Besides, paper was too precious a commodity here to waste on practice. So she smoothed the ground in front on her, brushing small rocks aside with her hand. With a stick she drew a circle in the dirt. She handed Ngalia a stick and pointed to the ground. "You make a circle too." Ngalia made a similar circle, and Sara's first attempt at teaching art began in earnest.

By lunchtime Ngalia was ready to begin applying lines, circles, and shadings to real objects. Sara looked about for a good first project.

"See the palms over there?" Sara pointed at the trees in questions. "Try your hand at drawing one of those."

Ngalia had a good eye for proportions, and set to work immediately. The tree's trunk lines were sketched quickly, and the palm fronds took on shape in the dirt. "Should I include the workers?" she quipped mischievously, quite pleased with her success.

"What workers?" Sara looked puzzled. "The workers in the top of those palm trees."

"What workers?" Sara repeated, staring intently at the palms. Suddenly a palm nut dropped heavily to the ground, creating a dull thud in the soft earth. Sara looked swiftly at Ngalia with wide eyes.

"They're gathering palm nuts to make oil," Ngalia's eyes danced with privileged knowledge.

"You can see workers in those trees?" Sara asked incredulously.

"It's easier to see what you know than what you don't know. I know men were to climb those trees today to get the nuts."

"That's cheating!" Sara declared. "Let's break for lunch. I want to see how those workers will get down."

Ngalia was reluctant to erase her first recognizable art project so they left the earth just as it was, palm drawing intact.

The girls kept a safe distance from the dropping palm nuts, but found a good place to view the descending workers. They didn't have to wait long before a man shimmied down the trunk of the tree.

"They climb down like monkeys!" Sara exclaimed. "No wonder folks think we came from apes."

Ngalia stared at Sara for a moment – intent to read her face for signs of mischief. "You making joke, yes?"

"Yes and no. People who don't want to believe God made us and everything else too, try to explain creation in some pretty comical ways."

"Comical?"

"Funny, humorous, silly."

Ngalia shook her head as if to clear such thoughts. "From apes? Really!" Sara grinned at her indignation.

Apol had lunch ready for them at Baba's. Paipi was squatting next to a pan of water Apol had set out for him to splash in. Between splashes he was happily floating nutshells and blades of grass, cooing about his successes.

"Thank you, Apol, for watching Paipi this morning. Sara and I had a good study time. I can draw good palm trees now," she added shyly.

"Show me."

Ngalia led Apol to a patch of bare dirt and smoothed the surface with her hand. Then using a small rock that lay nearby, she carefully sketched a palm tree with several nuts lying at its base.

Apol seemed satisfied and nodded a curt approval. "Time to eat," she stated, and scooped up Paipi on her march back to the kitchen.

The rest of the day was spent doing chores and preparing for the next day. Baba arrived home for the evening meal and settled in for the night.

Darkness came earlier than usual as dark clouds blocked the beauty of the sunset. Rain began pelting the area and puddles pooled in low spots. The warmth and crackling of the fireplace was soothing and for once everyone sat about quietly reflecting on the events of their day. Lightning and thunder crashed nearby and the front door swung open flooding the room with cool, wet air. Sara looked up to see wet angry soldiers flooding into Baba's house.

"You're under arrest," shouted the leader. He grabbed Baba's arm and yanked him to his feet. Ngalia muffled a scream into Paipi's neck, clutching the tiny boy to her and rolling protectively over him.

"Why do you arrest me?" Baba demanded, pulling up straight to his full height.

"You smuggled guns to the enemy."

"I was cleared of those false charges."

"Not by me!"

The angry soldiers grabbed Vincent and Amu, Sara and Ngalia and began shoving them towards the open door. Baba calmly but sternly demanded the children be left behind. "Those children must continue their schooling. The girl is deaf and dumb; she can not harm you. She needs the boy to care for her." The terror on Amu's face faded away as the child slumped to the floor, the soldier holding her kicked at her limp form in disgust but she felt nothing. Vincent seized the distraction to twist free, bolt out the door and disappear into the rain.

Baba was shoved out the door and the girls were forced out after him. No one chased after Vincent. Amu lay on the floor where she'd fallen.

Baba's shoes remained next to his rocker where he'd set them.

Chapter Thirty

Cool rain soaked quickly through Sara's dress, but she barely noticed. Baba was being pushed and shoved as if he were a young man. Time and again he stumbled and fell, only to be yanked up and pushed on. Kama quickly faded from view.

Sara and Ngalia tried to move forward in the line of soldiers to reach and help Baba, but they were deliberately held back. Occasionally they collided into each other; somehow it was comforting. They took turns carrying Paipi.

Baba fell again, and a frustrated soldier pointed his gun at the back of Baba's head, yelling at him in Swahili. Sara screamed and Baba looked back towards the girls and frowned. Purposefully he stood and pressed on.

It was morning before the men were willing to stop and rest. There was no food. Baba's feet were caked with blood and mud. Sara wished she could slide her own shoes onto Baba's feet, but they were many sizes too small for the tall man. It was the only time she ever wished for bigger feet.

Somewhere in their march through the night, the rain slacked and stopped. When they were joined by a second band of soldiers pulling four captives bound at the wrists, Apol slid into the group. Sara nudged Ngalia and nodded towards Apol who shook her head meaningfully at them. So they remained quiet and accepted her appearance as if nothing had changed. Vincent must have gone straight to Kilongo and Apol's house for Apol to be able to follow them so quickly. Finally the march was halted and the girls grouped as close to Baba V as they could manage.

"Why are you here?" Sara demanded of Apol in a whisper.

"I go where Baba goes," Apol answered quietly. "I take care of Baba and you three. Kilongo care for Vincent and Amu." Ngalia lifted Paipi from her back and handed him to Sara.

"I bring Paipi's father too." Apol announced calmly.

Sara and Ngalia exchanged looks of shock and protest, but Apol didn't seem to notice and bent her back to smooth an area for them to rest on. She motioned them to sit and turned to make her way to Baba. The soldiers tried to stop her, but she held her ground quietly repeating, "I help Baba. I help Baba." Finally they stepped aside and let her pass.

When Apol had done all she could to make Baba comfortable she returned to the girls and settled down beside them. "Sleep," she advised, and was soon snoring softly.

The soldiers moved about the makeshift camp, building a fire and setting up the guard schedule.

Several cast luring glances at the girls and Ngalia shrunk closer to Sara. When the soldiers started laughing and pointing at one another and the girls, a familiar form separated from a nearby tree and stationed himself between the girls and soldiers. Feet apart, arms crossed purposefully across his chest and rifle, he faced the cajoling soldiers.

Sara looked at Ngalia and nodded at the man's back. "I think he's come here to protect us," she whispered. Ngalia stared at the man's back for a moment and then curled up next to Paipi and Sara, keeping the two of them between herself and Apol.

"That would be a miracle from God," she muttered just loud enough for Sara's ears. The ground was cool and damp from the rain, but both girls were exhausted and hardly noticed. Paipi was fast asleep, never having awakened, and the warmth from his little body spread to the two cuddling him on either side. Sara pulled her feet up into the folds of her skirt and longed for the mosquito netting over her bed at Kama. Her arms were covered with big red itchy welts but she resisted digging at them.

"Ngalia," she whispered softly.

"Yes?"

"Could we pray together out loud?"

"Okay," Ngalia seemed hesitant but willing. "Dear God," Sara began, "You know what's going on here. Please protect and strengthen Baba, Apol, Ngalia and Paipi, all those at Kama, the captives and me too. We're frightened, we need your strength and help. Pleeeeassse and thank you in Jesus name, Amen."

"What she said, God, thank you. Amen."

The soldier standing guard over them quietly cleared his throat. Ngalia grasped Sara's hand, and added. "Oh, and God, thank you for bringing Paipi's soldier father to help us," she shuddered involuntarily. "Please keep him safe and protect him, and help him to accept you as his Savior. Amen, again."

Paipi's father cleared his throat again, a little louder, glanced over his shoulder at the girls, shuffled his feet slightly and resumed his stance in silence.

Sara squeezed Ngalia's hand. "That was good." Ngalia responded by shrugging her shoulders. Before long both girls slept.

Shouts in the camp awakened everyone at daybreak. The four young men tied at the wrists were delivered to the center of the camp and forced to kneel. Two soldiers advanced on them with rods and beat on their backs for several minutes. The girls watched in horror. Finally camp broke and everyone funneled back onto the path. Apol stationed herself next to Baba, assisting him when needed. He seemed to have gained strength in the night and did not fall as much with Apol to act as his eyes. As they progressed along a lead soldier fell back and noticed Apol guiding Baba along.

"You hid this man from the morning beating," he barked at her, "so you will take his beating!"

Apol sank to her knees and the man beat her with a rod. When Sara and Ngalia with Paipi tried to reach her, Paipi's father stood in their way and shook his head at them. They clung to each other and cried, unwilling to watch as Apol was beaten. Finally the man's anger was spent and everyone pushed on.

Softly spoken words drifted back to the girls as Apol took Baba's arm, "I'm okay, Baba, I'm strong. Such a beating would have killed you." Sara marveled that the day could be so crisp and clean when mankind was so vile.

Two soldiers dropped out of line and Sara watched them slip out of sight with mixed feelings of hope and envy. She heard gunfire from time to time and feared for anyone hiding in that jungle. At midday the procession came upon a small deserted village and halted to rest. Before long the missing soldiers strutted into camp with their bounty of two small monkeys dangling from their shoulders.

Apol was instructed to cook the monkeys; the girls were to help her. After locating the village cooking pit, the girls gathered small twigs and dried grass, and piled them on top of the cold pit. Then Apol began twirling one stick against another to spark a fire.

The soldiers stood back watching for several minutes until one muttered something then stepped in and applied his cigarette lighter to the task. Sparks lapped hungrily at the dried grass, then the twigs, and the girls quickly added small chunks of wood till the coals burned red-hot.

"What did he say?" Sara whispered to Ngalia. "He said he was hungry and couldn't wait all day."

"Figures," Sara muttered.

Apol had the monkeys skewered on a stick by the time the fire was ready, and they took turns slowly turning the meat over and over while holding it above the hot coals.

"I've never eaten monkey before."

Ngalia looked at Sara a moment before replying. "It tastes like chicken." A nervous giggle escaped from both girls. Ngalia quickly added, "We'll be lucky to get anything, so if offered, don't hesitate."

"Don't worry. I just wish we had water to wash it down with."

Water didn't come till later in the day when they crossed a small stream. Everyone got down to drink. Sara wished desperately for the water purifier in her backpack back at Kama, but her thirst overruled safety and she drank from the stream just like everybody else.

They passed through several deserted Villages. Sara wondered how the people knew when soldiers were coming near. Late afternoon saw the progression halting again, this time to apply the rod to the backs of the male captives again. When the leader advanced on Baba V, Paipi's father spoke up. Sara couldn't understand the Swahili spoken and again Ngalia translated for her.

"He is a man of God. You can not beat him without angering our superiors." Angry looks were exchanged, but the man muttered to himself and turned from the mischief he'd planned against the aged missionary.

For three more days they marched through the rain forest, stopping in deserted villages at night, drinking from streams, and eating whatever they could find along the way. On the fifth night they reached their destination.

A crude prison stood at the edge of this village adopted as headquarters for this battalion of soldiers. The building was locked up tight and no one was around.

Baba V sank wearily onto a bench that stood beside the building and stretched his full length along the board. "Wake me up when they get this prison opened."

One soldier was sent further into the compound to find keys and inform the commander of their arrival. Ten minutes later the Commander strolled angrily up to the prison. The soldier sent to fetch the key trailed miserably behind him.

"Why is this missionary here?" the Commander demanded in Swahili, Ngalia quietly interpreted for Sara.

"He smuggled arms to our enemies," the rebel leader smirked.

"He was acquitted! I will see you in my quarters. Now!" The words were spoken softly, but with such authority it got everyone's attention except Baba who appeared to be asleep. An unnatural quiet ruled over those left behind. No one wanted to make further decisions before hearing back from the Commander.

Before long a middle-aged African in brown shorts and a stained plaid shirt came striding up to the prison, his steps full of purpose.

"Baba V, Baba V, it is so good to see you, old friend."

Baba stirred on the bench, and accepted the man's offered hand to pull himself into a sitting position.

"Ah, Pastor Gonanoffy," Baba's voice was weak, but warm. "So they couldn't scare you off. Good man, good man."

"You are to come to my home, old friend. I knew the Lord wanted me here for some reason, though I couldn't think what it could be, now here you are. God works in strange ways, yes?" Baba just shook his head in agreement.

"What about my girls?"

"They must come too. The Commander . . ." His words were cut short by the sudden return of the rebel leader. Anger flashed in the man's eyes, daring anyone to speak. In silence he unlocked the crude prison and motioned the four captives accused of smuggling arms across the river to file in.

But Baba V, Apol, Sara, Ngalia and Paipi he ushered into the village to find refuge at Pastor Gonanoffy's house. When the rebel leader left, the pastor spoke again.

"The Commander is not happy with that man, and apologizes for your mistreatment. His officer will be dealt with accordingly. He and I have different political views, but the Commander is a Christian. His father is the pastor in his home village.

"Pastor Amuri was captured and brought here too. That rebel leader wanted to execute him, but when he kneeled to pray, they freed him. You are not a prisoner here, Baba, but now that you are here, the Commander doesn't know what to do with you.

I was told to keep you safe under house arrest until something else can be arranged."

"I thank you, friend. Tomorrow we shall talk." was all the response Baba V could give his pastor friend.

"Come, you are exhausted. You will sleep in my room. I am sorry I have no bedding. Everything has been taken, but at least you will be up off the cold floor." Baba offered no resistance, but followed Pastor Gonanoffy to his bed, and again laid his long form down on hard boards and was instantly asleep. Apol, Ngalia, Paipi, and Sara settled down beside the bed, on the ground, and were soon sleeping as well.

Unheard by them, a lone soldier circled the house throughout the night, his rifle held purposely across his chest.

⁂

Chappy was going over his safety list on the company chopper when Ross found him.

"Not good news, Chappy." Ross stated.

The old pilot turned his full attention on the younger man, crossed his arms over his chest and leaned back against the running board. "Okay, let's have it."

"The rebel forces have Sara and Baba V. Last night a band of rebels took them, along with a few others, off into a rainstorm. Vincent escaped, and ran to Kilongo, who contacted Bukavu on Baba's ham radio. He said Apol followed them to care for Baba and the girls. He's caring for the two children who lived with Baba V." Ross paused to catch his breath, and then continued.

"Kilongo has no idea where they've been taken, and by the time Apol can send word back to him, Captain Kyassa will have taken over Baba's house and he won't have access to the radio after that." Ross fell silent.

Chappy's frown deepened, a low, quiet whistle escaped his pursed lips. "So, what do we do now Ross?"

"First we pray, and then we plan." Ross bowed his head. "Father God," he spoke out loud, "We're feeling more helpless than ever here and I don't like it. But you are not helpless; I know you have people in the Congo who know and love you just as we do. Father, please bring those people around our loved ones to supply their needs and keep them safe." When Ross paused, Chappy jumped in.

"God, I'm still new at this, but I figure you love that little gal and Baba V more then either of us could even begin to, so I'm askin' you ta' bring your power into play here. You're the only one who can keep them from harm. They're in a powerful mess of trouble. I know you know that, but I figure since you created this whole universe, takin' care of this won't sweat ya much. So we're going ta' trust you to handle this for us. Just let us know when there's anything we can do. We stand ready and willin'. I'm asking in Jesus name. Amen."

"That was beautiful, Chappy." Ross commented quietly. "You blow me away! I'm going back into town to try one more time to round up government support, but so far my contacts aren't willing to stir up grief over one lone American girl. It'll be impossible to inspire a rescue squad when we don't even know where they are. So . . . . well I'm afraid I may as well go back to work until there *is* something I can do."

"That makes the most sense to me, boss."

"If you'll keep in touch with the Tarbell office, and bring me word of any changes, I'll gather my gear, and be ready to go whenever you are."

"I'll be ready in 'bout an hour." Chappy turned back to his safety list and started checking things off again. Ross turned on his heels and headed for the Banyon.

Chapter Thirty One

The morning sun was at work on Sara's face long before she awakened to new sounds and images. The floor grew warm around her, also from the sun's rays, and slowly she realized that Apol and Ngalia were no longer close beside her. Quickly she gathered herself up and joined the others in the adjoining room, trying to smooth her rumpled hair as she went. Pastor Gonanoffy was apologizing for his lack of hospitality. All he had to nourish them was clean drinking water.

"Usually, someone from my family slips in during the night and leaves me something to eat during the day. But last night they did not come. I think perhaps because one of the soldiers kept watch over the house all night."

Just then a knock sounded at the entrance to the mud house, and a young soldier bent to poke his head in. "May I enter?"

"Yes, of course Barnabus," the pastor rose to greet the man.

"This is Barnabus, though he's been forced into this rebel army, Barnabus is a Christian. He is a friend, and you can trust him." Baba must have told Pastor Gonanoffy that Sara understood French, but not Swahili, because he spoke in French.

Both girls, Apol, and Baba V nodded acceptance.

"Your voice is familiar to me, Barnabus," Baba V responded in French. "You came to our schools, did you not?"

"Yes, sir, I did." The man smiled warmly at the old man. "I very much appreciate my education too. I am embarrassed to be found in this band of soldiers, but they would have killed my family if I did not join them. Besides, it is better to know where and what your enemy is about, is it not?"

"I understand." Baba V responded warmly, and reached out his long arm so the young soldier could clasp his hand.

"I won't keep you, but I did want you to know you can rest in peace at night, Nondo has appointed himself your guard at night, and I will be standing guard over you during the day. I'm sorry this is necessary, but the captain of the squad hates white people, and their God. Now he's angrier than ever and will kill you if given the chance. Only disapproval from his superior's has kept him in check thus far.

"You two," he said pointing to Apol and Ngalia, "are free to enter the forest during the day to gather food. Be wary and careful, no one is truly safe."

To Baba and Sara he said, "Please do not try to smuggle any notes to anyone, or you will be accused of plotting with the enemy. But if any Christians wish to come here and visit you, they will be allowed." With a nod, Barnabus retreated and left those under house arrest to absorb all he'd said.

"God does supply our needs, does he not?" Baba beamed from the crude chair supplied him. Pastor Gonanoffy nodded.

"If you find my family in the forest, they will help you find food."

Apol nodded at the pastor, and rose to her feet, signaling Ngalia to join her. "We will go out together, safety in numbers. Sara, you will stay inside and care for Baba V and Paipi. Give whatever care you can to Baba's feet. I will see what you have done when I return. I will look for herbs in the forest." Ngalia followed Apol out and away from the house, away from the soldiers.

Sara began working to start a fire close beside the door, staying inside the structure yet reaching out to tend the flames. Pastor Gonanoffy brought her a pot of water and she balanced it on the three rocks centered in her fire. Soon she had enough warm clean water to soak Baba V's feet. *Lord, please help Apol find healing herbs for Baba's feet. They are so damaged. They must heal. Thank You.* She prayed silently but intently as she worked.

The sun was straight overhead before Apol and Ngalia returned, and Sara sighed in relief. Paipi had been a dear, easier than most toddlers Sara had cared for, but both were feeling hunger pangs. Baba slept in the chair, sitting up, his head leaning back against the mud wall. His soft snoring fascinated Paipi, but the child did not attempt to crawl into his lap or pinch his nose to interrupt the snores. Sara decided she must be experiencing the help of God's angels for the child to watch Baba so closely, yet allow him to sleep.

Apol placed three brown chicken eggs on the table, some leaves that Sara sincerely hoped were edible, and two papayas. The eggs were small, and didn't look all that encouraging, but the fruit was of nice size, and Sara could see six people sharing them.

Apol quickly set to scrubbing out the pan in which Sara had soaked Baba's feet. She scoured it with sand from the yard and rinsed it with clean water, filled it, put in the three eggs and water, and set it to boil over Sara's carefully tended fire. Soon a large leaf was placed before Baba V; on top the leaf was placed a generous slice of papaya and a peeled hard boiled egg. It wasn't much to replenish his strength, but he seemed delighted.

The remaining food was carefully split between the others. Sara missed the warm frothy goat's milk she'd come to enjoy at Kama. Some Klim to mix into the water for Baba and Paipi would have made her feel better about their fare, but they had none.

Everyone bowed their heads in prayer. "Lord, please bless this nourishment to the health of our bodies. Thank You for the safety of this home, the hospitality of our captors. Let us shine your light of love upon them, and show them a better way. Amen." Baba V wiped his hands together, rubbed them a bit on his dirty shirt and proceeded to eat with his fingers, showing great pleasure in the food set before him.

The others followed his example.

After the noon meal, everyone settled in to rest. The heat of the day was heavy and it was easy to fall asleep. Sara and Ngalia woke first, and spent their time quietly drawing and redrawing shapes in the dirt. Ngalia was eager to learn all Sara could teach her.

Everyone was awake before nightfall, Ngalia sat playing with Paipi. There was no evening meal to fuss over, just water to drink to satisfy their thirst. Sara thought it a good time to get Baba talking again. It would get everyone's mind off their hunger.

"Baba V, tell us more about your life."

"Well, we have no radio to listen to, do we?" he chuckled, and settled back in his chair. "Let's see." The room remained quiet while Baba sifted through his memories.

"Ah well, let's just start at the beginning. I was born Samuel Russell Vinton, December 3rd, 1907. My folks raised us kids on a farm near Pittsburgh, Pennsylvania. It was a good place to grow up. Dad was the superintendent of the coal mines for Indiana County, so I worked in the mines during the summers when school was out. What I experienced there has helped me understand the mines and miners around here. That knowledge became most useful during World War II, but that's another story. I'll get to that in a bit.

"As a young guy I worked hard to achieve the position of Eagle Scout. I hiked, camped, learned how to rough it in the wilds and adapt to any situation." Baba paused as if trying to remember something specific, quickly a smiled played across his face. "Always be prepared, that was our motto, a good one too. I was taught to expect the unexpected, to live in service to others, sacrifice to help others. You can see how my Eagle Scout training has been most valuable to me here in Africa."

"Oh yes, I see that! I wish I'd been privileged to more of that training myself." Sara agreed, but Apol and Ngalia exchanged a wide-eyed shrug between them. Why would one need to be 'trained' in survival skills they'd learned from birth?

Baba continued. "It was in 1927 I felt God's nudge to go to Africa. In March of 1928 I boarded an ocean-going vessel with an experienced missionary couple and sailed across the ocean. It took us a whole month to reach Dares Salaam, Tanzania. Enough time for them to teach me Swahili." Baba shifted his body on the hard chair and leaned forward, "We traveled by train to Lake Tanganyika, crossed that great lake by boat, and traveled by train to Kindu. From Kindu, we walked. Ten days we walked into the equatorial forest to Kama, and I was able to talk with the people along the way."

Baba paused a moment to breathe deeply as if the memory had made him short of breath, but he continued. "For two years I worked to evangelize the Walega people, only to realize how wise my friends and family had been when they said to get medical training before coming to Africa! Better late than never; I decided I'd better get that medical training.

"So I headed to Europe, studied French in Paris, and took the special one year tropical medicine course offered by the Belgian government. I just couldn't ignore the physical suffering of the people, and tell them how loving and kind God was without trying to do something to relieve their misery.

"In the meantime I'd sent for Marie Mikula to come to help out at Kama. When I returned from Belgium, Marie and I were married. That was April 18th, 1932. Ha, that was 67 years ago. It seems like only yesterday! I already told you the hassles we had getting married, but we finally got the job done. We built the first medical dispensary in Kama in 1932. Finally we could help the people with both their physical and spiritual needs. People hear what you have to say when your words take action and they know you really do care about them.

"Our first boy was born in 1933. I told you about that. Poor Mama. What an adventure we had getting her to Dr. Lewis. Our African friends rigged up a chair to carry her ten days to Kindu. We boarded a train in Kindu and rode four hours to Kibombo. A missionary from Tunda met us in Kibombo, loaded us up in his Model T Ford and drove us 130 kilometers, about 80 miles, to Tunda where Dr. Lewis had a little mud hut hospital."

Sara had already pried this story out of Baba, but hearing it again was just added fun. Good stories were worth repeating over and over again. Her mother taught her that.

"Did I tell you about the water buffalo in the road?" Baba chuckled, merriment dancing in his tired eyes. "That ol' buffalo wanted to fight us over road use rights. He rammed our bumper so hard he keeled right over. We jumped out, bent the bumper back into place, jumped back in and got on down that road. I don't know what happened to that buffalo, but he wasn't there when we came back through. We reached Dr. Lewis just in time for Sam Jr. to make his appearance. I wasn't allowed in the room when Sam Jr. was born. It was still an unaccepted practice to allow a man at a birth. Another day I'll tell you more about that." Baba paused again, and no one rushed him, but waited patiently while he considered how much to share with them.

"It was just grand returning to Kama with that tiny boy in his bassinet! The return trip was easier of course. Only five days from Kindu to Kama, we changed carriers twice a day. Sam Jr. was the first white baby the people in Kama had ever seen. There was so much excitement and rejoicing!

"We built our first burnt brick house that year. To us it was a mansion. We built in a bathroom, even had a shower. Then our second son, Fred, came along the next year. We opened our first school that year, 1934.

"A couple years after that we brought to Kama the first car anybody there had ever seen. George, came along in 1937. Three boys!" Baba shook his head. "Mama was so concerned she'd never get a girl, and we didn't till four years later, Betty didn't come along till 1941. By then we'd had our maternity clinic a couple of years, and the Leprosarium a year."

"All the while we trained the people, taught them about God, and new churches sprang up. Wherever there was a new church, a school was started as well.

"When the United States joined in WWII, I was appointed to be a U.S. representative in our Maniema County. We were cut off from any support from home. So we mapped out and constructed the tin mine camps, and we built homes for the miners. That's how God supplied funds for our family and our mission work through those war years. God is always so faithful."

Baba paused in his listing of events and Apol clamored to her feet. "I know you could listen to Baba's stories all night, Sara, but he is still very tired. This is enough for tonight." To Baba she spoke a bit louder, "Baba, you need your rest." Stepping to the door, she gathered the herbal water she'd been steeping in their only pot. "You girls take care of the necessary and we call it a day." Kneeling by Baba's feet, she washed and dried them as best she could, then motioned for him to get up and go to bed.

"Thank you, Mama." Baba pulled himself to his full height, and took himself off to the bed. Soon Apol, the two girls and a sleeping Paipi were positioned on the floor next to the bed.

Sara appreciated the effort Baba had made to speak English for her benefit. Still she struggled to understand every word. Baba had been gone from America so long, and his accent was heavily influenced by all the Swahili and French he heard and spoke daily. Hearing the stories they knew and loved repeated in English was good practice for Ngalia and Apol too. It was easy to see why Baba wanted her to teach English pronunciation at the school.

Spinning thoughts reflected back on the incredible experiences Baba had shared, and Sara had difficulty getting to sleep. She tried to imagine what it would have been like to be the first to do so many things in so remote a location as Kama.

The dirt floor was hard, the mosquitoes merciless, and a shadow resembling Paipi's father fell across the moonlight from the window at regular intervals as he circled the house. But as the air cooled and the forest noises added their own music to Baba's snores, Sara finally slept, only to dream of warm sudsy showers, toothpaste, hair brushes, frothy goats milk, and a nine-months-pregnant Mama V being galloped through the rain forest in a kitchen chair.

Their first day in captivity in Bikenge was behind them.

Chapter Thirty Two

The days passed slowly, or so it seemed to Sara as she remained restricted to the small mud home. The food situation varied as Christians hiding in the forest began to visit and bring them eggs, bits of cooked rice and greens wrapped in leaves, and occasionally fruit.

Sara and Ngalia found a block of time every day to practice drawing in the dirt. Pastor Gonanoffy allowed them to soften two small rectangles of hard-ened earth just inside the door to use as practice pads.

Apol asked if someone could run back to Kama and get the quilt Baba V's children had made and sent him from the United States, and it too was soon smuggled in to serve as a mattress on Baba's bed. Ngalia and Sara were delighted to find four pencils and a sketch pad hidden in the folds of the quilt, and knew that Vincent was surely watching out for them. Now Sara could have Ngalia carefully record her drawings and techniques on paper after perfecting them in the dirt. The precious paper couldn't be wasted on practice, but would serve nicely as an art textbook until a better one could be secured.

Along with the quilt and visitors came forest gossip. After Apol left to follow Baba, and before Kama's soldier's could realize Baba had been taken, Kilongo, Vincent and Amu had taken Baba's quilt, Sara's backpack, and whatever provisions they could carry from Baba's house. Kilongo sent word he had made contact with Bukavu on the ham radio before Captain Kyassa turned Baba's house into his new military headquarters. Kilongo and the children were now among others hiding in the forest.

Kilongo sent word that he missed his wife and friends, prayed them safe, and that one day they would be reunited. He also reported that Jeffrey, the head assistant at Baba's medical clinic and pharmacy, had closed up shop and vanished into the forest as well, taking as much of the medicine with him as he could. The murderous soldiers in the same band that took Baba and the girls had paid him a visit as well, demanding that he give them money. He had grabbed his Bible and began reading it to them. They thought he was calling down fire from heaven and ran away without harming him.

The news and supplies were received with thanksgiving and the hearers gathered together to praise God and pray His protection over their loved ones. Silently Sara added, *Thank you, God, that my power bars and water purifier supply will benefit my friends, Amen.*

The runner had been unable to retrieve any mosquito netting, and every time Sara rubbed the itchy red welts on her body she thanked God she had been forced to get all those horrible but effective immunizations before leaving home. Sanitation in the village left much to be desired; flies during the day and mosquitoes at night were relentless.

The rebels moved out on patrols from time to time, and when they were gone the villagers filtered back through their homes in hopes of finding something that would make their existence in the forest easier.

At these times, Baba would try to get out, stretch his legs, and visit with the people. Once or twice he got as far as the prison at the edge of the village. But each time he found it empty and wondered where the others were being held. On one of his walks, a man confided to Baba, that the reason the jail was locked up with no jailer when he first arrived, was because that jailer had recognized Baba, and ran away rather than have to lock up his beloved missionary.

Each day Baba's old skin hid fewer of his bones, as his weight and strength lessened.

"Baba, have you ever gone back home?" Sara asked one morning when all was quiet and she was again on Paipi/Baba watch.

"Ah, this is my home, child," he answered. "Okay, but have you ever gone back to the United States?"

"Oh sure, Marie and I visited the United States in 1963. We didn't stay long, because the work really needed us here. That was right after the 1960 rebellion, and there was so much to do to help put Kama back together. That 60s rebellion was perhaps even worsethan this war. Horrible, horrible things happened that should never have happened anywhere. Kama was overrun with the worst kind of rebel soldiers." Baba was quiet for a few moments, as if weighing in his mind how much of the history of Kama he could share with the young girl. Sara remained quiet and waited.

"We had lots of missionary workers at Kama with us then, at Kama and in nearby villages. The work was growing; we built roads, bridges, churches, schools, and medical buildings. We went on kusanyikos every weekend. You would call them safaris. Kusanyikos were such fun. Several villages would gather together and cook up food to feed everyone. Several of us missionaries would arrive in the big medical truck and kids and adults alike would swarm around us. . . . So much excitement and joy that we had come to visit them.

"I'd set up the medical clinic, and start right away treating the people, pulling teeth, immunizing the children, all that stuff. The other missionaries would meet with the pastors, teaching and counseling them. On Saturday evening we'd have a big church service, oh for two hours or so, with all the singing and preaching. Then we'd go outside to where we'd stretched a big sheet between two poles, and we'd show a Christian movie projected there on that sheet.

"Sunday morning we'd have three or four more hours of church, grab a quick lunch, and head back for home. Every weekend we did that. Oh, Mama V couldn't always go with us, but she would pray us safe over all those bad roads and bridges. Oh, how she would pray.

"Our son Sam and his wife Becky, came to Kama in 1956 as missionaries. All our kids went to America for college, you know. In 1958 our son Fred, and his wife, Lois, joined us, also as missionaries. Ah, it was grand having the boys and their families back home with us, working right alongside of us." Memories seemed to flutter across Baba's face as Sara watched him, and his mood lightened, then plunged again as he continued. Paipi had fallen asleep in Sara's lap, and she was glad he wasn't distracting her from Baba's history lesson.

"Then the 1960 Independence from Belgium rule was granted and the Congo rebellion started, the Congolese government mandated all the white missionaries leave the Congo. Sam and Becky and the grandkids, the Schoonovers, the Del Andersons, the Bahlers, the Ernie Greens, the Lee Greens, the Egemeiers, the Henshaws, all those wonderful folks were forced to leave the work here. And it really wasn't safe for them or their families any more. They had to go. I'm so glad they got out safely.

"Fred and Lois, with their baby boy, and Marie and I tried to stay on in Kama to continue the medical services, and keep teaching our pastors. But when the Prime Minister was killed in February 1961, we were taken forcibly by rebels from Kama to Kindu. I was severely beaten on that march. The soldier was drunk, and wouldn't stop. He cracked my elbow." Baba sounded irritated but grinned. "Ah, our work wasn't finished yet, and God got us all out of there alive."

The earth rumbled beneath them, as if it too were irritated at the violence played out on its surface. Someday she'd have to investigate the cause of so many quakes and tremors here, but the thought was buried so deep in her subconscious that Sara was not even aware of it. What she was conscious of was the horror she felt, and the chill that raced down her own spine. Memories of the beatings on the trail from Kama were still very fresh in her mind's eye, but Baba did not notice, and continued his narrative.

"In Kindu the United Nations placed us under protective care until it was safe to be released in May of 1962. A year after our release, Marie and I moved from Kama to Bukavu and opened a work there. We had become affiliated with the Worldwide Grace Testimony Mission back in 1948. Since then they've changed the name to Grace Missions International, the one my son, Sam Jr., now directs." Baba paused as his mind wandered to the work Sam Jr. was doing even as his father sat there under enemy control. Sara watched as he slowly smiled and his face softened for just a moment before he shook himself and returned to his story.

"Many officials knew me in Bukavu. The Belgium government had awarded me a medal in 1945, somewhere along there I was made an honorary member of the Order of the Leopard. That was a very high honor in the Congo. So people knew me. One Belgian merchant wanted to leave all the unrest and horrific memories behind, and I think he may have been fearful to stay. He sold us his wonderful mansion in Bukavu so cheap he practically gave it to us. We were able to get other buildings at good prices too. God is so good, so faithful to meet our needs. We moved in and lived there, worked from there.

"It made a wonderful headquarters, home, and guesthouse. Ha, it still does today. We were only forced out once then, for two weeks, when rebels overran Bukavu. We encouraged the Christian community there, started a Grace Church, a book store, a medical clinic, all the while organizing the rehabilitation program for the devastated villages in our Kama area. We had to get grain and seed for the people to plant, or there would be no food, and the people would starve to death." Paipi shifted his position in Sara's lap. She soothed him and he never woke.

"We had to round up medical supplies. Everything we had at Kama had been looted, burned, or destroyed. Rebuilding was a big work. Our six-month trip to the United States in '63 was necessary to ask for help for our people in Kama. We didn't get to move back home to Kama till 1966."

"*Another* rebellion in 1998 cost me the companionship of my grandsons. Bill and Sue came out as Missionaries in 1984. Rachel was born in '84, the first of several 3rd generation Vintons born in Congo. Fred Jr. and Karen and their kids, Steven and his Sue and their boy, all had to leave with their families to keep them safe. That rebellion had no leadership, it was a civil war spurred on by Rwanda, there was no protection, no structure behind it. But still I could not go.

This is my home, my life. I was glad we had capable people trained to step into Bill and Steven's positions at the schools and the pastor's school. Fred Jr. had to leave his medical ministry to the Muslims north of us." Baba paused and sighed. "It was so hard to see them go, and even harder to stand helpless to prevent the rebel soldiers swarming on Bill and Sue's home across from mine, and carrying away all the things they had to leave behind. I guess one of the soldiers didn't like me watching them steal everything, he grabbed my glasses off my face and stomped them." Baba shook his head at the memory.

"Baba?"

"Yes?"

"Didn't one of the missionary houses in Kama use to have two stories?" It was an honest question, an eye less trained than an artist's might not have noticed the telltale marks still on that home. But Sara was just such an artist, did notice, and was curious. "What happened?" Horrible pain flashed across Baba's face and Sara knew instantly that she'd asked a wrong question. Baba's silence stretched on for several more minutes. Finally he sighed, steadied himself and gave her a straightforward answer.

"We tore the second story off that house. The rebels used it, Sara, to horribly torture many of my dearest African friends to death."

"Why Baba?!"

"Because they wouldn't renounce their faith and belief in Jesus Christ, Sara. They were martyred."

"How could you go back there after that? I would be so angry!"

"Oh, child. God tells us not to let the sun set on our anger. Of course I was angry, hurt, I loved those dear people, and it was so senseless. So cruel." Baba shuddered. "But forgiveness, Sara, forgiveness is a wonderful tonic. Forgiveness frees us to move forward. There is no benefit in staying mired in the past.

"God is very wise, Sara, He gives us instructions to better our lives. If we allowed ourselves to stay mired down in the hateful muck of revenge we couldn't have rebuilt our ministry to all the wonderful people God gave us to serve here in Africa. Think of all those precious babies that might never have survived birth; or all the churches and schools that might never have been built, 600 churches, 300 schools for 30,000 students. Think of all the rotten teeth I might not have had the privilege to yank, or all the lost souls that might never have heard the good news of God's Salvation, if I had allowed anger to fester in my soul.

"No, Sara, God forgave the very men that pounded nails into the hands and feet of His Only Begotten Son, and lifted Him up on that cross to die. And Jesus, in all his agony and anguish, begged his Heavenly Father to forgive all those who cried out for his death on that cross. He said, "Father forgive them for they know not what they do."

"God has already forgiven those rebel soldiers. Am I better than God, that I can afford to carry around my hurt and anger? No, child, forgiveness heals." Baba's voice deepened with compassion as he continued. "You must let go of your anger, Sara child, and forgive the ones who killed your loved ones. You *must* in order to heal. You must rest in the knowledge that God is the only one who *can* judge righteously—He *will* judge righteously in his own time. We don't have to carry that weight around on our backs. God is so good and faithful. Let Him carry that burden for you. You have so much life ahead of you to invest in more important things, use your life wisely, Sara. Make it count for all eternity."

There it was. There was the answer Sara had traveled to Africa to find.

Chapter Thirty Three

Slowly the days turned into weeks, and Baba still did not regain his strength. Everyone was losing weight, but it showed the most on Baba's long lean frame. Members of Pastor Gonanoffy's family moved back home, and permission was given to house the old missionary and his people in the house next door to the pastor's house, but they were not allowed to return to Kama. Still people smuggled them eggs, and cooked rice folded neatly in leaves. Apol drew water from the village well, and they each got to wash up a little each day, though there were no showers or tubs to soak in.

Ngalia helped Sara with her long auburn hair by carefully braiding each inch tight against the scalp, all the way down to the tips, then pulling all the tiny braids into a swirl fastened at the back of Sara's head. Sara laughingly called it her built-in pillow and occasionally had Ngalia pour a bucket of water over it to flush out the dust gathered while sleeping on the ground.

Barnabus came to Baba at the beginning of his patrol one morning with a somber message. "Baba V, the captain plans to execute all the prisoners tomorrow morning. If you have any ideas of how to save them, now would be the time." So Baba requested an interview with the Rebel Commander in the village.

"How can I persuade you to free the captives you are holding? You know they did not transfer arms for me, all I had to give them was medicine."

"Ah, Baba V. Even though that's true, how would it look if I just set them free? They are our enemies. They fight against our cause."

"Okay, what would it cost me to speak with those young men before you execute them?" Baba asked.

"I see you are a businessman. A wise man. I tell you what. You get me a goat to roast and feed my men, and I will allow those prisoners to come to you to say their goodbyes."

"How am I to get a goat?"

"That is between you and God, Baba. That is my deal."

"Okay." Baba agreed, and returned to the house with Barnabus assisting him.

"Spread the word, Apol, and Ngalia, tell everyone you can that I need a goat. I will pay for the goat. If anyone has a goat, and will sell it to me today, I will buy their goat."

So Apol and Ngalia went into the forest with a new mission and word went out that Baba V needed a goat that day, and that he would pay for it. Before nightfall a large goat was led into the village and to the door of Baba's hut.

"I bring goat for sale. What you pay?"

"I will pay you 8 million Zaires for your goat." Baba answered.

"You have money?"

"No, I have no money. I am under house arrest by these soldiers far from my home. But you know I am good for the money whenever I am free to get it to you."

"Okay, then price of goat is ten million Zaires."

"I will buy your goat for ten million Zaires. Thank you, friend, I will get you the Zaires as soon as God allows me to do so." Baba signed the bill of sale for ten million Zaires for the goat.

Again Barnabus assisted Baba V back to the Commander's headquarters, leading the goat along beside them.

"Commander." Baba called out when they reached the right hut. The Commander came to the door and looked at the old missionary with the goat.

"I should have done business with you sooner, friend. We've not had meat to eat for much too long. The men will be released to visit you as agreed. You may see to this, Barnabus."

Barnabus led Baba back to his hut, and helped him onto the bed with his quilt.

"I don't know why I am so weak, Barnabus."

"Are you sick, old friend?"

"I don't know."

"I will go tell the guards to release the prisoners, Baba. Can you see them now?"

"Oh, Yah. I will be fine. Send them over."

True to his word, Barnabus delivered the Commander's message to the guards at the makeshift prison. However, as soon as the young men were released, they shagged out of there like the wind, and vanished into the jungle.

Back at Baba V's hut, Barnabus apologized to the old missionary. A weak but hearty chuckle lifted from Baba's bed. "You'd think they'd at least come by to say thank you, wouldn't you?"

Pastor Gonanoffy and Apol stood beside Baba's bed.

"I don't like the shaking. He's not getting better. His fever is climbing. I am afraid he is going to die." Apol spoke just loud enough for the Pastor to hear her. "I'm afraid he has malaria.

We are not finding anything in the forest to help him, and I don't have any medicine here to treat him. You've got to do something."

"I will go and tell the Commander. I'll take Barnabus with me."

Sara and Ngalia watched the exchange from the main room of the hut. Fear clutched at their hearts.

Outside, the pastor motioned for Barnabus to fall into step with him. "We must talk with the Commander. If we do nothing, Baba will die. How have your talks been going with Paipi's father?"

"I think Nondo is very near accepting Jesus Christ as his Savior, Pastor. He can't understand why Baba stays here in Africa and works with all the people, good, bad, sick, evil, all of them alike. . .and getting that goat to free the captives. . .that really made him think. First that Baba would do it, and second that the goat owner would trust him with no collateral but his word—for ten million Zaires! He just couldn't get over that. He said it had to be of God. He loves that baby boy. His wife was raped and killed by enemy soldiers, you know. It made him angry. They'd had no children. That's partly why he participated in the rape of Ngalia, that and the drugs given the soldiers to make them more aggressive.

"Now he is so sorry. He would like to take care of Ngalia and the boy, but knows he needs to be forgiven for what he did. He struggles with that. He struggles with the whole love and forgiveness issue. But he's very close, Pastor, very close."

Chapter Thirty Four

"The old missionary is very sick." Pastor Gonanoffy spoke carefully to the Commander.

"He is very ill, Commander. He shakes with a fever. I fear he has malaria," added Barnabus.

"What can I do about this?" demanded the officer.

"We have no medicine. The women have been unable to find anything in the forest that has helped him."

"Then we must get him over to the old gold mine. There's a Catholic hospital close by there in Kampene, but that's 60 kilometers (about 37 miles) of nearly impassable roads."

"If you will allow me sir, we could strap a chair with arms onto the bicycle, tie him into the chair, and with three men, one on either side to guide and push, one behind to help brake, we could get him to Kampene. I'd need six men. Three men to control the bicycle, and three to act as guards . . . . we will have to trade off positions regularly. The priests will take care of Baba if we can just get him there in time."

For a moment the Commander pondered his options. "What about the American girl?"

"I think she can keep up. The old missionary would be grateful if you helped get the young girl to safety." Barnabus held his breath, praying he had not pushed too hard.

"Do you think such a plan would work?" demanded the Commander of Pastor Gonanoffy.

"I don't know of any other option, sir," was all the pastor could think to say. "I think you should allow your men to try."

"I don't think it will work if he is as sick as you say, but I will allow it. You may take five men with you Barnabus, choose them wisely."

Pastor Gonanoffy and Barnabus bowed out of the Commander's hut before he could change his mind.

"Who will you take?"

"Nondo will want to go I think, and Kawaya is strong. He would make a good brakeman. I'll have to see who else is willing. Do you think Baba has a chance of surviving such a trip?"

"Only if God wills it."

When the men got back to Baba's hut, Pastor Gonanoffy's wife was waiting for them. "Our man in the forest says he's learned where one of Baba's medical assistants is hiding. He says he smuggled out some medicine when he fled Kama. If we tell him where, he will meet you."

"God is so faithful!" both men chorused with a grin.

The bicycle was immediately customized to fit an armed chair to accommodate Baba's lanky frame, and word was sent where they would wait for the medical assistant to join them. Baba was wrapped in his quilt, and strapped into the chair while Nondo held it steady. Kawaya and three others arrived to participate in the adventure at hand.

Apol gathered all the provisions she could, and the strange looking caravan moved out. Paipi was asleep in the sling tied about his mother's body. Ngalia, Sara and Apol had to trot at a steady pace to keep up. Sara couldn't believe what was happening. Baba had smiled weakly at her before they started out, and said, "Life is never boring when you are God's servant." She did not argue the point, as two men, one of either side of the bicycle began pushing the bicycle down the path, and another ran closely behind ready to grab the fender to slow them down as needed.

The men rested and switched positions every hour or so. For six hours they traveled over the torturous roads. Twice they had to lift the bicycle, Baba and all, over fallen logs blocking the trail. Finally they reached Kibundila. Baba was untied and carried into the hut of Apol's choosing.

"Lay him there," she told Nondo, making direct eye contact and smiling encouragement, while gently guiding him toward the inner room where she'd found a raised platform. Nondo seemed flustered by the kind gesture and hurried to comply with her instructions. Water was drawn at the well, and a fire started. As soon as the water had been boiled and cooled a bit, Baba was made to drink as much as they could get down him. Then everyone else took turns getting some boiled water to drink. It took time because they had only the tin cups the soldiers supplied.

It was nightfall before Baba's medical assistant, Jeffery, arrived. He had run the whole distance from where he got the message, but after checking the old missionary over, he wasted no time hanging an IV bag and beginning the process of rehydrating him. A shot of chloriphine was administered immediately and repeated three times over the two days they remained in the Village.

Baba flinched when the needle was jammed under his skin and into his vein. "Ouch! My, that does hurt a mite, doesn't it?" he grimaced. "Why yes, Baba, it can hurt."

"You know, Jeffery, for all the thousands of times I've given or ordered IVs, I've never had one myself before." His confession amazed the hearers.

"Well," the medical assistant stated, "What's good for the patient, is good for the doctor too."

"Yes, I hope that it is." Baba was made as comfortable as possible and left to rest while the IV dripped into his veins. Everyone waited, rested, munched on whatever they could find, and waited while Baba was continuously treated for his malaria and dehydration.

The forced layover lasted two days. On the third day Baba began to get some color back in his cheeks, and his fever fell. It was decided they could delay no longer. He was again wrapped in his quilt and tied into the chair strapped to the bicycle.

The group bid farewell to Jeffery, who took a moment to pray over Baba and embrace his beloved mentor. "God goes with you, Baba. My prayers will follow you. You come back to us when you are strong again. Go with God." Sara noted the tears in the man's eyes as three soldiers took up positions around the bicycle. One soldier ran ahead to lead the way and warn of difficulties in the trail. Apol, the two girls and baby fell in behind the bicycle, and the two remaining soldiers brought up the rear, their rifles ready for trouble.

Chapter Thirty Five

All through the day the caravan forced their way through the jungle trail. At one stream a single log spanned the water. The lead man halted the procession long enough to investigate the depth of the muddy stream with a branch he pulled from a nearby tree. He determined the stream bed was shallow and that the soldiers could navigate Baba and bicycle onto the single log and walk in the water on either side without too much difficulty.

Sara watched nervously for crocodiles to appear as the men splashed noisily, but none came, and the rest of the group balanced on the log to make their crossing. Had the water been clear, they would have paused to drink. Everyone watched for runoff water, or a spring, and their diligence paid off. They found a spring from which to drink.

Food was another matter. They gathered fruits when spotted, and shared them immediately. Once they stopped in a village populated with Mai Mai families. Baba was given a place to lie down and rest, and everyone was offered food.

When the strange looking caravan was spotted moving along the trail, it caught people's attention. And when they realized it was their own Baba V who was being helped by the soldiers, they came out of hiding to share their food and water.

Ngalia became less nervous around Nondo and even began allowing him to play with Paipi when they would stop. Nondo seemed less angry, and Paipi was drawn to the soldier who couldn't seem to take his eyes off him. He was shy at first, but then began hamming it up to make the soldiers laugh. Any laughter was welcomed, and Paipi loved being the center of attention.

The fifth rest stop along the trail, Nondo, with Barnabus coaching, positioned himself near Ngalia.

"May I speak with you, Ngalia?"

Sara shifted herself to be looking away from the two, as if that gave them some privacy to talk, but she was too weary to get up and move away. Nondo didn't seem to mind, and graciously spoke in hesitant English so as not to shut Sara out.

Ngalia must have nodded, because Nondo continued. "I have become a Christian. I have accepted your God. He is a good and faithful God, Ngalia, a forgiving God. I know that now. I am sorry I hurt you. There is no excuse for what I did, but I need you to know why I could be so evil."

"I will listen." Ngalia allowed Nondo to continue.

"My wife whom I loved very much was raped and killed by enemy soldiers. We had no children. I joined the Mai Mai rebels to seek my revenge. They gave us drugs to make us better soldiers. I did not know the drugs were evil, and would make me do wrong things. I realized it too late, after I hurt you. I do not take the drugs anymore. Now I know what they do to you. Can you forgive me?"

Ngalia was quiet for several minutes before she responded to Nondo. Finally she answered him. "Baba V says we are never to allow the sun to go down on our anger. He showed me God's words in his Bible. It is God's wisdom. Satan makes evil things happen to all of us, to try to keep us from loving God. But God promises to turn everything that happens into a praise to His Glory if we love Him and let Him work in our lives. God gave me Paipi to comfort me, and now I think God is helping you. I watched you protect Sara, Paipi and me, I believe your words."

"Thank you, Ngalia." Nondo, raised his head to look directly into Ngalia's eyes. "You are proof to me of God's greatness."

The call was given and everyone forced themselves to get up and fall into line. Baba on his bicycle had been propped up against a tree in such a way that he could even rest his head against the cool trunk of the tree. Quiet snores came from the old missionary, and for a moment the soldiers just stood looking at the peace on the old man's face. Everyone grinned at one another, shook their heads in disbelief, and the caravan continued on with a lighter step. The very young and the very old both slept peacefully while the rest did their best to make their journey as easy as possible.

At nightfall, the caravan arrived at the Catholic Mission in Biunkutu, two miles shy of Kampene. The priests came out to see what was causing all the commotion, and welcomed Baba V with open arms and hearty, though gentle, hugs. It was quickly realized they were old and dear friends, even though they were of different religious backgrounds, and served different counties. The soldiers looked from one to another in amazement.

"You can not stay at the hospital, Baba V; it is too far away from us! You must stay here with us at the mission, in a house of your own. We will bring the doctors and nurses to you. You will be cared for in your own private house. Your girls can stay with you. You must stay here, Baba, you must stay here."

All the priests were so adamant that Baba accepted the offer, and was shown to a small house up the hill behind the mission. It had a living room, a bedroom, even a real bathroom.

Everyone had a looksee through the small house, and Baba was settled in to rest. Runners were sent to the hospital to ask the doctor and nurses to come immediately to the mission.

"We will feed your soldiers, Baba, and give them a place to rest. Food will be brought up to you and your girls. You rest now, old friend. We will take care of you."

True to their word food was prepared for all the caravan, the men were shown where they could clean up, then they were all sat down to a hearty meal and later shown to a place they could all sleep.

Apol, Ngalia, and Sara quickly realized the little house had no hot water, but still they enjoyed washing up. Though the water was extremely cold, they were at least clean.

But it was too much for Baba. With his malaria he could not stand to dip even his fingers into the cold water. So Apol went down to the house below and was given a pot of hot water, which she carried back up the hill. The mission staff had given her a big sponge as well, and she set about sponging the trail dirt off the old man. There was much to sponge, it was the only bath for Baba since leaving his house arrest in Bikenge village.

Less than an hour passed before a knock on the door announced the arrival of the hospital's doctor and two nurses.

"He had four shots of chloriphine and two days of a glucose serum IV at Kibunbila," Apol communicated to the doctor. "He has lost at least 30 pounds in the last six weeks, I would guess. The soldiers brought him on a bicycle, strapped on a chair. We have been traveling all day."

"It is a miracle he has survived. God must still have work for him. How old is this missionary?" the doctor asked.

"He is 91." Sara answered. "He has been here in the Congo since 1928, he is a medical missionary too." The doctor just shook his head and turned to his medical bag. Sara and Ngalia were standing back against the wall by the foot of the bed, to make room for the doctor and two nurses that had come with him. The doctor motioned for them to step into the other room while he made his examination. They obeyed, but it was with reluctance, and a stern look from Apol, who refused to leave Baba's side.

When the doctor and his nurses were done with their examination, they stepped out of the bedroom with Apol and spoke in the living room. "He is very weak. If he had not had the medical care along the way, I have no doubt he would have died before getting here. But if we are diligent and God wills it, I think he has a chance of surviving the malaria. It certainly seems God is on his side.

"I am leaving these two nurses here at the mission. They are Peace Corp volunteers, and are capable of caring for Baba V." The doctor turned from informing Apol and the girls and directed his instructions to the nurses. "You are to massage his legs daily, try to keep atrophy from setting in. It will be a while before he has the strength to get up and move around of his own accord. Get as much food down him as possible, and lots of liquids. I am leaving medicine here for you to administer regularly. Shots for the malaria and vitamins that I hope will build up his strength. Continue to do as Apol has done, and bathe him in warm water only. Keep sponging him off, but don't let him get chilled." Soon the doctor was leaving, and the nurses went down to the mission house to request housing.

From habit Apol, Ngalia, Paipi, and Sara positioned themselves on the floor beside Baba's bed and slept.

The following morning, the soldiers came as a group and knocked on the door.

Barnabus spoke. "We have been well fed, allowed to clean up, and have rested. Now we must return to Bikenge. It will be easier traveling without the bicycle, so we are going to leave it here. Baba may need it again. Please tell Baba goodbye for all of us. I can tell by the snoring that he is still resting." Everyone grinned.

Nondo hesitated when the others turned to go. "May I hold little Paipi one more time before I go?" he asked Ngalia. Apol nodded to Ngalia, as if to assure her that it was safe, and she in turn nodded to Nondo. Paipi was more than a willing participant until Nondo tried to hand him back to his mother, then he cried.

"I will pray for you, Nondo." Ngalia said as she pried her son from around his neck. "Thank you for protecting us."

Nondo seemed uncertain of what to do with what Ngalia had said to him. Finally he blurted out, "I shall be praying for all of you too." Tears clouded his eyes as he turned away, and he stumbled, almost falling. Ngalia quietly watched him go until he caught up with the others and they were all out of sight. Sara embraced both Ngalia and the crying, reaching, boy in her arms and they all cried together.

Chapter Thirty Six

Life at Biunkutu took on a routine that almost passed for a sense of security, but everyone remained aware the Mai Mai soldiers were still in control of the area, and neither Sara or Ngalia were allowed to venture out alone.

Apol and Ngalia no longer had to forage for food in the jungle forest so Ngalia and Sara volunteered to work in the mission garden, weeding and gathering food for the central kitchen. Sara especially appreciated the chance to get out and enjoyed feeling useful. The sunshine and open spaces contributed to her sense of well-being.

Food was brought to them at their little house on the hill, and slowly they began to regain their strength and energy. Apol shared Baba's feeding schedule with the Peace Corp nurses. She fed Baba breakfast and allowed the nurses to feed him lunch and supper.

Paipi shared fruit with Baba anytime he could get his attention. But most of Baba's time was spent sleeping until the medicines and rest began to restore his strength. Morning and afternoon his feet, legs and arms were massaged and exercised, gently at first, but with increased intensity as he was able to stand it.

The Peace Corps nurses brought a hairbrush and tiny bottle of airline shampoo for the girls to enjoy, and found them all extra clothing they could wear on the days they laundered their own clothes. Sara no longer cared her outfit wasn't fashionable, but appreciated it being reasonably clean. Shoes were found for Baba and tucked away in a safe place until such a time as he would have need of them.

One day when Ngalia and Sara were working side by side in the mission's garden they began talking about how remarkably faithful Apol was to Baba.

"Do you know why Apol is so devoted?" Sara asked Ngalia.

"Aside from the obvious you mean?"

"Yes, is there reason beyond what you or I would have – and maybe everybody else in Africa." Sara laughed.

"I think so. Apol's mother was a sickly person. She had sickle cell anemia as an infant and was thrown away by her parents. Mama and Baba V rescued her and raised her in their own home. They loved her and allowed her to live in one of their outbuildings when she grew up. She worked for them too, cooking and cleaning, much like Apol does now. Then of course when Apol came along, she must have felt like Baba was her grandfather. She probably played on Baba's lap of an evening like Paipi does."

"Baba has sure impacted the lives of a lot of people."

"Impacted?" Ngalia cocked her head in question.

"Um, helped." Sara answered.

"Ha, that so! I like to know how many babies Baba bring into this world! I bet he delivered four maybe five generations of babies in some families."

"Baba said that when he first came to Africa the men weren't allowed at births, what happened to change that?"

"I hear Baba tell that story," Ngalia said. "Babies and their mothers were dying all the time. Baba V tried to teach the midwives about washing their hands and using only boiled water to clean birthing cuts, because they didn't have clean-water wells back then, they got their water from the river. Baba and Mama V taught the people that twins were a double blessing from God, and not a curse, as ancestors' superstition taught them. So people stopped killing all the twins. So things got better.

"Then one day the chieftain's favorite wife had a baby they couldn't get out. The midwives couldn't help her. She was in much pain and they feared she and the baby would die, and the chieftain would be angry with them. So they sent for Baba, they said, 'you have healing hands, Baba, you come and save this mother and baby. If there is trouble, we take care of it.' So Baba went, and he was able to turn the baby and deliver him safely. Both mother and baby lived, and the chieftain was so grateful not to have lost his daughter and grandson that he said Baba could deliver babies from then on. And Baba has done so for generations!"

"When did you get clean-water wells?"

"I don't know when, they been here all my life. But I know how. Money was raised by the missionaries' families and friends in churches in America, and outsiders came to our villages and dug the wells and made them safe.

"Baba started such a big work at Kama, so many people come to help us. Most not stay as long as Baba, he has been here forever.

"But we have benches and tables and chairs because people came from America and brought big tools, one time a whole sawmill, and they taught us how to use the tools, and how to make strong furniture.

"We learned how to make good bricks from our clay pits, and burn them to make them strong, and then mud them together to build churches and schools and hospitals. There is little money here, just what comes from the government. Our government pays teachers $20 a month, I don't know how much doctors are paid. I know missionary money comes from America, their friends and families support them. All we can give them is love, and devotion, and food when we have it. Sometimes parrots from our jungle, things like that."

"Ngalia, does Baba ever get to see his family?" Sara couldn't imagine being so far away from one's own children, and it seemed Baba didn't go back to the United States very often.

"Baba's sons come often. Dr. Sam Jr. comes and does kusanyikos almost every year, sometimes twice a year and he bring other people with him. Sometimes he brings pastors from America who teach our pastors while they are here, and he send young missionaries to help Baba, they come and learn how to help people Baba style." Ngalia laughed. "You are learning some of Baba's style!"

"How do you mean?"

"You come to Kama and overnight you are a school-teacher-in-a-dress. And you teach English, and you teach me how to draw things. Did you think you would do that?"

"No! But I'm learning, Ngalia. Baba has walked with God through sooo much. He is very wise. He seems to know just the right moment to teach what you're the most in need of and ready to hear! You've taught me a lot too; I'm glad we are friends." Sara paused to see if Ngalia heard how sincerely she meant her statement. Ngalia looked over at her and grinned, so Sara asked, "Who else comes to help Baba?

"Baba's son, Fred, comes every year to fix broken machines. He very good with cars and lorries, eh…trucks, anything with a motor. He bring Baba supplies from America. Now he also bring supplies to his son, Fred Jr. and Fred Jr.'s family in Kipaka. When we not under rebel control, Baba's grandson,

Fred Jr., work in Kipaka, at medical clinic, and he teaches people about God too.

"Baba is so proud of his children, and grandchildren, and great grandchildren, soon he have great great grandchildren helping people in Africa. People who can't come in person send supplies and money to help Baba with his work. God makes all this happen because Baba lives to do God's work."

"Baba is a humble man." Sara sighed.

"No, not humble, Sara," Ngalia responded, "he *is* very wise. He truly know all this not done in his own strength. He **knows** it is God who make everything happen, who brings others to Africa to work like Baba has worked. Baba loves being God's man. Baba knows we are in a bigger fight than with soldiers and rebels, and governments. Baba says the real fight is between God and Satan. Satan had a stronghold here, and he still want to control all the people and keep them from knowing God. But God brought Baba and others here to break that stronghold and free us from bondage. Baba loves being that man God can use."

Sara remained quiet for a few moments, just thinking about all Ngalia has said. Finally she said, "It's not been an easy life, has it?"

"No. But because of Baba's work, *I* know God, and His forgiveness, and His love. Paipi will grow up knowing about God. Even soldiers like Nondo learn about God, and God is giving me the strength to forgive Nondo." Ngalia paused and Sara picked up her thought.

"And there are thousands of people just like you who know God because Mama and Baba V obeyed God's call to Africa. It's hard to wrap my mind around it all." Both girls were quiet, and slowly realized that the weeds weren't pulling themselves. The sun was nearly straight overhead and the day's heat was at its peak. "We've been talking and not pulling weeds." Sara let her guilt express itself in her voice tone.

"Well, the weeds thank us, and they will live to see another day." Ngalia said, pushing herself up off the ground. Sara followed her example. The girls linked arms and headed back to Baba's new house.

Chapter Thirty Seven

Days turned into weeks, and weeks into a month. Word was gotten to the Sanchezes in Bukavu that Baba and Sara had been moved to the Kiunkutu Catholic Mission Compound, that Baba was very ill but recovering, and that there was still no way to get them back to Kama or on to Bukavu. The Mai Mai rebels still controlled the whole area around them, and no one was allowed in or out.

Baba's strength gradually increased and he was able to sit up and visit with the mission priests. When he was strong enough to walk, he and the girls would take some of their meals with everyone else down in the central house. It was during one of these lunches in the cool interior of the mission, that their quiet conversation was shattered by the percussion of rocket and gunfire.

"Get back from the windows!" Shouted the Father Vyisti. Apol and two of the priests helped Baba to lower himself to the floor beneath the heavy dinner table, Sara, Ngalia and Paipi, and the Peace Corp nurses scrambled to join them there. The kitchen staff ran in shouting that the Mai Mai soldiers were fleeing and taking everything they could carry with them. The percussion of gunfire continued to split the air and grew closer and louder.

"The rebels are stealing all the hospital mattresses!" Cried one of the cooks, but there was nothing anyone could do to stop them.

When the gunfire had passed beyond the mission, and everyone was collecting themselves off the floor, the front door to the mission was thrown open and soldiers filed into the room. The Captain spoke in French.

"Greetings, Fathers. The Mai Mai Rebels are gone. We now control this area. Tomorrow we will take all of you to Kindu."

"Why must we go to Kindu?" One priest questioned.

"We have our orders from headquarters down there. We are to bring all of you to our headquarters, you are our prisoners now, and we are responsible for your safety."

"But Kindu is 150 kilometers away," stated one of the Peace Corp nurses. Sara quickly calculated in her head between kilometers and miles, and came up with around 93 miles. "We have people here who can not travel that distance."

"Do you have any vehicles?" ask the captain. "We might still have some bicycles," answered one of the priests. "And Baba V was transported here on a bicycle with the help of three men."

"Well, see what you can put together to ease your travel. We will collect you in the morning."

When Baba and his household returned to their house on the hill, it was to discover Baba's bicycle, chair still attached, had not been taken by the fleeing rebels. Everyone rejoiced that Baba's new shoes had been safe on his feet. It didn't take long to gather their things together for the morning.

"I'm not certain my shoes have another 120 miles of tread left on them," Sara confided to Ngalia. "But if God could make the Israelites' shoes last 40 years in the desert, I guess

I'll trust Him to hold my shoes together." Both girls giggled, and Ngalia just wiggled her sturdy bare toes in Sara's direction.

Morning found everyone gathered in front of the mission house. Baba's bicycle and chair held the interest of the soldiers in charge of delivering everyone back to Kindu.

"How did this work?" the captain inquired of Apol.

"It takes three men to operate Baba's bicycle." She explained. "One on either side to push and hold Baba upright, and one to follow close behind to keep the bicycle from gaining too much speed on the downhill runs."

"I was afraid that was the case." The man shook his head and grinned, then chose out three of his soldiers to do the honors.

The two nurses carried backpacks which included medicines for the trip, should Baba have a relapse. The mission's cooks had stayed up all night preparing what food they could, and packaging it for easiest transport. No one minded carrying the food, for everyone knew how little food there was to find along the trail.

Soon the new caravan was organized. All bundles of belongings and food were distributed, and they pushed off leaving the Kiunkutu Mission behind. Apol and Ngalia balanced heavy baskets on their heads. Sara carried Paipi in Ngalia's sling around her own body, and a basket of food balanced on her hip.

Nights along the way were spent in deserted villages as often as possible. The soldiers would choose a hut, clean it out a bit, and then invite their captives to enter and sleep inside, while they slept outside the housing. They were less threatening to the individuals in their care, and seemed as curious about Baba's history as Sara. Soon the newly assigned soldiers had him talking and telling stories about his life.

"Were you here before the elephants were driven away?" one soldier asked.

"Yes, the elephants caused much trouble in our villages. They would come in angry and smash huts and people. The government gave me license to kill one elephant every month to feed the people. I didn't have time to go hunt elephants, so I would give my license to one of my men there. He'd go and hunt for elephants to feed our people, and the lepers. But he always came home with **two** elephants!

"I would say, why do you kill two elephants when we have license for only one? He'd say, Oh Baba, I feel so bad, but I had to kill the second one in self defense, he was going to kill me, so I killed him.

Ha ha, poor ol' Mubuli, he was really a wonderful fellow."

"Did you ever hear the message drums?" Another soldier asked.

"Oh yes. That was how we knew when an elephant was charging a village, and how Mubuli let the village know to come carry home his kill. And drums were beat to scare the elephants away, but sometimes it didn't work."

"How did Mubuli kill the elephants?" Sara wanted to know.

"Oh, he killed them with a spear, on a big long handle. The men would follow along behind the elephants, and then spear them in the groin, and push it in, and keep pushing the spear further in until the elephant fell. The elephant would take maybe a day or two days to die. By then the men from the village could get there to help carry the meat home. But that's all finished now. Elephant hunters are no more. Now the elephants are all gone off to the jungles, there is plenty of jungle there where they can hide for the next 50 years in the jungles out there."

"Baba is tired," Apol would tell everyone. "He must rest." And that would be the end of Baba's storytelling for the night.

Another night one of the soldiers wanted to know where Baba got his medical training.

"I went to Antwerp, Belgium, to tropical medical school. The Lord closed and opened the doors for me. The Belgium government sent an order around, all you foreign missionaries who don't have training and a clinic for tropical medicine have to get out.

I had no training, so, if I have to go, I have to go." Baba shrugged his shoulders, holding his big bony hands out in front of him. Sara could tell the soldier's were in for a long story fest this night.

Ngalia caught her eyes and with a silent nod they slipped away from the group and moved out of earshot.

"As much as I love that story, I'd rather you help me with my drawing." Ngalia giggled at the face Sara made.

"I love Baba's stories. But I'll teach you. I love doing that too!"

Apol allowed the soldiers an hour of uninterrupted stories before stepping in to remind everyone that Baba was still recovering from his illness and needed to rest. With reluctance his audience took their leave and everyone settled in to sleep.

"Sara," Apol spoke softly from close by.

"Yes?"

"Ngalia and I must return to Kama tomorrow. The food supply we carried is small enough to be transferred to you. Every day we continue on we are that much further away from home. The nurses will care for Baba and watch over you." Apol's voice had a hiccup to it, and she coughed to cover it up. "I know you will take good care of Baba too."

Silence screamed into the night, and Sara's heart felt constricted. Tears filled her eyes. She couldn't speak; couldn't find any words to say. She hadn't thought about Apol and Ngalia and Paipi ever being gone from her life. Of course it made sense, of course it had to come, but could she bear it?

Baba stirred in his quilt and rolled to his back. Soon his snores filled the air with familiar sounds and the jungle noises filtered back into Sara's conscious awareness. Paipi snuggled closer against her, and Ngalia reached across him to grasp Sara's hand. Sara squeezed Ngalia's hand in return and allowed her tears to roll onto the ground unchecked. *Why God, why does loving and losing someone have to hurt so badly?*

Chapter Thirty Eight

Everyone was all business the next morning. The women fixed a quick breakfast of the food at hand and bundled all remains after everyone had eaten. Apol thanked the soldiers, the priests and Peace Corp nurses for their hospitality and care for Baba and party. Then she turned to Baba.

"I must return to Kama, Baba," Apol spoke calmly and firmly to the aged missionary. "You go to America, you visit your family, you get strong again, then you come home to us." She wrapped her arms around him and they held each other for several minutes before she turned away.

"I love you Baba." Ngalia took her turn, and tears coursed down her cheeks. "You come home to teach my Paipi. We will be praying and waiting for you." Both women turned to hug Sara. "You make sure he gets his sleep, Sara." Apol instructed gruffly. "And if God should lead you to come back to us, you know you are always welcome. We will make you a home. Live well with God, Sara."

"I won't forget what you've taught me, Sara, and I will teach your art to others. Make your peace at home, choose your path carefully. Send word. Don't forget us." Ngalia pressed the hairbrush the nurses had given them into Sara's hand. "You take this. You need to look your best in big city."

Sara accepted the brush but clung to Ngalia and Apol till one of the nurses gently laid her hand on her shoulder. "Bye, thanks for everything." She choked out. "Keep safe. I'll pray for you everyday." She allowed Apol and Ngalia to walk away without trying to hug or kiss Paipi goodbye. Too fresh in her memory was Paipi's parting with Nondo, and she couldn't allow their parting to get anymore difficult. Through her tears she could see Paipi's grinning face and childish wave as he looked back at them from his sling, and she returned his wave.

Again the nurse squeezed Sara's shoulder and gently turned her towards Kindu. Sara realized they would have to run to catch up with the others, and soldiers stood waiting to follow them. "I'm ready." She stated with resolve and hoped that she truly was.

Day four on the trail to Kindu was well underway when a sharp bang had everyone ducking for cover, rifles ready to respond. Baba's bicycle handlers veered to a sudden stop, grabbing for Baba to keep him from pitching over the handlebars.

"We've lost a tire, Captain." One of the men called out, and the Captain made his way back to where the handlers stood holding the bicycle upright, Baba perched on top looking more comical than usual.

"Oh, Baba what do we do now?" Puzzled, the Captain walked around the bicycle, scratching his head and taking the whole situation in. "This bicycle is done, and we are still three days from Kindu. Get Baba V down from there and let him rest." He instructed the handlers.

"You there, and you. Find me two good pole trees, we will carry Baba the ancestor's way."

"That will require four men, Captain, it takes four men to carry my chair like that." Baba pointed out.

"Well, I'll give you another soldier. We'll get you to Kindu, Baba, don't worry, I have my orders. We'll get you there whatever it takes. You rest a little while, and we'll look around."

Baba was lowered to the ground, and the nurses moved in to help him walk to a fallen log beside the road, while his handlers worked to untie his chair from the discarded bicycle. Sara followed, and sat on the ground near him. The nurses preferred to stay standing, one behind Baba, allowing him to lean back against her, the other urging Baba to drink water from her canteen.

Suddenly Baba started pointing down the road, "Say, what is that coming there?"

"It's not possible! It's not possible!" came from the Captain as he moved down the road to see better, then to intercept a man peddling his bicycle towards them. "Can we hire your bicycle, or borrow it, sir. We have a missionary in need of it here."

"What missionary do you have?" demanded the rider. "Where is he from?"

"He's from Kama."

"You have Baba V?"

"Yes."

"Oh, take my bike, he's our missionary, I am honored to help."

The two men walked the bicycle on to the group watching and waiting.

"Baba V, this man says you may have his bicycle. He says you are his missionary. He is from Kama."

"Oh, Baba, it is so good to see you safe," exclaimed the Kama man. "We have worried and prayed about you."

"God takes care of me," Baba grinned and reached out his hands to grasp the hands of the newcomer.

"God must *really* love this missionary," mumbled one of the nearby soldiers. "Look, He gives him a bicycle in the middle of the jungle; brings it right to him the minute he needs it!" The soldier spoke French, and Sara grinned at the nurses also hearing his mumbling.

"We all agree with you," they replied to the soldier, and he just shook his head.

"Well, praise God and call the men back, we won't need poles now." instructed the Captain. "Thank you sir, for this bicycle, we will transfer Baba's chair right over and sit him back in it and be on our way."

"May we leave my old bicycle for my friend here?" Baba suggested. "Replacing one tire is easier than replacing the whole bicycle." The captain agreed and was happy to comply considering the circumstances.

In short order the whole caravan was back on the road. The priests were chattering away to one another and laughing as they followed along behind the girls now. Sara couldn't catch their words but had a fair idea that they were discussing how much fun they were going to have telling and retelling this story to others.

Sara hoped their rescuer was headed for Kama, and would tell everyone there what had happened and how God had provided. Apol and Ngalia deserved to know and have a good laugh too.

That night Baba had a new story to share with his rescuers. "Many years ago, probably before any of you were born, during another of our awful wars, Pastor Philippo's village was in the path of some murderous soldiers. The lookouts saw them coming and warned the people, so the village was empty long before the soldiers got there. Pastor Philippo led his people towards the river, but the soldiers were still coming behind them. When they reached the river they had no way to get across, and stood together praying for God to deliver them. Suddenly one of their young men started shouting, 'canoes, canoes,' and the young men jumped in the water and swam out to capture the empty canoes that were floating down the river as they prayed. Everyone was put into the canoes and paddled safely across the river and escaped the soldiers."

"Where did the canoes come from?" asked one of the men.

"Oh, God provided them."

"How?"

"A village way upstream posted no lookouts, and when the soldiers came into their camp, they cut all the canoes loose so no one could escape. The canoes floated downstream to arrive just when they were needed to answer the people's prayers."

"We did not even have time to pray today before God provided you another bicycle!" The soldier who had been muttering earlier exclaimed.

"Ha ha, ha ha," Baba laughed. "God knows what we need before we ask. He just likes us to be polite and ask sometimes." Everyone laughed.

The remainder of the journey to Kindu held its challenges of bad roads and broken bridges, not enough food to go around, and general hardships, but the full 93 miles were completed in a total of seven days.

"You have faith in God, Baba?" said the Captain more than once. "Have faith in us too."

If there was one thing Baba was not lacking, it was faith. God really was in control. He moved where and when He deemed best. Sara did not miss the obvious.

Chapter Thirty Nine

Kindu was a sizable city and teeming with life. Boats came down the Congo River all the way from the Atlantic Coast to dock at Kindu, the port city at the end of the line.

The soldiers delivered their charges to the Catholic Mission where they were welcomed with open arms. Word was gotten to Pastor Wabula, serving at the Grace Bible College in Kindu, who in turn got word to Tom Sanchez in Bukavu that Baba and Sara had arrived safely in Kindu, and would be flown on Monday aboard a Catholic plane to Kalima, 60 miles closer to Bukavu. After a one or two-day layover, everyone would be flown on to Bukavu. Tom called the Tarbell Office in Douala and left word for Ross Mann.

Sara missed the guidance of Apol, friendship of Ngalia, and the comforting comedy of Paipi. She tried to focus on following the example of the nurses. They were each old enough to be her parent, maybe even grandparent, and Sara had great respect for the choices they had made to leave the comfort of their homes in Italy to serve the Congolese in a war zone.

The hardships of their journey had taken its toll on each of them, and no one minded time to simply relax and rest. Baba's spirits were high, but his body was weak, and needed the rest. Sara welcomed that time to curl up in a chair nearby and sleep.

Ross was bone tired when he returned to camp to find Chappy leaning against his chopper.

"Hey, Chappy, have you brought me word of Sara?" he called out before jumping off the truck. Pushing off from the chopper and wiping his hands on his pant legs, Choppy strolled towards the advancing Ross.

"The government army rescued a whole bunch of folks at the Catholic Mission at Biunkutu. Baba V and Sara, Ngalia, Paipi, and Apol were among them. They were taken to Kindu, and are in transport to Bukavu. Grab your stuff, Tarbell's granted you family leave. I've got a plane waiting at Douala. Let's go!"

Tom and Michelle Sanchez were waiting impatiently at the tiny airport across the border in Rwanda when Chappy's plane landed and taxied off the runway to a spot out of the way of other flights. They saw Ross climb out of the plane, and walked over to greet him.

"Welcome back, Ross," Tom stretched out his arm to shake hands with the ruddy-bearded construction boss. "I'm so glad God has brought all our people out safely and we can return your niece to you in one piece."

"Hi Tom, Hi Michelle." Ross shook hands with Tom and hugged Michelle. "I agree with you, Tom. I'm so grateful they're all okay that I'm not even feeling the need to educate that niece of mine!"

"Oh, I think she's gotten quite an adequate education already, Ross. I'm quite certain Baba has done considerable educating in these past three and a half months!" Tom laughed. "You may not even recognize the young lady, I'll bet the pigtails are gone and a matronly braided bun may be in their place!" All four laughed at the image suggested and Ross motioned towards Chappy. "This is Bill Chapman, fondly referred to as Chappy. He's the pilot who made it possible for Sara to get her hard earned education!"

"Delighted to meet ya, Chappy." Tom pumped Chappy's hand. Michelle nodded and smiled warmly at the pilot.

"Sara's bold confidence in her God got Chappy here reflecting on his life," Ross gently prodded his friend.

"Really?" Tom caught the prod and played along. "How's that?"

"I made a decision to join God's team. I'm a Christian now." Chappy announced with confidence.

"Hallelujah!" Tom and Michelle both exclaimed in unison. "God is so good!"

Chappy locked his plane and chocked the wheels. Then the four walked over to the shaded seating area provided to await the plane bringing the others.

They didn't have to wait too long before the Catholic Mission plane landed and taxied up to them. Stairs were wheeled over to the plane and put into place after the side door snapped open. Baba was assisted to the top of the stairs, and Ross rushed up to assist his shaky descent. Sara quietly followed, uncertain how to greet her uncle. As soon as Tom and Michelle took charge of Baba and started walking him carefully to their car, Ross turned and embraced Sara in a bear hug.

"Welcome to Africa, little thing. Sorry I wasn't here to meet you when you first arrived."

"I'm sorry I've made so much trouble, I needed to see you to tell you. . . I just couldn't tell you over the phone . . ."

"I know child, I know." Ross comforted Sara for a moment then pressed on to matters current. "Do you have any luggage?"

Sara grinned and held up the tiny brush Ngalia had pressed into her hand at their parting. "This is it."

"How about Baba?"

"Just the clothes on his back."

"Okay, then. Chappy and I brought your belongings from the hotel in Douala."

Sara hadn't seen Chappy standing off to the side, and suddenly spotted him. "Chappy, is it really you?

Hello, again!" Sara embraced the pilot in a big hug, then turned her attention back to Uncle Ross. "Can we cross the border into Bukavu without passports?"

"I think we can go into Bukavu with no trouble, but we'll need your passport to get you back to the United States. Please tell me you left your passport in Douala in your suitcase." Ross bent to pick up the two cases he had set aside when he ran to help Baba. Sara squealed in delight when she realized Uncle Ross did indeed have her suitcase in his hand.

"Clothes, real clothes and toiletries, oh guys, you're the greatest!"

"Passport?" Ross prompted.

"Yes, should be. I wasn't thinking I'd need it in Kama. It's just as well, my backpack and everything in it was left at Kama when we were taken. I'm lucky I was still dressed when the rebels barged in. Baba wasn't, he was barefoot and in his pajamas. So he doesn't have his passport or documentation of any kind. But surely people here know him."

"It will take some doing to get through all the red tape, but Baba should be able to get whatever paperwork he'll need. Tom and Michelle will be able to help him with that."

The three did not have to rush to catch up with Tom, Michelle, and Baba. The priests and nurses waved to them as they climbed into the Catholic Mission Van.

"We'll be in touch." They called to Tom, he nodded and waved.

Chappy made the rounds of each person, taking more time with Baba than the others, then Sara, and excused himself. "I've got a work order over in Tanzania that'll take me a few days. I'll come back by to collect Ross and Sara on my way back to Cameroon. So glad I got to meet all of you. Perhaps I'll see you all again. I hope so. Ross, keep an eye on that Sara girl. Don't lose her again." He teased.

Bukavu was bigger than Sara had expected, but the guest house was exactly as she had imagined it.

"The first thing on my agenda," Baba declared with all the authority he could muster in his weakened condition, "is an hour-long soak in a bathtub filled to the top with hot sudsy water. There's crud on me three months deep."

"We can arrange that for you, Baba, but first I'm going to feed you. You are nothing but skin and bone, and Sara, you're not much more than that! You know this look would cost you thousands at those fancy spas in the states. Here you got it for free!" Everyone chuckled.

"You'd better eat first, Baba," Tom chimed in, "Michelle has been cooking for two days. She intends to put some meat back on your bones."

Baba was settled into an overstuffed armchair in the spacious living room. Sara paused to hug Baba before following Michelle out to the kitchen. "May I help?"

"Of course. I'll get you settled into a room after supper, but you'll want to freshen up. The bathroom is just down the hall there. There are washcloths and towels in the cabinet. Take your time, but don't dillydally."

It was all Sara could do to keep from jumping into the shower and putting on all clean clothes from her suitcase, but Baba had spoken up first, and she wasn't going to cut in line. She quickly washed as needed to be presentable in the setting out of food, and returned to the kitchen.

The dining room was set up, ready for service. Sara helped carry Michelle's feast to the table. The smell of roasted meat and fresh baked bread made Sara's mouth water. Two tall glasses of cold milk stood in the middle of the table.

Baba was retrieved from the living room, Tom on one side, Ross on the other, and settled in the armchair at the head of the table. Everyone else gathered around the table, clasped hands and bowed their heads to pray. Baba did not hesitate.

"Thank you, Father, for bringing us safely to this beloved home in Bukavu; Thank you for bringing Sara to share these past few months with me and your people. Thank you for Tom and Michelle, and their family, here to minister to your people in Bukavu. Thank you for bringing Ross to share our reunion. Now we ask your blessing, Father, on this food, cause it to nourish our bodies and rebuild our strength. In Jesus' precious name, Amen."

Amen's echoed around the table. Chairs were pulled out and everyone sat down with a show of gratitude and eagerness to dig into the savory feast Michelle had set before them. The milks were passed to Baba and Sara. Tom and Michelle settled on either side of Baba, filling his plate, cutting his meat, and helping him in any way they could.

Sara soon realized that as delicious as everything was, she couldn't eat much. Two thirds of her chosen foods were still on her plate when her stomach refused to absorb even one more bite.

"Eyes bigger than your stomach, Sara?" Uncle Ross teased.

"I'm afraid there's more truth to that than I like!" she acknowledged as she poked at a bite of her meat, eyeing it longingly. "Can I save this for later?"

"Of course you can. Don't worry, Sara. Your stomach will stretch out again with proper encouragement." Tom sympathized. "For now we'll settle for baby steps." He turned his attention to Ross. "How long can you stay with us, Ross?'

"I've arranged to stay over a few days as needed, but I can't be gone from work too long. We're nearing the completion of the pipeline, and I need to get back. We're close enough to the end that I've been able to get permission for Sara to stay with me till we complete the job, and then we'll both be flying back to Los Angeles to wrap up Sara's affairs there. I don't think I'll let her out of my sight for a while. No more solo jaunts crossing paths in Paris!" He deliberately sounded gruff and Sara kept her gaze in her plate missing the twinkle in her uncle's eyes as he stuffed a bite of meat into his mouth.

"Are Rich and Kathy still manning Radio Kahuzi?" Baba changed the subject diverting everyone's attention away from Sara.

"Yes, and Kathy wants to see you before we leave for the States."

"Oh, I can't go off to the States," Baba protested, "I need to get back to Kama!"

"We know that is your desire, Baba, but it is not safe now, and we have no way to get you back there without angering the powers that be. Besides, it will take time for you to recover sufficiently enough to return to the work." Tom spoke quietly but with a decidedness that brooked no argument.

"Besides, Baba," Michelle added gently, "Your children have been worried sick over you. They need to see you, to know you are really okay. We've been in touch with them. Tomorrow we'll get in touch with them again, and let them talk with you in person. Then when you are strong enough to make the trip, I will personally deliver you to your son George, in Texas. You can use your time in the States to visit with all your family and the churches that support your work here. The people who survive this war will need to start over again, rebuilding, if and when this war is ever over." Aggravation sounded in Michelle's voice and Baba patted her hand.

"We've done it before; in God's strength we'll do it again."

When the evening meal was concluded and everyone pushed away from the table, Tom enlisted Ross's help to assist Baba down the hall to the bathroom. Michelle had excused herself from the table moments before and gone to run Baba's bath of hot sudsy water and it was now ready for him. Tom assisted Baba while Michelle showed Ross and Sara where they would each be sleeping.

"It will seem odd not sleeping on the floor beside Baba." Sara told Michelle. "It seems as though I've done that my whole life."

"You've had quite the adventure, haven't you?"

"It feels so surreal. I guess it will take a while to process everything I've experienced and learned in the past three months. I miss Apol and Ngalia so much. And parting from Baba won't be any easier." Sara spoke so softly Michelle could barely hear her and she realized Sara was close to emotional exhaustion and tears. She sat down on the edge of the bed and motioned for Sara to sit beside her.

"It will be alright, Sara. Our time here on the earth is so short, and we have hard work to accomplish for our Heavenly Father. We will have all of eternity to be reunited with our loved ones. The key thing we need to remember is that God is The Only Constant, unchanging, unfailing force in our lives. He's the same yesterday, today and tomorrow. He's the same in

America as He is here in Africa, or Brazil, or Mexico." Michelle paused to gently command Sara's full attention.

"God is the same everywhere. He cares the same everywhere. He promises that those who diligently seek Him will find Him. And He will work through the lives of those who open their lives to Him for that purpose. You've just spent three and a half months with a man who has fully trusted God for 70 plus years under the most trying of circumstances and had a ball, loving every challenge and opportunity God entrusted to him. You're truly one of the lucky ones, you've seen with your own eyes how Baba does things 'God's way.' God has mighty plans for you, Sara; don't let yourself be bogged down by clinging to things, to people, or to a comfortable life." Michelle had wrapped her arm around Sara's shoulder as she spoke and now gave her a gentle hug, but did not remove her arm.

"Remember every true friend is a gift from God, and rejoice in the truth that if they're Christians, you'll see them all again, if not here or now, later – when we're all together in eternity. It's all gain, all gain. And you are most definitely one of the lucky ones." Michelle gently hugged Sara's shoulders again, and quietly left her with her thoughts.

Sara continued to ponder all Michelle had shared with her. It was a lot to process, a lot to remember, but somehow she knew it would all benefit her if she could hold onto it. Then she thought again of Baba, and went to the kitchen to find Michelle and ask, "Does Baba need medicine tonight?"

"Tom will have examined Baba by now; he'll take care of him. Tom runs the Grace Medical Clinic here in Bukavu, and has everything he'll need to continue Baba's recovery."

"Oh, of course, I was forgetting he's a medical person too."

"Are you sure you want to wait till Baba is done soaking before you sleep?"

"No, I think all the excitement of the past several months is finally catching up with me. One more night of crud won't kill me. Do you mind?"

"No, I think the sleep is more important for you now. Baba is in good hands, your Uncle Ross is here, and you have a real bed all to yourself tonight. Go sleep, Sara. Tomorrow you can enjoy a long hot shower and fresh clothes. Good night, hon. Sleep well."

Chapter Forty

Sara woke refreshed and moderately eager for the new day. The bed felt so wonderful, she could have stayed there all day but for the pull of a shower. The household was still quiet, so she gathered what she would need from her suitcase and made her way to the bathroom. A long hot shower with soaps and shampoos, a daisy shaver, toothpaste and toothbrush, clean fluffy towels and a real hairbrush and mirror. . . .plus clean, fashionable, well-fitting, suitcase-rumpled clothing, all made her feel like she had morphed into a land of great luxury.

Yet, she realized she'd trade it all just to know her loved ones at Kama were safe and had enough food. She would never take life comforts for granted again, she was certain of that. And Sara paused to thank her heavenly Father for His provision and to ask his protection over Ngalia and Paipi, Nondo, Apol and Kilongo, Vincent and Amu, Pastor Gonanoffy, and so many more. *Lord, help Ngalia and Apol benefit from those things left in my backpack,* she added to her prayer.

She quietly finished up and volunteered her services to Michelle who was already busy in the kitchen when she came out. Michelle put her in charge of the scrambled eggs. "Eggs are one commodity we can enjoy here. People come by with produce, fish, fruit, and I buy what I can. Even though we are in the city, there is not a tremendous bounty of food. We've too many refugees. Rich and Kathy McDonald, who you'll meet today, run Radio Kahuzi, and broadcast Christian radio throughout Congo, Rwanda, Kenya, even further in some places."

"How do people hear the broadcast? Surely it's hard to get batteries, even if you have a radio, and I didn't see any mud houses with electrical outlets."

"Oh, not a problem," Michelle smiled. "A Canadian based company makes and supplies them with handheld, solar powered radios, which are tuned to only the one station, Radio Kahuzi. They hand out thousands of them, to university students, children, refugees, military personnel, anyone who will take one. Folks who don't have one will crowd around the person who does and they listen together. That's how radio clubs start. Radio Kahuzi not only puts out the gospel and educational programs, but they help separated families find each other. Radio club representatives will bring in a list of all the people in their club, and where they are; Rich reads them over the air and people find one another. It's amazing what God is doing through their work." Michelle stopped to catch her breath and carry dishes to the dining table. She returned and continued.

"Last I heard, they had 210 radio clubs just in the past month. The university students are hearing this Christian programming and a short while ago, three men from one of the Bukavu universities met with Richard and said that a group of professors and students decided that they needed to have a regular daily Bible Study. They actually voted to include this decision in their statutes. On their own, they have begun to tape the programs in French and translate them into Swahili for their own use and for the station to broadcast.

"Richard gave them a supply of the small booklets in French entitled, 'How to Know God.' That club is made up of a very diverse group; some are Catholic, some Muslim, plus several other denominations. Richard would like to supply them with the book of Romans, but he doesn't have them yet.

"Don't let the eggs burn, Sara." Michelle handed Sara a big bowl to scoop the eggs into and continued. "A large group of refugees have been organized into radio clubs. In one club there are approximately 400 widows, orphans, dispossessed and handicapped, 'the nonvenerable.' Richard is involved in compiling lists of those needing special assistance. In cooperation with the NGOs they are helping to set up "Nutrition Centers" to feed the weakest. Many are dying from malnutrition. I've seen plenty of them myself."

Anguish crossed Sara's face, but Michelle was so concentrated on getting breakfast together, while talking, that she missed it and continued to share what had become her routine life experience. She spoke with genuine pride and gratitude for the work they could accomplished to help those in need, and didn't dwell on the fact that the need was far greater than the available solution.

"Radio Kahuzi has become a local partner with Food for the Hungry, helping to alleviate the malnutrition of hundreds of people left without gardens or tools to garden with after the wars. Above and beyond the operation of the radio station Richard and the staff are distributing tons of beans and corn. One ton of seed yields 50 tons in three months." Michelle paused to look over her table to see what was missing. "Sara, would you please pour two glasses of milk from the fridge, and set them on the table?"

Sara complied and Michelle continued as if never having interrupted the thought flow.

"The people are planting near a swamp which provides moisture year round even in the dry season. They get three crops harvested per year. They are also starting 20 nurseries with 40 kilos of seed which will feed 4,000 families with 10 grams each of seed: carrots, cabbage, tomatoes, etc. Action Against Hunger is providing the gardening tools to work the gardens. It may sound like 'social work,' but it is vital to sustaining life here. We all suffer from the lack of good food because of these wars. Listen to me going on and on!"

"Is Radio Kahuzi close by?" Sara asked.

"I'd say its close by. Rich and Kathy live just the other side of our back wall. Unfortunately you have to go around the block to get to them, or them to us, because of the wall, but that's close. Kathy grew up in the Congo. Her parents were Fred and Millie Baylor.

They worked alongside Baba V in the 1950s until the 1960 Rebellion forced them out of the country along with so many others, so Kathy has known Baba all her life."

Breakfast was ready and the others were congregating around the dining room table. Sara helped carry the last of the food, and everyone set about putting the table in order. Again Baba had been set at the head of the table, and again he bowed his head, raised his large bony hands and prayed.

"Thank you Father for this house, for its keepers, for comfortable beds, bathtubs filled with hot sudsy water, nutritious food and the hands that prepare it. Amen."

"Seems Baba's appetite is coming back." Tom muttered and everyone chuckled. Sara was careful to take less food and did her best to eat it all.

Michelle and Sara had finished cleaning up the breakfast things when Kathy and Richard McDonald arrived for their promised visit. With them was a middle-aged African woman who kept her eyes downcast, and tried to stay back out of anyone's way. Baba reached out his long arms to Kathy from the overstuffed arm chair he'd been placed in, and wrapped her in a warm embrace.

"So how is my little Kathy?" he wanted to know as the tall, thin, dark haired woman sank into the chair set next to Baba for her. Sara noted that Kathy was smiling and her manner was soft and comforting towards Baba.

"God is faithful, Baba. We are still broadcasting, in spite of Satan's opposition and harassment. But we will catch you up on all that news when you are more rested. Have you been hearing our broadcasts?"

"No, I ran out of your little radios long ago, I sent the last one to an isolated zone and a work that needed it more. I had the ham radio to call Tom and check on things."

"Okay. We are hoping for another shipment of radios from Galcom, but you know how that goes. The radio clubs have grown to more than 250. Our journalists read their letters on the radio, and their locations, and we hear families are being reunited."

"Ah, that is very good."

Baba nodded but Sara sensed he still had questions.

"What haven't you told me, little Kathy?" The question evoked sudden sobs from the shy African woman standing back against the wall. Tears flowed down her cheeks and Richard moved to her side and gently urged her to come sit by Baba as Kathy rose to make room for her.

"This is our friend Mama Hyota, Baba." Richard explained. "She has seen horrible things and we thought if she could talk with you about them, perhaps it would be easier for her to get past them."

Uncle Ross sat very still, afraid to shift his weight in the chair, lest he distract from the events unfolding right before his eyes. Sara moved behind his chair and quietly massaged his shoulder and neck muscles. It gave her a release from the tension in the room and she hoped it would work the same for her uncle.

"What is it, Mama Hyota? What did you see?" Baba turned his head ever so slightly to catch sight of Hyota in his limited peripheral vision.

"The soldiers line up whole groups of people . . . some my dearest friends, and others I knew," Hyota choked out the words, "and shot them all. Their bodies were thrown into the lake . . . and there was nothing I could do to stop them." Hyota buried her face in her hands, her shoulders shaking with her sobs. Baba leaned forward and reached out to her, patting her on the back as if to comfort her.

"Cry it out, Mama Hyota, cry it out. Let it go. Let it go."

Michelle and Sara wept openly. The men cleared their throats and shuffled their feet. Baba began to pray. "Father, we need your comfort. You have watched your creation over the ages kill and devour one another. You've seen your precious babies sacrificed alive, aborted, even just thrown away for convenience sake. Yet you loved mankind enough to forgive us, and die for us. We are only human; we do not have your strength. Help us to forgive. Forgive and move on and minister to the very ones who do such evil. You alone know the depth of our hurt, yet You love every one of these people. Only in your strength can we do the same. We ask for that strength, Father, all we need to finish our work here, in Your Precious Son's name, Amen."

To Mama Hyota Baba said, "You will be okay child, God is still God, no one can take that away from us. Just call on Him, lean on Him for all that you need. He is a very big God, only He can soothe your hurt." Baba turned his attention back to Kathy.

"My dear little Kathy, your parents must look on you with such pride from heavens gate. You know from whom our strength comes to do this work. We must grieve our losses. But those who are gone grieve no more, their work is done. But we grieve deeply, and then move on. We still have much work to do." With that Baba patted Mama Hyota's knee again, and motioned for Ross and Tom to come and help him, "I think I should lie down for a while now."

When the two men had Baba up on his feet, supporting him on either side, Kathy stepped close and whispered in his ear while handing him a package of underwear they had brought for him. Baba felt the package and grinned from ear to ear. "These are like gold! Thank you my dear ones. Thank you!" Kathy wrapped her arms around the neck of the old man and hugged him. "I knew you would be happy to have them, Baba. Go rest now." She stepped out of the way so the men could assist him down the hall to the bathroom and then on to his bed.

Kathy looked at the others with a red face and shrugged her shoulders. "No missionary likes to return to America in dingy or no underwear."

Michelle stepped to Kathy's side and gave her a hug. "How about a piece of cake, it's chocolate. I figured having Baba and Sara safe out of the jungle was reason enough to dip into the special occasion supplies."

Kathy nodded and the four women moved to the kitchen to set out the special occasion treat. Mama Hyota's face still showed signs of her tears, but a new peace seemed to be settling around her eyes, and she no longer looked only at the floor.

Afternoon found Ross growing restless. Sara had retired to her room to catch a nap, and Ross waited for Tom to return from the Medical clinic. Michelle worked about the house cleaning and preparing the evening meal.

"I hate to rush in, grab Sara, and disappear so quickly," Ross spoke to Michelle, "but delaying won't make it any easier on Sara to part company with Baba V. I know your hospitality would cover any stay, but the food supply is limited and you have your hands full with Baba, getting his passport and papers, etc. I'm glad you're taking him back to the states. I think that is the right move, and I have no doubt God will restore his health and he'll come right back to the Congo to encourage his people here."

"He's 91 years old, Ross." Michelle reminded him gently.

"Oh," Ross answered gruffly, "He's got a good six years left in him." He grinned sheepishly at Michelle's stern look. "Ah, mark my words," he refused to back down, "God isn't done with Baba yet. He's just needed in the States for a short while, that's all."

Michelle shook her head, "You're probably right. He sets a mighty high standard for the rest of us to imitate!"

"Yes, he does." Ross acknowledged. "May I use your phone? Sara and I should really call California and set those folks minds at ease."

"Certainly."

Ross waited till Sara woke from her nap, then called Hope Mission and handed Sara the phone. Sara couldn't decide if she was more excited or more nervous to talk to folks back home, but she knew she had to speak with Mrs. Schaffer.

"May I speak with Mrs. Schaffer please." She asked when an unfamiliar voice answered the phone. Mrs. Schaffer came on the line and nearly squealed Sara deaf when she recognized her voice. She called everyone into the kitchen and put Sara on speaker phone. "Are you alright chil'?"

"Yes, I'm fine."

"What were you thinkin'?" Sara grinned and knew she wouldn't be able to satisfy Mrs. Schaffer's indignation across the miles.

"I've so much to tell you! I taught English in the school at Kama, and I taught Ngalia to draw. Baba V and just everybody has taught me so much. I'm ready to come home now. I know I have unfinished business there. Uncle Ross is here, and I will be going back to Cameroon with him till he completes that pipeline to Chad. He says to tell you he'll bring me home in a couple of months."

"Couple o' months? Sara, are you really okay?"

"Yes, Mrs. Schaffer. I'm perfectly fine. I told you God would take care of me! We're calling from Bukavu, at the guest house, international calls cost a'plenty, so I'll call you again from Cameroon. I've got to go now. I love you all." Sara handed the phone to her uncle and stepped back.

"She really is fine, Mrs. Schaffer. She's grown up a bit, but it's all good. I'll bring her home as soon as I can. You all take care now. Bye." He hung up the phone and grinned at Sara. "Oh are you gonna' have some explaining to do!" Sara had the grace to blush and shift her gaze to the floor.

Tom came home early that evening with the express purpose of playing host to his visitors. "I know you've seen Bukavu, Ross, but this is Sara's first visit. It would be a shame for her to leave without seeing some of our sights." Sara agreed and was looking forward to a quick tour before the sun set and everyone retired to the relative safety of their homes.

The first stop was a scenic overlook of Lake Kivu. The beauty of the huge lake, with its mountainous frame, caught Sara's breath. She could have sat there for days sketching the beauty around her. How anyone could massacre people and shove their bodies into a lake as beautiful and serene as what lay before her was beyond comprehending.

"Have you noticed any of our earthquakes?" Tom asked of Sara.

"Yes, but I'm used to earth quakes, being from LA."

"I'm certain you are. Our whole area here is underscored by huge faults. At the head of the Lake, just beyond our sight there, above Goma, lies Mt. Kahuzi, an active volcano. It's rivers of molten lava sent people fleeing for their lives while you were busy inland. There is never a dull moment here in God's Country." Tom would have laughed out loud had he caught the look Sara flashed his way.

Another vantage point allowed Sara to see some of the expanse of the city, but Tom turned their vehicle towards home without attempting to take Sara down into the city. The sun was low in the sky, and no one was safe outside their homes after dark. Besides, Michelle would have supper waiting for them.

Ross broke the news of their morning departure to Sara just before they retired for the night. "Chappy's back and Tom will drop us off at the airstrip on this way to the clinic tomorrow morning. We'll have breakfast with Baba before we leave. Pack your things, have them ready to go." He leaned over and kissed the top of Sara's head, squeezed her arm reassuringly and left her to cry herself to sleep.

Chirping birds woke Sara just as the morning sun was making its appearance. She quietly made her way to the bathroom to shower and fix her hair. She packed her bag, carefully tucking away the tiny brush Ngalia had given her, and went to the kitchen to help Michelle.

The conversation between them was light and cheerful. Breakfast was the same. When Tom pushed away from the table, Ross followed suit and assisted Tom in getting Baba to his chosen chair. Then Ross spoke to Baba.

"Well, I'm going to take my niece now and return to Cameroon, old friend." Ross reached for and grasped Baba's hand in a gentle but firm shake. "Thank you for taking such special care of her for me. Let me know when you're back in country again. We'll get together somehow. Maybe I'll even bring Sara with me!" Ross managed a convincing chuckle.

Sara stooped to Baba's side and put her arms around his neck. "Thank you Baba for all you've taught me. Lord willing, I'll be back." He patted her on the back and she stood to thank Tom and Michelle for their hospitality. "Take good care of him," she managed before her voice choked and Ross turned her towards the door. He saluted his hosts, and Baba, though Baba could not see it, and collected the suitcases which he used to nudge Sara out the door and to the waiting car.

"I get it, Father God, I get that I have to go home and deal with matters there, but I surely will come back if You're willing to use me here, Father" Sara's whisper was a hopeful prayer, *"I surely will come back."*

Epilogue

Sara Calhoun has shared with us the memories and adventures of *many* people who had the privilege of learning firsthand from BaBa V's life. While Sara, as a person, is fictitious, the adventures she had are not.

BaBa V on the other hand is the genuine article. He is truly one of the heroes of our century. I have listened to his stories since I myself was a child. I have been blessed by the ministry of his coworkers, children, and grandchildren.

In 1999 I was privileged to interview BaBa V in the living room of his son, Fred, and daughter-in-law, Lois. Baba had returned to the States to complete his recovery from malaria after being held hostage for three months by a wild band of Congolese rebels. He used that time to visit the churches and people who supported his work at Kama, but his heart and desire was to return as quickly as possible to rejoin the spiritual battle for the hearts of those he left behind in the Congo.

I have included in this epilogue what BaBa's eldest son has to say of his Dad's life. Dr. Sam Vinton *Jr.* often joked with friends about his own retirement. He'd say, "I don't have the nerve to retire – my dad is still at it." What Dr. Sam knew of his Dad touches my heart, and I hope it will also touch yours.

Young Baba V

Baba's medal of honor

Completing the Task
By Sam Vinton, Jr., Executive director of Grace Missions International

How does one come up with words that can adequately explain 75 years of missionary service in the Congo? How does one in a page or two, describe what made Sam Vinton, Sr., leave the United States of America on March 12, 1928, and serve God faithfully even to this day? What are the main things that characterize the life of this remarkable man? In the next few paragraphs I will try to put down on paper what I believe are the three great characteristics that make him not only the longest-serving Protestant missionary (75 consecutive years), but a successful and beloved spiritual father to thousands of Congolese.

As a teenager growing up in Congo, I was one day leafing through some of my father's books when I came across his first prayer card—the one given to his friends and family before his departure for Congo in 1928. Under his picture he had this verse that I read and have never forgotten – "I was not disobedient unto the heavenly vision" (Acts 26:19). In this pithy statement of the apostle Paul is found the first thing that characterized my father's life and ministry. It is the word obedience.

Obedience to the Call of God

How do you account for 75 years faithful service? A characteristic that touches the very core of my father's life is obedience to the Call of God. When Paul stood before King Agrippa as a prisoner, he could say in all honesty that he had obeyed the call of God and it was this obedience that brought him, humanly speaking, into being a prisoner. Almost 2000 years later, because of his obedience to God's call, my father could write: "Like Paul I can tell of episodes – prison – looting – being forced to walk for three days through the forest at gunpoint with little food and unboiled drinking water…but because of the prayers of God's people, God worked. He gave me supernatural strength to endure the difficult safari through the forest by foot and by bicycle – He let malaria get me down knowing there was not antimalarial medicine where I was being held under house arrest so I would be released and sent to the Kampene Hospital where I received the proper treatment."

People have often spoken to my father with awe and praised him for his sacrifice and willingness to endure hardship and suffering. But as far as he is concerned he has not suffered or sacrificed – he has simply ***obeyed***. (The only sacrifice he has been willing to speak about has been separation from family.) It is a sign of the sorry state of the church today when people like my father and Mother Theresa, for example, are put on a pedestal when in reality they are simply living a life of obedience the way all Christians are supposed to live. This does not mean that every Christian would end up in Congo, but every Christian should understand the teaching of no longer living to self, but to Christ, in total obedience.

Commitment to the Call of God

About 30 years ago, my father chose another of Paul's statements to characterize his life and ministry. From that time on he has had these words printed on his stationery: "However, I consider my life worth nothing to me, if only I may finish the race and complete the task the Lord Jesus has given to me—the task of testifying to the gospel of God's grace" (Acts 20:24).

If obedience is the first characteristic of my father's life, the second is commitment. Not only did he obey the call of God and leave America to serve in Africa, but he has never lost the awe of being called by almighty God. This has produced in my dad a life of commitment that places God and God's demands on his life to be worth more than conveniences, security and safety—yes, even his life. His love for God and people has led him to attempt great things for God with great sensitivity to the culture and feelings of the Congolese with whom he worked. And he did so years before cultural anthropology became an important aspect of missionary training. He taught by example-the way he lived and worked and cared for people. People saw God working through him— so much so that when the midwives came to him one night from the forest where they were having difficulty delivering the baby of the chief's wife and asked for his help, their response to my father's hesitation (he knew that in their culture it was a taboo for a man to deliver a baby) was this: "We know God works through your hands so come, we'll bear the consequences."

This commitment also causes him to have a strong desire to finish the race (cf. 2 Tim. 4:7) and complete the task of testifying to the Gospel of the Grace of God. Implied in the words "finish" and "complete" is the idea of "reaching one's goal or finishing one's work." This is why at 95 he is still looking for more challenges from the Lord because he believes that his work is not yet completed.

Contentment in the Call of God

The third characteristic of my father's life that has made it possible for him to go through the "ups" and "downs" of missionary work is the word contentment. Many times he mentioned to me the importance of living in the light of Philippians 4:10-13. With Paul, he could say that, "I have learned to be content whatever the circumstances." He also could say, "I can do everything through Him who gives me strength."

There is no question that Sam Vinton, Sr., has had an extraordinary life and ministry in Congo that is an example for each of us. But there is a catch to this kind of life. The catch is **obedience**, **commitment** and **contentment**. Sam Vinton paid the cost and is still paying the cost. The question you and I must answer is this, "are we also willing to pay the cost in obedience to God?"

[This article was published in the GMI (Grace Missions International) Impact magazine in March of 2003.]

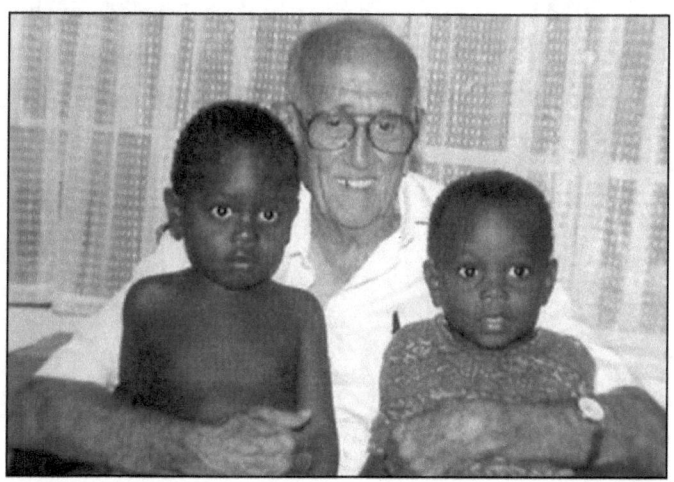

BaBa V did indeed recover from the events told in this book. Following his recovery his children desired for him to stay stateside and not return to the dangers in war-torn Congo. But BaBa laughed and said, "People said I couldn't go to the Congo when I was 19 because I was too young. Now I'm 91 and you say I can't go to the Congo because I'm too old.

Well, God will decide." And God did decide. At age 93 BaBa V returned to help his friends in the Congo recover from the tragedies they endured during the war, and to plant new fields for food, and rebuild their lives, homes and churches. God continued to use him to the end of his life. They say God has the best retirement benefits going, and in January of 2005 BaBa V retired to join his beloved God, and beloved wife, Marie. He was 97 years old.

What about Sara? What has become of her? I don't know yet. But I'm certain that if we are to learn of her future, God will indeed let me know and when he does, I shall do my best to get it all down on paper so I can share it with you.

May God richly bless your reading of "The Only Constant".

Lynne Warmouth

Patina!

Stories from the Heart
of God's Tender Care

By, Lynne A Warmouth

In life's journey, sometimes you have a take a look back in order to move forward. In Patina! I share the memories God sent my way to remind me that the "good" outweighs the "bad" in a life committed to serving Him.

Each memory came in such vivid, vibrant detail, that I could not rest until I had set each one to paper. As I shared these pages with friends and family, I was encouraged to preserve and share them all in one single collection, thus the writing of "Patina!"

www.ingramcontent.com/pod-product-compliance
Lightning Source LLC
LaVergne TN
LVHW041751060526
838201LV00046B/972